SONNY'S SECRET

John Aiken

Sonny's Secret

ISBN 13: 9780692746615
Library of Congress Control Number: 2016944763

Story by
John Aiken

Cover Designer
LoMar Designs

Printed in USA
Go to our website: www.kingdombuilderspublications.com

DEDICATION

To Elva who put up with all of my long hours of writing and to
my daughter Pamela who took all of that writing and made it
into this book.

CONTENTS

	Dedication	iii
	Acknowledgments	v
1	The Box	6
2	The Fishing Trip Ploy	48
3	The Wiretap	78
4	The Bottle in the Bag	96
5	The Chase	112
6	Pedro's Reprimand	133
7	Sonny Heads for Charleston	153
8	The Chain Gang Escapees	174
9	Jack Sims Gets Fired	226
10	Round 'em Up, Brand 'em and Put 'em in the Corral	248
	About the Author	258

ACKNOWLEDGMENTS

To Travis for his moral support and many hours of editing.

THE BOX
Chapter One

"Sonny, it's gonna fall! Come down!" Tommy and Brian yelled as they ran from the debris spewing out of the busted pipe.

The rusty gutter-drain on the old warehouse he was climbing had broken loose and he was hanging two stories up, several feet from an open window. Bits of metal, dirt clods, and dust rained into his face and eyes.

Sonny made a strong push, got his left arm over the window ledge and pulled himself closer. He held on tightly with his left arm, turned loose the pipe and grabbed the window ledge with his right arm. He pulled himself into the open window and fell on the floor of the dark, deserted warehouse. Too frightened to make a spitting noise to get the gunk out of his mouth, Sonny stuck his fingers in and scraped it out piece by piece. Barefoot, wearing short pants and no shirt, he wiped his eyes with the back of his grimy hand.

Once he got his voice back, Sonny stuck his head out the window and whispered down to Tommy and Brian, "I'll come down and go out the back door."

Sonny turned to find the stairs and reality hit him. He was all alone in a huge, spooky, long-deserted cotton gin. He took a few steps away from the open window and froze. How could he get up the courage to climb down the narrow, creaky stairway to get out? The idea of exploring the warehouse sounded exciting in the outside light, he knew then that he would not be alone. Now, it was different. He had to either move through the dimly lit building, or hang out the window and drop. The cotton gin's tall ceilings made the two-story drop much farther than that of a normal building and Sonny realized that going out the window was not an option.

Sonny stepped carefully and tried not to make a sound, but the rotting, warped boards made eerie, squeaking noises. Adding to the horror, pigeons and sparrows littered the floor. Had they flown in and died? Or had they been killed by vampires! He picked up the pace and made it down the stairs. He was headed for a small door in the back when he heard someone pushing open the front door. His heart pounded, his knees trembled, and he was certain that the warm liquid on his leg was blood. Sonny dove into a coffin-size crate, slid the lid over and prayed. He sunk down into large clumps of musty cotton that had lain rotting in the box for more years than Sonny had lived.

As the footsteps and voices got nearer and louder, Sonny scrunched down deeper into the box that he was now sure would be his coffin. He was lying on something in the bottom that felt like glass bottles. What else could be in the box with him? Were there rats that would gnaw his ears, or, "Oh, my God! Snakes?" Sonny was certain that whoever was around would feel the building shake from his pounding heart. Not only that, he wasn't sure that he could stay still much longer. Upright long neck bottles in the bottom of the box pressed into his body. The powdery cotton on top of him was itchy and scratchy. "Oh please, Lord, don't let me sneeze."

Soon there were at least two men standing within several feet of the box. One of them said, "It's only two o'clock and Gus won't be here until three. Help me shove this crate over by that window. We'll have a drink and deal a few hands of five card stud."

Sonny's fear turned to terror. As the box began sliding, the bottles under him clinked together and cotton dust filled his mouth and throat and burned his eyes. He felt like he was suffocating. He was praying that this was a dream and he would soon wake and run to the safety of his mother's arms.

Sonny heard a chilling voice say, "Reach down into that crate and get a bottle of that Crown Royal and hand me a paper cup."

Just as the lid started to slide, another voice said, "Hey, never mind, we've got a bottle of Jack Daniels already open on this desk. It's *smooooth* stuff." The lid over Sonny slid shut, and he heard the bottle slam onto the edge of the box.

"All right, sit down and pour us a drink. I'll deal." Sonny thought he couldn't be any more terrified than he already was, but now his blood turned to lead powder: the voice was that of JT McGloughlin. Mr. McGloughlin was the superintendent of county schools, and highly feared by students, even in a crowded school building. Here the fear was on a scale with vampires and swamp lizards. Sonny tried to make himself become invisible so he could sneak out to Tommy and Brian.

"Tommy and Brian? My God, where are they? Are they still waiting for me to open a door or window? Can they even imagine that I'm in a large coffin, with JT playing cards right on top of my trembling body?"

Tommy and Brian heard the voices in the warehouse and ran for the bikes. Brian jumped on his bike and his handlebar bumped the wall.

"What was that?" Yelled JT.

"I don't know but it came from out back. I'll check it out."

8

The voice belonging to "I'll Check it out" sent Sonny's body rag doll limp. That voice belonged to Garland Webb, Timmonsville Chief of Police. Sonny knew that when they found him, they wouldn't even have to look for a gun to shoot him with; Garland carried a pistol that hung down to his ankle.

Garland stomped back over by the box and spoke loudly, "I didn't see nobody out there, but that Sims boy's dog was roundin' the corner like he was followin' somebody in a hurry. I bet that little turd was messin' roun'."

"Well, we can handle Sonny Sims. Look out front and see if Gus's here yet. We've got to get that stuff loaded and on the way before dark."

Sonny could feel the floor shake as Garland's boots carried his 300 pounds of ugly fat to the front window and back. "Nobody's here yet, deal me another hand."

JT drained the last sip of bourbon, made a smacking sound, and poured several fingers of the brown liquid into his cup. Sonny knew that JT was chewing on a cigar even before he lit it up. He always had a cigar clenched in his teeth, and often cigar juice was on his chin. The kids laughed about it at school, but no one ever talked about it unless there was complete privacy. Even in the closed box, Sonny could hear the Zippo lighter flick open, and he could imagine the sickening smoke smell when the flame ignited the stinking Cuban tobacco.

How much more could Sonny stand? He had endured more in this one hour in the box than he had endured before in his whole life. Now he had to add the fear of getting sick and vomiting from the stench of the burning tobacco. Sonny could visualize JT chewing on the burning wad of leaves, all dressed up in a suit, tie, and vest. No one ever saw JT when

9

he wasn't dressed up like he was going to a funeral. It was a town joke that he was born in that suit, and it just stretched to fit as he grew. The suit wouldn't have had to stretch much sideways—JT was hoe-handle skinny, but he went upward like a milkweed searching for sunlight.

Sonny could also visualize Garland standing by the box. He, too, always wore the same suit, but his was a uniform. The kids joked that Garland had stolen it from a doorman at a cheap New Orleans hotel. It had twisted rope braids on the shoulders and several ribbons above his badge like the army generals wear. What he called his "Peace Machine" hung on his belt, and looked like a cross between a Civil War musket and a twelve-gauge shotgun. No one had ever seen him draw the odd looking pistol because he took too much delight in smacking heads with his "noggin knocker." Most of the time, he didn't even have to use that; the sickening jail smell on his uniform was enough to make most folks steer clear of Garland Webb.

Sonny couldn't believe that he was in a box and the two most feared men in the county, his school superintendent and the chief of police were drinking and playing cards just inches above his head. It was early September in the Pee Dee part of South Carolina, and the heat and humidity were bad enough to make chickens lay boiled eggs. In the box, he guessed it was hot enough to burn his tongue black. He was afraid that he had sweated so much that it was running out the bottom of the box. He feared they might think the liquid was from a broken bottle and start digging down inside. What if they planned to load the box on a truck? Worse, what if they were loading something that was in the box?

Tommy gave Brian a brotherly slap across the face and

threatened him with a much worse beating if he didn't shut up. They were hiding in the corner of the dark closet in Tommy's room. Tommy was every bit as scared as Brian, but he was older and had to be the tough one. "What are we gonna do?" Brian said between sniffles.

"I don't know yet, I'm thinking, so shut up the snivelin'."

"But Tommy, Chief Webb wouldn't have been sneaking into the building unless he's searchin' for some murderers. What if they've already killed Sonny? What if they kill the chief? What're we gonna do? I'm scared, I'm gonna tell Mama!"

"Hush! You ain't telling nobody nothin' till I say so. Just sit there and suck your thumb."

"But I told you there was vampires in there," sobbed Brian, "Now Sonny and the chief are both dead."

"Ain't nobody dead less I say so. Keep your mouth shut— Mama'll hear you."

Garland shifted his cards around, and tried to hide his face from showing that his highest card was a nine and he had only one of those. He sucked in a big drag of Camel, laid it on the box with the glowing end hanging off, and when he spoke, clouds of smoke drifted from his nose and mouth. "I wonder what Gus'll have today? I hope it's more whiskey."

McGloughlin rearranged his cards; "It's set up to be either a load of Scotch liquor, or a truck-full of army weapons. Either one'll bring a good haul from Antonio. Course, those Lucky Strike's last week weren't a bad day's doin' either. Whatever it is, it'll be tax free, and money that nobody knows we've got. Now, deal me two cards; one down, and one face up."

Garland threw him the two cards, and said, "The

dealer takes three."

"I can't see that. I'm folding. You already took me for eighty dollars, and I just got here," said a new voice.

"Easy come, easy go; quitcha bitching" McGloughlin said, as he threw three Jacks on the table. Garland flinched, laid his cards face down on the box, took out a red bandana, and wiped sweat from his eyes. JT took a big drag of cigar, spit out a piece of tobacco, and shoved the pile of twenties into his vest pocket.

Sonny finally recognized the new voice as that of Dalton Sellers. He was terrified to hear someone there that he didn't even hear come in. "Have I already started the dying process? God! What if I'm already dead? Even if I'm not, I'll soon be. This group of people gets worse all the time. What kind of meeting would have the superintendent of schools, the police chief, and a gambling club bouncer, together in a deserted warehouse?" Dalton was a loudmouth, one of the most violent people in the county—except to Garland, McGloughlin and Gus Segars. He was always playing up to them, and he bragged openly about his being close friends with them. Nobody took the friend part seriously; it was more like a snake snuggling up to a mama crocodile so he could steal eggs.

Sonny had been in the box for over an hour. He tried pinching his leg to see if he was alive. He was so cramped from being in one position that he couldn't even feel the pinch. Sonny's mouth and body were dried out, the cotton was making him itch, and he was terrified. He was thinking that if he were already dead it would be better than getting killed later. Whatever was going on was something illegal. He knew that if the chief of police and the superintendent of schools were in on it, they surely wouldn't let killing a ten-

12

year-old kid stop 'em from getting away.

Sonny knew that if Dalton Sellers was involved, Gus Segars was in on it too. Gus ran the gambling club outside of town, and Dalton Sellers was his bouncer and whatever else Gus wanted him to do. Rumors were that they were part of a New York mob, and they had killed an undercover cop. The story was that the cop had been sent in by some federal folks to investigate the hijacking of Government property. There had been a rash of trucks hijacked in the area, all of them belonging to the military. Most of them were bound for the PX system at the Charleston Navy Base; but one of them had been carrying military weapons.

JT heard a noise outside, "Look out and see if that's Gus, he should be here by now." "It is, and there's a truck right behind him with a load of somethin' that'll make us rich." Gus came in and told McGloughlin, "Pour me one of whatever you're having, it smells good."

"It is, Gus. It's Jack Daniel's, from Tennessee. A whole *hellava* lot smoother than that gut rottin' stuff that you call whiskey out at the Vet club."

Sonny heard the door open again and a voice that he didn't recognize walked over fast. Whoever it was sounded agitated. "I had to rough up that dumbass driver. He kept trying to keep me from gettin' in the truck."

Gus was disturbed. "*Wadn't* he told you were comin'? Antonio was supposed to have it set up."

I don't know, but he didn't act like he knew. I tried to climb in the truck, and he kept trying to pull me back. I had to whack him with an ax handle. He was still lyin' there when I drove off. I shoulda brought him with me so we could take care of him. Now I don't know if he was just tryin' to make it look like he was doin his job, or if Antonio hadn't

13

told him we were gonna lighten his load.

Gus turned up his cup, finished it off, and pointed at Garland, "Drive over to the pit, find that driver and check him out. Find out what he knows, and if he can identify Cecil. If he can, you'll have to put him in the jailhouse we've got behind the club."

Garland's lit Camel made a shushing sound when he dumped it into the whiskey-wet paper cup. He blew a big puff of smoke, popped several peppermint lifesavers in his mouth, and shook the building as he stomped out the door.

Tommy got face to face with Brian and gave him the ultimatum, "Either you come with me to look for Sonny, or I'll tie you up, gag you, and leave you here in the closet."

Brian was trembling and sniffling, but he agreed to go. Big brother Tommy was his hero, and Brian wanted to please him.
As they walked down the street, Tommy saw Mrs. Stevens standing by the curb. "Hi, Mrs. Stevens, we're playing a game with Sonny, and he's hidden from us real good. I don't suppose you've seen him in the last hour or so?"

"Well, no, I haven't, Tommy. Before lunch, when he rode by with you and Brian, was the last time I saw him."

"Thanks, Mrs. Stevens, we'll find him." Mrs. Stevens was the wife of the postmaster, and she always seemed to know everything that the kids in town were doing. She was nice, and she was always pleasant, but she didn't hesitate telling a parent if one of the kids didn't meet her standard of behavior. Mr. Stevens had married her when he was in the army in New Jersey. She was from a family that ate garlic at every meal, and you could smell her going down the street. Mr. Baroody ordered the stuff directly for her, cause none of his other grocery customers ate garlic.

Tommy and Brian rode by Sonny's house and his bike wasn't there. Now they would have to go looking for him, and hope that he was still alive. When they got close to the warehouse, Brian had a panic attack and started crying. Tommy pulled Brian's ear and screamed, "I said, stop crying."

Brian's voice was quivering, "But, Tommy, I'm scared."

Tommy rubbed his little brother's head and spoke gently, "Everything's gonna be all right, Little Brother. Sonny's probably home by now."

As they got near the back of the warehouse, Tommy saw the big truck parked by the loading dock. He noticed that Sonny's dog, Troubles, had come back, and was standing at the back door. They also saw that Sonny's bike was still lying in the tall bushes. Tommy was having a hard time being brave now. He was beginning to feel like Brian; maybe something bad had happened to Sonny. They kept on pedaling, and stopped behind a giant oak tree a block from the warehouse. Tommy stuck his head out from behind the tree and whistled. Troubles, Sonny's half collie and half something else, looked, but didn't move. Now they knew Sonny was still in there.

JT, Dalton, Gus, and the other person they were calling Cecil walked over to the side door that had a loading dock. Sonny heard the door open and close and it got quiet. "Am I alone? Oh, God, are they gone?" Sonny hadn't been much for praying in the past, but now he was saying more prayers than a bunch of hungover Baptist Deacons at a Las Vegas convention. Sonny had been so sure he was a goner that he didn't even think of prayer until the loading door shut, and then he got a slight feeling that he might get out of this alive. "But how do I know if they're gone? It's quiet in here, but did anyone stay? What if I try to get out and my legs are too weak to get me out the door?"

Sonny realized he had to try and get the lid open enough to see if anyone was there. Before he could move, he heard the loading door slide. JT was bragging, "This is the biggest haul we've had yet. Get yourselves a cup, boys. I'm gonna pour us a celebration drink."

Dalton was gloating, but he was as nervous as a barefoot boy on a hot tar road. "You want me to start separatin' the load. JT, we need to get shed of that truck."

"Nah, have a *snootful* first and then we'll all get it loaded." JT poured them a cupful, and Sonny could hear them slapping the cups together. Sonny imagined they were toasting like the folks do in the movies. JT made his slurpy, smacking sound, slammed the cup on the crate, and said, "Let's get at it."

Once again, the big door to the dock opened, and Sonny couldn't hear anyone inside. He reached up, slid the lid a little, and listened; all quiet. He had lain in one position for so long that he couldn't get out of the box. He crouched down in a different position and wiggled his toes. He tried to get enough blood circulating to make a move to the small door in the back. Finally, he dragged himself out of the box, limped over behind a stack of old newspapers, and rubbed his legs. Once he got some feeling back in his legs he went as fast as he could to the little door. Sonny had to make a thumping noise getting the slide bolt unhooked, but once out he sucked in the fresh air and rejoiced. Troubles ran over and licked Sonny's face and Sonny gave him a big hug.

He left his bike and took off in a run that would have been funny on a regular day; he was hopping and skipping on one leg, and dragging the one that still had no feeling.

The group loaded the stolen haul into farm trucks that Dalton and Cecil had brought over earlier, then came back in for another celebration drink. JT walked back over to the box Sonny had been hiding in, and when he picked up the bottle, he hollered, "What the Hell! This box was closed when we went outside. Did any of you come back in and open it?"
Everyone assured the others that they had not gone into the box. JT was almost yelling, "Somebody's been messing around in here. Dalton, search the building and see if you see anybody snooping around."
Dalton picked up a metal hook that years ago had been used to drag cotton bales. He went up and down the stairs, and when he got to the back door, he screamed, "Come over here. This door's unlocked, and the last time I checked it was bolted."
Gus said, "Well, we're probably just a little jumpy from the excitement. Lock it back, and let's get the stuff out of here. Dalton, you and Cecil get that haul up to the meetin' spot with Tony's boys. I'll take the truck over to Lynches River, and put it in a place that it won't be found for a while; Garland knows where to pick me up. Look around, and when you come back make sure nothin's been disturbed. I'll have Garland keep a close check on the place."

Tommy and Brian rode by Sonny's house again and Troubles was laying on Sonny's top step. "See what I told you, Troubles wouldn't have left the warehouse if Sonny wasn't with him. I told you everything was gonna be all right."

"I don't see his bike," Brian sobbed.

Tommy decided not to stop by Sonny's house yet, but told Brian he had an errand and would see him back at the house. "If you say anything to Mama, I'll whip your can every day for the next two months." With that promise, Tommy rode over to a patch of woods where he could hide and see if there was any activity. After a wait with nothing going on, he rode casually by and checked out Sonny's bike. "Oh my God, it's still there, maybe Brian's right, maybe we will have to tell Mama. First, though, I'm gonna go over and knock on Sonny's door and see if he's home. Since Troubles is there, he's got to be. Maybe he just left his bike and ran home."

Garland drove up to the AMVETS Club just as JT and Gus got there. The club was four miles from town, and surrounded by woods. Gus still called it an AMVETS Club, but in reality, the AMVETS folks had taken his charter away months ago. The veteran's organization didn't approve of the way Gus ran the club.

The group went into the back room, and Garland stomped in, "I found that dumb, damn driver. Cecil gave him a few good licks but he wadn't in bad shape. He was pretty scared. He said Antonio told him that I would be the one to get the truck, and when somebody without a uniform tried to get in, he wanted to know what was goin' on. That's when Cecil smacked him. I took him over to Florence and told him to get the hell out of town. He's gonna say that he didn't report this because he was knocked out and didn't know where he was or what had happened."

JT pulled a pig foot out of the salty brine in the kitchen store house and between gnaws said, "Well, we'll be OK there, but I'm still wondering if that little piece of crap, Sonny Sims, was messing around. Garland you lean on him tomorrow and see if he acts suspicious. If so, we'll deal with him."

Tommy went around to Sonny's room and tapped on the window. "Sonny, it's Tommy, you in there?" Not a sound. Tommy knocked louder. "Sonny, it's Tommy, open up." Finally, Tommy heard a moaning sound. Sonny opened the door to the little screen porch that was off of his room, and then unlatched that door so Tommy could come in. Sonny got back down between the bed and the wall and talked in a sniffling whisper. He was hugging a small teddy bear.

"Tommy, Mr. McGloughlin, Chief Webb, Gus, and Dalton Sellers, are doing some kind of illegal stuff. It sounds like they might have even killed a truck driver to steal his load of liquor. I stayed in a crate full of moldy cotton on some bottles that was stolen whiskey. I just barely was able to get out. Where's Brian?"

"I had to send him home. He was wettin' his pants and snifflin' so, he was getting' on my nerves."

"Well, I'm more scared than he is. Garland saw Troubles and has a suspicion that I was messin round. Tommy, those folks are dangerous. You know that story about Gus Segars and Dalton Sellers killing that undercover G-man? Well, I believe it. They didn't seem the least bit concerned that the one they call Cecil may have killed a truck driver. If he ain't already dead, then Garland's gonna kill him. Either way he'll be dead, and they think I know somethin about it, JT told 'em. We can handle that little Sims piece of snot."

19

Tommy's eyes were as big as his elbows. "Sonny, maybe we should call the FBI."

"Huh! Even though we're Junior G-men, there ain't no way they're gonna believe us. When we tell 'em that the chief of police and the school superintendent are robbers and killers, they'll just laugh at us and then go and tell JT and Garland the big joke. The agents all come over and cater to JT, 'cuz he's married to Senator Furman's daughter. Heck, they could get by with killing me without even having to go to jail. I'm scared to leave the house. Mama'll be home in a little while and think I'm sick and give me a dose of salts if I don't go outside and play. I'll have to take the salts, cause I ain't going out and get seen by that bunch."

"I know what we can do Sonny. We don't have to have no help from those G-men. We've got our own G-man kit with the disguises and the black powder to take fingerprints with. We can go over to the warehouse after they're all in bed, get a bottle that they were drinking from, and take fingerprints. That kit has a magnifying glass in it, and we can look for clues. That's what Melvin Purvis would do."

"I ain't never going near that warehouse again, and I sho' as hell ain't goin in there in the night. You're as crazy as that bunch of crooks."

"Well, have you got a better idea?"

"I sure do. I'm gonna stay right here in this room until I'm eighty years old and I know those murderers are all dead."

"You know your Mama ain't gonna let you stay home and miss school unless you've got a fever high enough to burn a billy goat. We gotta think of somethin, but right now, I gotta go check on Brian. Mama'll see him cryin' and he'll tell her what happened and she won't believe us either. She'll laugh and call your Mama, and they'll think we've been seeing too many James Cagney movies. Only movies they'll let us see any more will be those stupid musicals."

Gus held his glass high in a salute. "All right boys, drink up, there's more where this came from. We're gonna have enough money soon to buy this town. We'll tell anybody that don't cater to our wishes to move out. Here's to Antonio, he's got us in the midst of a wonderful opportunity. He knows the schedule of every truck that leaves the loadin' dock in North and South Carolina, and he knows which drivers are willin' to make some side money; course the one today's on the run, he sure as hell won't go back and face Antonio. He'll be bathed in cement and used for an anchor on a Charleston loadin dock.
But we still have to be careful."

JT was in his thinking mode now; he had abandoned his smelly cigar and lit up his briar-bowl pipe. Most people liked it when JT was thinking, cause his pipe tobacco had a pleasant aroma.

"We've got to make certain that that little Sims brat didn't see or hear anything today. I don't feel comfortable about that back door being unlocked and seeing his dog hanging around. Also, if he was messing around, we know those Buddin boys were in on it too. Sonny never goes anywhere without those two trailing behind him."

Garland patted his peace machine. "This thing we got goin' is too big to be messed up by a couple of nose snots, like those road bumps. I think we need to lean on 'em hard and find out if they got anything to hide."

Dalton had a rusty or probably bloody switchblade knife almost as long as Garland's "peace machine." He was digging gunk from under his nails that looked like dirty chicken fat. He was a nasty sight. All he ever thought about was cuttin', hittin', or chokin' on anybody that he didn't take a shine to. Actually, the only ones that he did take a shine to were those that could help him pull off some type of crooked caper. "I say let me have a shot at those three. I'll show 'em this little tenderizer, and they'll put their fuzzy tails on a freight train before tomorrow mornin'."

"Well, we're gonna do something, but I don't think we need that yet." JT puffed on the pipe and actually looked like a school superintendent. Well, at least one from the early part of last century. "I think we'll let Garland get 'em in a corner and see if they're overly nervous. If not, we can forget about 'em. If so..."

Tommy was walking the railroad track that ran through town. He looked up and Garland Webb was sitting in his police car staring at him. Tommy started to run but took a deep breath and tried to act normal. Tommy was shaking, but he kept his head down and concentrated on looking at the rail he was walking. He heard a horn beep beside the track and jumped when he saw it was the police car. Garland was wiggling his index finger for him to come over.

"Hop in, Buddin, I got a little problem I need to talk with you about." Tommy thought about running, but he knew, you can't run from Garland Webb.

Tommy eased over to the car and stood there. Garland pointed at the car door and said, "Get in." Tommy froze. "Come on, you know I wouldn't hurt you. You don't have nothin to be scared of, do you? If you ain't done nothin wrong, then you don't have to be afraid of the law."

Tommy was terrified, not of the law, but of the lawless that wanted him to get in the car. He didn't have any choice but to get in; if he refused, he knew Garland would get him. His only chance was to try and act like he wasn't any more afraid than he usually would be. That's a lot of fear, because all of the kids were afraid of Garland.

Garland walked around to the passenger side, opened the door, pointed at the seat, and said, "In!"
Tommy sniffed back the tears and looked around. He saw that Dr. Babb was looking out of his drug store window, and Mr. Waldrep was checking oil in his DeSoto right across the street. Tommy figured that if they knew he was getting in the car, Garland would have second thoughts about doing anything to him.
"Settle down, Buddin, I just wanna ask you a few questions. Somebody's been shooting out town streetlights with either a slingshot or a BB rifle. You got any idea who's doin it?"

"No sir, I didn't have nothin to do with it."

"I didn't ask you if you had anything to do with it, I asked if you knew who did it."

"No sir."

"You mean to tell me that you know every kid in town, and you don't know which one's been shootin' out the lights."

"No sir, I mean yes sir."

"Well, what the hell do you mean, do you know or not?"

"No sir."

"Why you so afraid? You got somthin' to hide?"

"No sir."

"What about that Sims boy you're such good friends with, did he have anything to do with it?"

'No sir."

"Whadda you mean, No sir. You said you don't know nothin bout it, so how can you know that he didn't have nothin to do with it?"

23

Tommy was sitting on his hands so the chief couldn't see them shake. He was glad he had his "Dodgers" ball cap pulled down to soak up some of the sweat that was pouring out. He was not only scared, but in the hot car with Garland the tobacco juice and jail smell was sickening.

"Well, you didn't answer. Is there a reason?"

"I don't know nothin about no lights gettin' shot out. I swear."

"Well, do you know anything about anything else that I might need to know? Like anybody breakin' the law. You know I don't like people that break the law. And you know that I deal with that in whatever way it takes. You do know that don't you, Buddin?"

"Yes sir."

"I want you to keep your lids up and let me be the very first one to know if you see any kind of mischief goin on. You know how mad I'll be if you were to tell somebody else bout some problem that's goin on in my town. I'm the chief, folks 'spect me to know what's happenin'. That's why folks believe in me and trust me, 'cause they know that I always do whatever it takes to keep peace in this town. We understand each other, boy?"

Tommy just sat there with his head down, staring at all the junk on the floor of the car. When Garland cranked up and the car started to move, Tommy looked over and hollered, "Where are we goin? I gotta go home. Mama told me not to be late for dinner, and I gotta go to Mr. Baroody's and get a loaf of bread for Mama."

"We're just gonna drive a minute. I'm gonna show you those lights that got shot out; you sure you didn't have nothin to do with it? There's one right on this corner. We need those lights to be burnin' at night so I can see what's goin on. You think I need to talk to yo' Mama about them lights? Maybe your little sidekick brother and that pimple ass Sims boy had somethin to do with it. You listenin' to me boy?"

"Yes sir. I know they didn't do it, 'cause that would make Mama mad."

"Well, I'm glad to hear that you care about whether yo' mama gets mad or not, cause if I have to tell her you were involved in some devilment she's gonna be upset. So you better keep straight; and you sho' as hell better make sure I'm the one you tell if you see anybody breakin' the law."

"Yes, sir, can I go home now?"

"I guess so, but you tell that little snothead Sims that I wanna talk with him. In fact, you tell him I want him to come and talk to me right away. Where is he anyway? You two are almost always together."

"I think he's sick. He's got a fever."

"Well, you tell him if he don't get well enough to come and see me by tomorrow mornin, I'll have to visit him at home. You tell him that. Tell him that I don't cotton to folks makin' me go to them. You hear me boy."

"Yes sir."

"All right, get your little tail out of my car; I got serious work to do. I better hear from you if you have anything to say bout any doings goin on in my town."

Gus told Dalton he'd take the call on his phone in the back of the club. He lit a small wooden tip Cuban cigar, picked up his gin and tonic, and walked to the back booth. Dalton held the extension phone until Gus picked up and then he gently laid the receiver down. "Hey, Antonio, what's goin on?"

"I heard from the driver on that last load. He's mighty

25

scared. His wife wanted to know how he got all those cuts and knots on his head, and she made him go to the emergency room and get stitches. He's trying hard to make it all go away, but the cops have pushed him hard about losin' his load. He just keeps sayin' he don't remember nothin bout it. He thinks they don't believe 'em."

"Do we need to do anything about him, Tony? If he's gonna spill his guts to the cops, we better make sure his guts are loaded with concrete."

"Well, I don't think he will, Gus. He's more scared of my guys than he is of the cops. Our big problem is his ole lady. She's suspicious of somethin. She must have overheard some phone calls, because she keeps tellin' him to level with the feds. She's a nosey bitch and I'm concerned, but I don't think we should move on her yet. If he doesn't talk to her, and plays his phone calls tight, we shouldn't have a worry."

"Tony, the cops have been lookin round the site where Cecil grabbed the load. I don't know what they've got, but they hauled off a ton of dirt and debris. Everybody knows Cecil smokes them funny little filtered weeds, and I'm sure there's a lot of those in the debris that they're picking up. How you reckon they found out Gilbert lost that load at the sandpit. He was 'sposed to tell 'em it happened when he pulled off of Highway 76 for a pee break."

"I don't know, Gus, but I don't think the driver tole 'em nothin. I'll get to Cecil, and have him quit smokin' if we have to. He can swear he hadn't had a cigarette in months. How can they prove otherwise? In fact, how could they prove they're his, even if they suspect it? I don't think fingerprints would stick on a weed butt."

"Well, you keep watch, Tony, and let me know if you need some muscle from here. Dalton can't wait to light into somebody."

Garland shook the tables and rattled the catsup bottles on his way to the back booth of the club. Gus motioned for him to have a seat. Garland didn't always wear his Royal Mountie type hat, but today he had it on. He laid it on the table, pulled a handful of napkins from the molded silver container, wiped the sweat from his head, and lit up a Camel. "Gus, I leaned on that older Buddin boy yesterday, and it's hard to tell. He's always like a little sneaky snake when I ask him a question so I'm not sure if he was more scared than normal. He did tell me though, that the Sims boy has a fever. Could be he's seen somethin that's scared his temperature up. I told Buddin to have him see me right away, or I'd go to his house and see his mama."

"He didn't tell you anything about the warehouse?"

"Well, I didn't ask him outright, Gus, I just hassled him enough to let him know that I better not get no surprises."

"What are you gonna do about the Sims boy, Garland, are you goin to his house?"

"Well I'm hopin' I won't have to, but I'll do whatever. If I can catch that younger Buddin boy alone, he scares easy. Sims and the big Buddin try to be tough guys, but he didn't look so tough yesterday when I was puttin' a little muscle on him. I'll know somethin soon. That little Buddin boy goes over to Truet's Texaco for candy every day. If I can catch him, he'll be runnin' his mouth like a hound dog on a coon trail."

"Let me know soon as you find out, I gotta get back on the phone and see if that last load payoff is at the site yet. If so, you can pick it up in your town car. That way, if somebody sees you, it'll look like official business. Gus bit the end off of a real Cuban stogie and lit it with a fancy Ronson lighter. It ran through Garland's mind to rib Gus about lightin' up with a woman's lighter, but he thought better—it's not a good idea to get on the wrong side of Gus Salters, even if you're a police chief. "Heck, he took care of a federal undercover cop; no way he'd think twice about stuffin' a small town chief in a meat locker."

As Garland left the club he noticed that Dalton was playing one of the slots with change from the register. He just played at the club to practice up, 'cause he knew Gus wouldn't give him a payoff, even if he won.

Garland drove around town and saw Brian. "Hey, little Buddin, get your backside over here." Garland's voice sounded like a mad bull snorting at a red fire truck. Brian stopped and froze in his tracks.

"I said over here, butt brain." Brian just stood there. He tried to run, but his legs wouldn't move. He felt the warm fluid on his leg, but that still didn't thaw him enough to run.

"Hey, I said get over here, or I'm comin' to getcha." Brian started sniffling, and shuffled a few feet closer. Garland reached over and pulled him to the car. "What the hell you so afraid of boy? You done peed in yo' britches. You been up to somethin bad? Tell me, have we gotta go and talk to yo' mama?"

"No sir."

"Well, what you doing peein' in your britches just 'cause I wanted to talk to you? You gotta be into somethin. Where's that turd face brother and sorry friend of yours?"

Brian's eyes pushed all the skin off of his face, and he stared down at his feet, "I don't know."

"You always round 'em, how come you not with 'em today?"

"Tommy said he was going over to Sonny's, and he said

28

Sonny might have somethin contagious. He told me to stay home."

"Well if he told you to stay home, whatchu doin here?"

"I just was goin to Mr. Truet's to get a Mars candy bar, but I don't need it. I'll go on home now."

"No you won't, not 'til I say you can go home, now get in the car, boy."

Brian had tears running down his chest onto his shorts, and it was mixing with the pee stains. He looked like a sad sight. "Your brother told you I talked with him yesterday? Brian just stared into space. "You hear me boy? I'm talkin' to you."

"No sir, I mean Yes sir."

"Well, what the hell do you mean, boy?"

"He didn't tell me nothin."

"He didn't tell you I'm investigatin' to see who's been shootin out my street lights? You have anything to do with that? You better speak up; my patience is wearin' thin. Come on, I'll show you one of the lights, and you tell me who did it." Garland drove over to the edge of town nearest the cemetery. Brian was shaking and sniffling, crying for his mama.

"What you want yo' mama for boy, you shoot this light out up there? You know that light cost the town money. Yo' mama pays taxes, so it cost her money. She ain't gonna be happy when I tell her you done that."

"I ain't done nothin, Mr. Webb, I swear. I just wanna go home."

"Well if you didn't shoot out the light, what else you been up to? You know anything about anything goin on that I'm 'sposed to know?"

"No sir."

"What about that little rat ass friend of yours? He been

29

into anything I oughta know bout?"

"No sir."

"How you know he ain't boy? You said he had a fever and you ain't seen him. How come he ain't been deliverin' his papers this week?" Brian started crying so loud and shaking and trembling so, that Garland decided he'd better back off and let him go for now. He'd get it out of the Sims boy; if there was anything to know.

Sonny's mother, Hannah, went to Florence everyday to take care of her sister-in-law, Phoebe. Phoebe suffers from some type of memory disease and doesn't know anybody, including Sonny's mother, Hannah. Each day while Hannah gave her a bath and fixed her some hot food, Phoebe relived events that happened when she was a small child. To her, those times were actually occurring right then. She would holler out the names of childhood schoolmates and play like she was outside the old school and it was recess. She was afraid the bell would ring, and then, thinking Hannah was her schoolteacher, Phoebe would beg her to let them keep playing. Sometimes Hannah would tell Phoebe that she had to turn in her math homework, and Phoebe would get real quiet. Sonny's mama, Hannah, was a warm and friendly type of person and everyone liked being around her, and she usually played along with Phoebe's mind games. This day though, she he was rather reserved, and didn't tarry long with Phoebe. She wanted to get back home and check on Sonny.

Broom's drive-in, on the outskirts of town, was a gathering place for the dating kids. In addition to the booths and tables inside, they also had curb service. Most nights the back parking lot was full. The boys would order a hot dog with 'lots of onions' cause that was macho. They would then order a coke for the girls and a beer for themselves. Most of them ordered onions on the girl's hotdog and made sure she ate them. Otherwise the girls wouldn't want to kiss someone with onion breath.

In the daytime a crowd usually hung out at the lunch counter. There were eight stools and you could sit on one and twirl from side to side, or even spin all the way around. It was a cozy place. There was always a Roy Acuff, and Ernest Tubb, or some good old Bill Monroe and his Bluegrass Boys playing on the jukebox.

Dalton backed up to the door, got out, and pulled down the tailgate of his 1940 Dodge Ram pickup truck. He had brought a new model juke, and two of the latest model pinball machines. Mr. Broom leased the machines from Gus, and Dalton always brought him new models when they came out. There was some type of magic about the lights on the jukebox and the noise from a new type of pinball machine. The new models always created extra business.

"Hey, Dalton, whatchu got? Another new machine?"

"Yep, your customers gonna love these, Carlton. They got more bangs and clangs than a track full of freight trains."

"Lordy, I member when a juke box wadn't old 'til it wore out. Now they're old as soon as a new one comes in. Them pinball machines though, I'm glad they change those often, cause the kids learn how to cheat 'em after a while. Dalton, you need any help with that?"

"Nope, 'cept for you to hold the door open, Carlton." Dalton always liked to bring the machines in at lunchtime. That time of day a crowd was there to see the kind of muscle he had. He took great delight in being able to move a

31

jukebox as big as a piano. He would gently lift one side, rock it back and forth until it was in place, then he would lift the other end, swing it around and give a little slide to get it against the wall. When he did this heavy moving the crowd got a good view of his bulging muscles. If anybody ever had a second thought about not catering to Dalton, they got a chilling display of a good reason to stay out of his way. Dalton figured it was good to advertise that he was the strongest badass in town.

The only one that might have been a match for Dalton was another town strong man, Cleo Free. Everyone in town knew the story of Cleo and Carl Poston's flat tire. Carl didn't have a jack, and he was standing helplessly by his 1940 Ford when Cleo came along. He told Cleo he didn't have a jack and Cleo said, "Carl, that ain't no problem." Cleo just backed up to that fender, picked the right front side off of the ground, and held it there while Carl changed the tire.

It was always a fantasy of the town folks to see Cleo and Dalton tangle. It would have been a gruesome fight, 'cause Dalton would use anything he could get his hands on to put the lights out on his enemy. Cleo, a gentler giant, usually was content to whip his opponent with his fists and strength, but he wasn't above pulling out his knife if the situation demanded. After he finished with the first one or two he always wanted more. He would look the crowd over after a fight, and yell, "Anybody else want a piece of me? What about you? You want some of me?" He would stalk around to every table, and glare at anybody that he thought might be even thinking about it. Luckily, Dalton had never been around when Cleo put out a challenge. Maybe it was more than luck, because Dalton no doubt knew that if anybody could punch out his clock, Cleo would be the most likely one.

Once Dalton got the machines in place, he scanned the room to make sure that all the customers saw his muscle. Then he ordered a Black Label beer and chugalugged it without the slightest bit of a frown on his face.

Carlton followed Dalton out to his truck. "Did you hear about that load of Army rifles and pistols that was hijacked over at the sand pit? Somebody made off with a nice haul. The feds are scourin' the area now, and I think they done hauled off half the dirt in the sandpit to look for clues."

"Nah, I don't pay no 'tention to what them fed asses are up to. If I had my way, we wouldn't let 'em in the county."

"Well, I don't know if they found anything, but it sure is excitin' havin' somethin like that nearby. All them *fedies* have been in here orderin' food and cokes and it was like a windfall to have all that outside business. I had to drive over to Florence today and get me a new batch of rolls and wieners. I sold more this week than I do after a high school prom. Them prissy pants don't drink much beer, but they put down cokes and eat hot dogs like little kids."

"Well don't let 'em play music on the juke and put nickels in the pinballs. Next thing you know they'll be drinkin' beer and wantin' to stay here forever."

Gus was not at the club when Dalton got back, so he opened up a PBR and stretched out in a booth. Lacy, the waitress, came over and sat down. "What's up Tiger, you look like you been ridin' a porcupine bare back." Lacy was one of the few that could joke around with Dalton and live to tell it. He liked her because she kept her nose out of his business. Also, she was able to pass on a lot of information she picked up from bits and pieces of conversations.

Customers would get to playing the slots, or betting a hand of blackjack, and not even realize that Lacy was around.

Gus came in just as Lacy answered the phone. "Gus, you got a call; it's Antonio, you wanna take it in the back?"

"Yeah, give me a minute, and bring me a rock and vodka." Gus sat close to the oscillating fan and cooled the sweat off. He lit a Lucky, took a long drag, and picked up the phone. "Hey, Tony, what's up?"

"Gus, you in the back?"

"Yeah, what's goin on, Tony?"

"Well, we're gonna have to hold back on grabbin any loads for a while. Them damn feds are gittin' itchy. They've got that driver in jail that Cecil worked over, and I'm afraid he's gonna break. His wife's telling 'em that he knows somethin."

"Can't one of your boys get to him, Tony?"

"Not now, he's in their custody, and they won't let anybody see him."

"What about Sterling? All he has to do is shout that they can't hold his client without lettin' him talk to his lawyer, and they'll let him in."

"We were hoping not to hafta do that, Gus. Sterling says those feds put the prisoner and his lawyer in a room that they bugged. Sterling'll hafta be careful what he says, cause this guy's not very stable. He may not understand what Sterling's sayin' without him gettin too graphic. If they are recording, we'll be worse off than we are now. But, it may be our only way to go now. I'm gonna talk to Sterling again, and see if he can't go over and get through to Gilbert. Maybe he can get bail set up. We need to get that boy in a place that we can show the real world to him. He either takes what the feds hand out, or he takes what our boys hand out. I think he'll realize the difference in methods."

"Well, let me know if you want Dalton to talk to him. He's ready to bust loose on somebody."

"Sonny, me and Brian are scared. I'm not sure Brian's goin to school tomorrow. He just sits around and mopes and Mama's on our case to know what's goin on. If he doesn't go to school, Mama 'll either kill him or find out everything. When Garland got me in his car, he didn't mention the warehouse, but he kept trying to scare me by bringin' up other things. He told me he thinks that I've been bustin' out streetlights, and he even told me he thought I one time stole a bicycle. What are we gonna do? He said if you don't go see him, he's comin to your house."

"I don't know. I'm scared too. I'll hafta go and see him, cause if he comes to the house Mama'll skin me unless I tell her. Even then, she won't believe all of this. She'll believe the chief. I'm thinking about running away to Mexico. I'll go see him today, but I'm gonna do it after it gets busy downtown. I want it so that if he tries to kill me, there'll be other folks around. If you don't ever hear from me again, you tell Mama what happened. If I've been kidnapped and killed, then she might believe you."

Sonny finally got up the nerve to go see Chief Webb. He pushed the huge door open enough to slink into the jail office. Chief Webb was lying way back in his well-worn chair, the fan was on full blast, and Garland's Camel was burning on the edge of the desk. Not only was Sonny terrified, but the smell of the smoke and the nasty jail was dreadful. Garland eyed him up and down, but didn't move for a while. Then he picked up his Camel, took a long draw and leaned down and blew smoke in Sonny's face. Sonny wanted to gag but he held it back. He was sweating, his tummy was growling, and he was shaking all over.

Finally, Garland said, "Come on in and shut the door, Sims." Sonny pushed the door part way, and Garland boomed out. "I said shut that damn door, boy. Now!"

Sonny pushed on it, but he was so weak he had to use both hands to close it. "Tommy said you wanted to see me, Sir." His voice sounded like a shipwreck survivor that had been on a raft with no water for three weeks. His words cracked, and the pitch was so high it sounded like a basset hound in a thunderstorm.

"He did, huh. Well that's the first thing that little turd patty's done right since I've been in this town. He told you what I wanna see you 'bout, boy?"

"Yes sir, He said there was some broken street lights, but I ain't broke no lights, Chief, I swear."

"That's easy to say Sims, but can you prove it?"

Sonny just stood there. Tears were running down his face, and he didn't know what to say.

"I said, can you prove it?" Garland was yelling. He got out of his chair, leaned over toward Sonny's face and said, "If you can't prove you didn't do it, and I say you did, nobody's gonna believe you. They gonna believe me. I'm the law in this town, and a little piece of crab crap like you ain't gonna be able to get out of this. What else is it that you don't know nothin bout, Sims? Is there anything going on that you think I oughta know bout? You better fess up now, so I don't have to come down hard on you. I don't like lyin little snot balls. I got more respect for dog slobber than I do a lyin little turd. You hearin' what I'm sayin' boy?"

"Yes sir." Sonny's words trailed off. Garland towered over him, lit another Camel, leaned down, and blew more smoke at Sonny's nose. Sonny coughed, his eyes were already wet from crying, and he had to hold his breath to keep from throwing up. The smoke made him want to run out into the street, but he couldn't make his legs move. Garland put his hand on the back of Sonny's neck and pulled him away from the door.

At that time Mayor Coker walked in. "What's going on, Chief? What's Sims doing in here? You been into trouble, Sims?"

"No sir."

"He's been crying. What's he so upset about, Chief?"

"I been askin' him about some street lights that's been shot out. He tells me he didn't have nothin to do with it but I don't believe him."

"Well, Garland, why do you think he did? Do you have any evidence that he was involved? We've never had no big trouble with Sonny have we?"

"We never have caught him, but that's the kind that does this sort of thing. They think they can get by with it by goin to church and not doin nothin in front of me."

"Well, Sims, you go on home and we'll get with you later. I've got somethin important to talk with the Chief about."

Sonny ran the three blocks to his house and got under the bed. His body was heaving and he started crying out loud. He wasn't even concerned that his sister, Jackie, was home. Jackie heard the crying and stormed into the room.

"What's the matter with you? Why you hidin' under the bed, and whatchu cryin about? Did Grover Caldwell beat your butt again? Quit being such a crybaby. Come on out and let me see you. If you don't I'm gonna call Mama."
Sonny slid out and tried to quit sobbing, but he couldn't. His whole body was in a spasm.

"I don't see no marks on you. You been acting like this for two days now. What's wrong with you? I told mama I thought she needed to take you to Doctor Holman. She said she was, if you weren't OK today."

Sonny didn't say a word, he just trembled and sobbed, and looked like a ghost in a windstorm.

Garland hated Mayor Linwood Coker. As far as Garland was concerned, Linwood thought being mayor of a little town made him a big shot. Garland couldn't wait for the day when he had enough cash to get the hell out of this one wagon town. He hated the fact that Coker controlled his life and could fire him if he chose to just on the spur of the moment. He listened as Mayor Coker talked about some idiot plan to have the grammar school students come by the station and meet with him and the chief.

"It'll be good PR for the town Garland, and it'll give the kids a chance to see that we're on their side. Maybe then they won't get scared and run when they see your police car. If we can get them to trust us more, we'll have less of the little things that you and Sims were talking about: fewer shot out street lights and fewer windows covered with messages written in soap. What do you think?"

"Well Mayor, I'll do whatever you say, but I think it's a mistake to coddle these kids. If we make it too soft for the little brats they'll begin to take over the town. Next thing you know they'll have no respect for the law."

"Well, Garland, let's you and me get this straight. This is what we're gonna do, and you damn well better believe it's a good idea. Furthermore, when the kids come by, I expect you to act like you like nothing better than showing them your office. Speakin' of your office, I want it neat and clean when they come by. I'm gonna talk with JT about the student visits. He'll have to OK letting them leave the school grounds for a town hall and police department tour. He'll more than likely want them to visit a grade at a time. I'll see you later and let you know when JT says they can come. We'll talk more at that time about your future as chief here."

Garland sat and seethed while Coker went out the door. His Honorable, as he wanted to be called, ran a seed and feed store; he thought that gave him the experience to run the town. "Well, by God, Garland Webb runs this town, and with the help of my buddy JT, no smart ass seed salesman's gonna stay in my face for long."

As soon as Coker cleared the door Garland was on the phone. "Hey, JT, Mayor Smart Stuff is on the way to your office. He has some half-a-loaf scheme to let the school kids come by the police station and learn bout respect for the law. He came in while I was squeezin' down on Sonny boy, and Sonny was lookin like an elephant with an earache. Soon as he leaves, I need to talk with you. Call me."

"OK, I'll put shoe prints on that idea. Don't worry about it."

Half the town folks were at the clay pit watching the federal guys look for clues. This was the nearest thing to excitement they'd had since Melvin Purvis shot the famous mobster, John Dillinger. Even though that happened in Chicago, Melvin was their very own boy. Born and bred right here in the middle of Timmonsville.

"Hey folks, there's not gonna be anything exciting here. Why don't you go on back home and we'll let you know what we find? If you do stay around, you'll have to back up to those markers over there."

The folks shuffled back a few steps, but nobody moved to leave. This was just like the movies. The real G-men were right in town, they all had those official badges, and every one of them knew their boy, Melvin.

The guy doing the talking was dressed in a suit and tie and the folks got a kick out of that. "That fool's in tropical heat, walking around a hot sandpit, and he's dressed like he's ready to head out for Sunday school. Heck," the crowd was thinking, "He's as crazy as our school superintendent." The man got a beep on some kind of little radio he had in his hand, and he walked over to the back part of the lot.

There had been four major hijackings within twenty miles of this spot, and each one of them had connections to Antonio's Longhauler's Union. There were a lot of suspicions about Antonio but so far, there was nothing concrete that he could be charged with. If they took him in, he would holler for his lawyer and next thing you know he's home. They had to find enough evidence to make something stick. They knew he had accomplices in the area, but they had not been able to get more than just speculation. One thing for sure, the FBI didn't let Garland Webb know anything about what they were doing. He had to find out just like the other town citizens. Often when the FBI worked a case they involved the town law enforcement; not so with Garland. The agents didn't trust Garland at all, and most thought he had something to do with the hijackings. In fact, they hoped so, because each agent wanted to be the one to flash the badge, handcuff him, and stuff him into the back of a squad car. Just his looks gave law enforcement a bad name.

Nobody, and certainly not Garland, knew why they were looking for evidence at the sandpit. How did they know that's where the transfer went down? Soon a group of the agents that were digging started pointing, and one yelled out, "We found something that looks like blood over here, Sir, and several sets of footprints right beside it. This may be the place the driver fell after he got cracked in the head."

"Get some pictures of it and check and see what blood type it is. I bet it matches our boy. This is not where he said he was hijacked, so if it is the place, what was he doing here? This could be just what we need to put more pressure on that driver. If we can link this to Antonio and his mob, we'll have some good size fish.

"Inform all the agents that no one is to give out any kind of information without my OK. Some of the folks that are watching us hang around the AMVETS Club. Tell them to also be especially careful at the hot dog stand down the road. Some of those regulars in there have asked a lot of questions, and some of them have ties to Gus and his AMVETS club."

"Yes Sir."

Garland was in the jail bathroom sneaking a drink of Seagram's VO when the phone rang. He put the cap in his pocket, held the bottle in his hand, and ran up front to answer the phone. "Garland, your best buddy, Coker, just left here with his dull-blade scheme to get him some PR from the parents. He thinks if I let the kids out of school to come by his office and visit the jail it'll help him get re-elected. Course he didn't say that, he tries to make it sound like he wants to make the kids learn more about the law and politics. I told him that an event such as that had to be planned in advance and this year we would not be able to let the kids participate. I had a little fun with him though and we put it into a schedule for next year. He looked like a little puppy chasing a mama skunk and couldn't figure out whether or not to catch her."

"Thanks, JT. If that SOB had got that to lord over me he and I might have had to tangle. I can't wait 'til we get a few more loads, so I can get the hell out of here."

"That may take a while, Garland. You know Antonio has to be very careful with those fedies on his case. So you just give that dear old mayor friend a fresh, smiling face, and we'll get his butt one of these days. In fact, I've got a plan to get Woody McKay to run against him. With my support, and indirectly that of Senator Furman, we can't lose."

"I can't wait."

Garland laid the phone down and took a leisurely swallow of his "nerve" medicine. As he started toward the bathroom to put the bottle back in his secret hiding place, the door opened, and in walked Emily Coker, the mayor's wife.

"Garland, have you seen Linwood? He told me he was going to stop by here today. What are you doing with that bottle? Are you drinking?"

"Of course not. This is evidence. I found it in one of the cells, and I'm sendin' it to the sheriff's department for fingerprints. I'm gonna find out who brought it here, 'cause I search all of the prisoners when they come in. Somebody had to slip it in between the bars."

"Well, Garland, if you're going to get it fingerprinted why are you holding it in your hand? You should be holding it gently with a towel? You're supposed to be a police chief, and I've learned more about maintaining evidence from watchin' Humphrey Bogart movies than you have by being in law enforcement."

"Well, it would seem that way, but I wanted to make

sure that I didn't drop it and ruin the evidence completely. I was just holding on to a small corner of it, and besides, it may not even be whiskey. I'm gonna have the lab check it for the contents when they run the prints."

"Garland, I sure hope you don't drink the evidence. Anyway, Linwood'll want to know exactly where it came from, and what progress you make in finding the person who brought it to the jail."

"I'll find 'em all right."

"If you see Linwood, tell him I need to talk with him. His clerk down at the store has just gotten a draft notice and must report to Fort Jackson in Columbia next week for a physical. Linwood'll need to find someone to mind the store while he's on town business."

"I'll tell him if I see him, Miz Coker, but when he left here he was going over to see JT at the school administration buildin'. He may still be there now."

"Garland, please don't handle that bottle anymore, and call Linwood as soon as you get the lab results."

"I'll do it."

Gus and Dalton had Lacy bring sandwiches to the storeroom in the rear of the club. When she left, Gus closed the door and they dug into the food. Watching Dalton eat was not a pretty sight. His hands were grimy, and he made slurping noises when he stuffed the double-thick cheeseburger into his big mouth. He had a piece of lettuce stuck on his chin and there was so much catsup smeared on his face he looked like he had been in a fight with a vampire and lost. Fortunately, that didn't bother Gus. Gus was raised on the docks of Newark, New Jersey, and he was used to strong, grubby guys like Dalton.

Gus was a little more refined in his eating habits than Dalton, but he constantly talked with his mouth full. When he got excited, he was subject to blowing food across the table. Dalton wouldn't have cared, even if he noticed.

"Dalton, those damn G-men are becomin' a nuisance. A lot of people that I don't know have been comin' into the club lately for a drink. They have AMVETS cards from other towns, but I feel like they're more of those snoopy cops like the last one you caught pokin' round. I saw one of 'em park in the very back part of the parkin' lot, even though it was early and there were almost no cars here. He was soakin' up land in the back, like he was lookin for any fresh diggings there. I know you covered it good, but if they get a warrant they could dig up the back and find their boy."

"Well, they gonna hafta dig a lot. I used the backhoe, then I got a truckload of leaves and pine straw from another part of the lot. I mixed that in with the top layers of dirt so it would look like it hadn't been disturbed."

"I hope so Dalton, because I don't like all these strangers nosin' roun. If they ask too many questions somebody might give the wrong answer. I don't think we have to worry 'bout JT; he'd be a tough nut for 'em to crack. Plus, with his daddy-in-law, Furman, the feds don't wanna mess with him. I worry bout Garland though. His marbles are a little flat, and I don't think he could roll out of the way if they got to pushin' on him real tough like."

"Yeah, Gus, I agree. That ranger hat he wears don't cover much that's useful. What about Cecil, how would he handle pressure?"

"Well, I've wondered that. He's a little smarter than Garland, but I don't know how much pressure he could take if they got one on one with him. Just keep your lid covers up, and tell Lacy to be particular what she says. I don't think we have to worry 'bout her as long as she don't try too hard to help." Lacy rang the buzzer in the back so Gus would know to look through the glass window that covers the front area. From out front the window looked like a picture of Babe Ruth standing at home plate waiting for a pitch. From the back, though, Gus could see who was in the club and get some idea of why they might be there. The reason for Lacy buzzing this time was obvious; a stranger was sipping on a beer trying too hard to look casual. He was moving his eyes all over the area taking everything in. Gus and Garland agreed he didn't look like he belonged in an AMVETs club. After the stranger drank his beer and left, Gus and Garland walked out and asked Lacy what she could tell them about the guy. "He don't *b'long* here. There's somethin fishy bout him. I think he's a cop."

"What was his name on the card?"

"Ed Thomas. I got suspicious as soon as I saw it was a Winston Salem card. I made special pains to remember it, because I knew he didn't look right when I saw him drive up. He was dressed in old clothes but his hands didn't have no work trails on 'em. Also, the Dodge farm truck he was driving didn't fit right with him."

"Well, I'll get Antonio to check him out at the Winston club."

Gus left Garland at the club and drove over to Florence to see his attorney, George Malini. George was trying to work out a settlement with Gus's wife, Gladys. She had filed for divorce and was kicking up a ruckus. Gus had never told her any of his business directly, but she had been to the club and she knew that the slots were paying off. She also knew where he got his non-taxed liquor.

George's office was in a well-kept Charleston type house that once had been his uncle's family home. Gus walked into the lobby, George came down to meet him and they walked up the stairs together. Like lawyers do, George knew Gus had done some shady deals, but he didn't know how shady. Anyway, that's what attorneys are for, to help people. Of course it entered his mind in quiet moments, that by helping Gus he was sharing in a lot of misery to other people. He had plans to confront Gus and let him know he didn't want to represent him in any way that was unlawful.

"Gus, that wife of yours has gone off the deep end. She called here today and demanded a huge sum of money, but she wouldn't say how much. She just said, 'If it's enough, I'll shut up, if not, you'll read what I have to say in the Florence Morning News and the Columbia Record. I'll holler loud enough to get attention; you can bet on that.' She demanded that I call her back tomorrow."

"George, you've got to get to her and find out what she'll take to blow away. I'm making pretty good at the club and if I have to pay her to shut up I'll just have to do it. You've got to figure some way though, that she'll have to stick to the agreement if she makes it. You lawyers are supposed to have all the answers."

"I'll work on it tomorrow, Gus, and I've got some ideas, but you know I don't get involved in anything illegal."

On the way back, just a short distance from the club, Gus saw a telephone lineman on a pole with a headset. "Is that a fed putting a tap on my line?" He'd worried about that for a while and now he felt the reality was there. He would have to find a phone he could use, but who could he trust that had a phone that wouldn't also be tapped?

Garland gunned his police Ford and headed to JT's office. On the way he ate sugarcoated doughnuts and the frosting crumbs dropped all over his clothing and littered the seat of his car. Now his car and clothes had a fresh mixture of sugar and Camel ashes. When he finished the last one, he threw the empty box on the floor, along with the Coke bottles and empty cigar wrappers.

JT was sitting behind his huge desk with a smile on his face when Garland walked in. JT's office was the nicest in town: he had a rug on the floor from Thailand, his desk had a highly polished finish, and the top was cleared of all paper. The walls were lined with pictures of Senator Tom Furman shaking hands with just about every person who had ever been in any kind of office in South Carolina. There were also pictures of presidential and vice presidential candidates that had come to South Carolina to court votes. In the background of each was a smiling, or at least a smirking, McGloughlin. JT offered Garland a real Cuban cigar, lit one for himself, took a big drag and blew a thick cloud of smoke.

"Garland, I've got the perfect idea for taking care of that Sims kid. You're gonna love it, but I'll have to tell you about it later. For now, I need you to plan on a fishing trip Saturday. Come by here after school is out and I'll fill you in."

THE FISHING TRIP PLOY
Chapter Two

The intercom system at Timmonsville Grammar School was little more than a bunch of static. It sounded like a squirrel convention in a pecan patch. Even though it was not a pleasant sound the teachers and students could understand it, they had listened to it enough to be able to get most of what was said. Now they heard the crackly voice of the principal, Marion Mellette: "May I have your attention please? Our distinguished superintendent, Dr. JT McGloughlin, has asked that all students and faculty report to the assembly room at once for an important announcement." Mr. Mellette, as usual, repeated the message, then headed for the assembly room.

There was a lot of apprehension from both the kids and the teachers. It was unheard of for the superintendent to call a special meeting to address the teachers and students. The assembly room was buzzing with a lot of discussion and speculation, but as soon as JT got to the podium a hush fell over the crowd.

"Students and faculty, I know that you all are happy that the summer is finally over, and you are now back to the business of school." JT's attempt at humor was met with silence but he continued. "Sometimes, you, as students, think that you are never recognized unless you either: make the Honor Roll, become a class officer, or star in the class play. Well, we're going to start an annual tradition here to dispel that notion. Starting now, and during the first month of school every year, we'll be giving an award to a student that: maybe hasn't become class president, hasn't been chosen to be in a class play, and has had to work hard to make good grades. In other words, it won't be the one who has necessarily achieved the most, but the one who has done the most with what he or she has. The one that wins this award each year will be treated to a special trip. The location of the trip might change from year to year, but this year it is a deep-sea fishing excursion on my boat in Charleston. The winning student will be honored with this day of fishing. I know you'll all want to win next year; if for no other reason than I'll be the one baiting your hook. Just think, this student who has shown extra potential will be able to brag that the superintendent of schools baited his fishhooks. It will provide the memory of a lifetime. In addition, the person that will be using the net to bring in the student's fish catch will be our own police chief, Garland Webb."

There was quite a commotion at this as the kids dreamed of having the not so loved police chief and the fearsome superintendent taking orders from them. JT allowed the students to cut up for a moment and then called the group back to order. "The award each year will be based on a number of factors. Grades, of course, will be very important, but not just the top grades. We'll look at grades that someone gets by using all they have and doing the best he or she can do. Outside jobs, school and community activities will be taken into consideration as well. The student chosen this year will have to get up early Saturday morning. We'll leave town at five a.m., and cast off as soon as we get to Charleston. I'd like now to call to the stage the winner of the new SUPERINTENDENT'S AWARD FOR MOST POTENTIAL; let's hear a lot of applause for this year's winner—Sonny Sims!"

The crowd sat in cemetery silence. For what seemed an eternity to Sonny the room was eerily quiet. All eyes were shifting toward him. Slowly, the cheering and shouting began. No one in the assembly room could comprehend why Sonny was the chosen one, but nobody but nobody argues with JT McGloughlin.

Sonny sat as still as a statue. The perspiration popped out, he felt dizzy, and he slid down in his seat. The crowd started yelling, "Get up there, Sonny, don't be shy." Those next to him started pulling on his arms to get him to go, but he was rooted down like a Cyprus tree in a windstorm.

JT bellowed out, "Looks like Sonny is a little stage struck, so instead of coming to the front now we'll have him come up after the trip. At that time, he can tell you about his experience and show off his prize catches. I know he's excited, so some of you get him some water and give him your congratulations. Next year the Superintendents award winner could be you, so work up to your potential at all times."

"FBI Assistant Director Pete Stokes" was known far and wide as Pedro. Even those closest to him didn't really know when or why that name started. Pedro also had a title that somehow just evolved. As the Assistant Director of Field Operations, Pedro made himself available to the field office supervisors whenever he was needed. If they wanted help on an investigation, he would visit the office, and pore over, or 'inspect' the contact reports and other investigative records. Even though the Bureau had no official title of Inspector, Pedro became known as Inspector Stokes. Over a period of time the informal title came into common usage. Hoover was certainly aware that agents referred to Pedro as Inspector, but he never made a comment about the title.

Pedro sipped the last of his coffee, punched the intercom

button, and asked Cornelia, everyone called her Connie, to bring him another coffee. He stared at the pictures and other information on his desk and pondered his next move. Pedro was deep in thought when Connie brought him his coffee.

"Thanks, Connie. Now I need you to get Joe Means in here right away." Connie closed the door and went across the hall to get Joe.

Pedro had been with the FBI, in his mind at least, since he was eight years old. He never even thought about any other job. His hero was Melvin Purvis, the famous G-Man who shot John Dillinger. As soon as he got out of college he applied to the Bureau; soon afterwards he was notified that he had been accepted. His appointment to the Bureau had been with the blessing of none other than that of United States Senator Tom Furman. Now he was looking at the photograph of Senator Furman's son-in law, JT McGloughlin. How was he going to handle it if further information backed up what he had now that McGloughlin was up to his beady looking eyeballs into a hijacking ring? Unfortunately, he didn't have many doubts, but as a professional investigator, he wanted all the facts before he made any judgment call.

Connie tapped on the door and entered. "Pedro, Joe Means is attending a task force meeting at city hall, but I got a message to him. He should be here within the hour."

"Thanks, Connie." Pedro stirred in his sugar and cream and stared back at the pictures.

Timmonsville was abuzz with talk of the "New tradition" that McGloughlin had started. No one disliked Sonny, and most thought he was a pretty good kid, but it was difficult to comprehend how he had been picked over some of the really obvious performers. Even though there were no brave souls that would dare question McGloughlin directly, it did cause a lot of whispers. Even the faculty was stunned that Sonny was chosen as the one with the most potential. Although none of them doubted that he had some potential, few of them had seen any of it really used. The only reason they were not more surprised, was that they had learned never to be surprised by whatever JT McGloughlin made up his mind to do.

Hannah Sims stopped by Mr. Baroody's Grocery Store on her way home from taking care of Phoebe. As always, when no customers were in the store Mr. Baroody was using his large feather brush to clear any dust from cans and boxes on the shelf. "Mr. Sam," as a lot of town people called him, took a lot of ribbing from the men in town about his constant dusting, but the women loved the way he kept the store neat and clean at all times. Hannah walked in, picked up a bag of Maxwell House coffee, and started toward the bread counter. Mr. Baroody stopped dusting and came over and put his arm on Hannah's shoulder. "Congratulations, Hannah, I know you're really proud of Sonny's selection as the one with the most potential at Timmonsville Grammar School."

"What? I've not heard anything about it. I just got back from Phoebe's in Florence. What happened?"

"Well I'm honored to be the one to tell you that your boy, Sonny, has won a new award presented by JT McGloughlin himself. I heard that it was called 'The McGloughlin Student Potential Award.' I know you've got to be one happy mama."

"Well, I'm happy alright, but I'm also stunned. Sonny's not been feeling right lately and I was afraid his schoolwork would suffer this year. Ring up this coffee, a loaf of Merita bread and a pound of hamburger, then I've got to get home and see my boy." Mrs. Sims pulled out her change purse, unfolded a wadded up dollar bill, straightened it out, dug out the correct amount of change and handed it to Mr. Sam. She grabbed her packages and hurried home.

Sonny had ridden his bike to school, but he was in a hurry to get home. He asked Francis Denham if he would take it to his house, and he would come by and pick it up later. Then he asked Mrs. Busbee to give him a ride home. "Sonny," Mrs. Busbee said as she cranked up her 1941 Mercury, "I'm so proud of you. I don't always agree with Mr. McGloughlin, but I sure do today. You're probably my favorite student, and I agree that you have an ocean of talent and potential. I can't wait to see the look on Hannah's face when you tell her. You don't mind if I stop by your house do you?"

"Actually, Mrs. Busbee, Mama's at Aunt Phoebe's house, and anyway, I feel sick. I think I've got some kind of germs. Maybe you could stop by later."

"Well, OK, but you tell your mama that I'm just as happy and proud as she is."

"Yes Ma'am, thanks for the ride."

Joe Means tapped on Connie's door and walked in. Joe was one of Connie's favorites and Joe was fond of Connie as well. It was not the kind of dangerous friendship that could develop into a relationship. First of all, that was an absolute rule of J Edgar Hoover: no employees could have any kind of personal relationship. Of course, that's not to say it wasn't done, but most didn't, because the risk was very much like kissing a crocodile. Joe and Connie just had a healthy respect for the professionalism of each other.

Connie was the perfect assistant for someone like Pedro. He was warm and friendly, but he expected the absolute most out of an employee that they had to give. She always knew where every file or memo was, and usually could show up at Pedro's desk with it before he even asked. Not only that, but she whipped the long investigative reports out of her Royal typewriter in record time. It was a Bureau joke that Connie could type a ten-page summary faster than Pedro could draw his 38 Colt Police Special.

Connie buzzed Pedro and told him Joe was there and Pedro got up and met him at the door. Joe Means had worked for Pedro for the entire time he had been with the Justice Department, and he considered him a close friend as well as his supervisor. "Well, Joe, how was the city hall task force meeting? Did Washington Metro Chief convince everyone that his department should take over the Justice department?"

"Chief Campbell is indeed a piece of work that never got finished, Pedro. He dominated the entire meeting. I was thrilled when I got your message that you needed to see me. I couldn't have stood him all day. Chief thinks that his department should be in charge of security for the Capitol Building. He's also convinced that the President would be safer if his city police were guarding the White House instead of the Secret Service. He's careful what he says about our agency though, because he's terrified of our boss, J Edgar."

"Well, if his department ever takes over providing security for the President, we won't have many people running for that office. Joe, I called you in, because I'm not sure if I can be objective on this hijacking case in South Carolina. As you know Senator Furman was responsible for my being appointed to the FBI and this case is leading more and more in the direction of his son-in-law, JT McGloughlin. Mark Hughley, the SAC in Charlotte, asked me to look over the investigative files. He's understandably uncomfortable because of the political overtones involved."

"Well, Pedro, I've seen you in the middle of some political operations before, and you were always objective and fair. I know you can handle this, but if I can help in any way, I'll be glad to do what I can."

"Thanks for saying that Joe, I guess I needed to hear someone shore up my objectivity. I would like, though, for you to go down to the Carolinas and personally debrief the agents working this case. I want you to get Mark Hughley to assemble his group for you, get their ideas on the case, and give me your assessment. You'll have to meet with them either in Columbia or Charlotte; Florence is too small to have more than one FBI agent meeting without the whole county knowing about it." Pedro buzzed Connie and in an instant she was standing by his side, steno pad in hand.

"Connie, work with Joe on travel arrangements for his trip to South Carolina and meet with Mark Hughley's agents. Joe, you and Mark can work out the best place to start, and then Connie can set the reservations. Get down there as quickly as you can."

"Right, Boss, and don't worry about this, it'll all work out. It may even turn out that the Senator's son-in-law is not involved."

"Thanks Joe. Connie can you stay a minute?" Joe left and Pedro closed the door. "Connie, I'd like you to get me all the files available on Senator Furman. Keep it on the hush, and get them to me as quickly as you can. Also, check with Bill Leake over at Senate Security, and see how many times the Senator has been to the Florence area lately. Don't talk with anyone but Captain Leake; this is a very sensitive issue. I didn't tell Joe, but there are some indications that the Senator himself may be involved in this. I felt Joe could be more objective if he doesn't know about the Senator's possible involvement until after he gets the interviews underway."

"Sir, regarding the files on Senator Furman, you know that Jerry Merrit has started a procedure in records that all file requests have to be in writing and signed by a supervisor. You want me to try without the written request?"

"Uggh, I forgot about that, Connie. No, I'll call Jerry and try and wrangle a favor out of him. This is not something that we want spread around: that we're looking at a Senator's involvement in a matter that has no formal charges. I've got a personal stake in this though and I want to do it as quietly as possible. I would rather not have to go into formalities at this time."

Jerry Merrit was a twenty-year veteran of the bureau, and was an outstanding agent. Several years earlier he was involved in a shoot-out during a bank robbery and a child nearby was killed. Even though ballistics tests proved that the bullet that killed the little girl was from the robber's gun, Jerry felt guilty for not getting the thug before he could fire. Jerry took a 38-caliber slug in the hip, but the real damage was the psychological. He had dreams many nights of the six-year-old lifeless little girl lying face down on the hot asphalt parking lot. The Director transferred him to records after that, and he has been there ever since.

Jerry was at his desk reading a case that the Supreme Court would soon be deciding. It dealt with the right of the Bureau, or any other police agency, to refuse to allow a suspect to view his criminal file. Jerry picked up the receiver on the first ring, "Criminal Records, Agent Merrit."

"Hi, Jerry, this is Pete." For some reason, Inspector Stokes did not mind others calling him Pedro, but he didn't feel comfortable using that name for himself. Pete "Pedro" Stokes had spent twenty-five years transferring from one state to another at the whim of J Edgar, but he still had that distinctive South Carolina accent. Even though he received several hundred calls each week, Jerry knew instantly which Pete was calling.

"Hey, Pedro, what's a high up like you doing calling a low life like me?" Pete and Jerry were close, and there was usually some of this type of banter when they talked.

"I just felt like I needed to be brought down to earth, Jerry, and nobody can do that better than you. Added to that, I need a favor. I need a file, but I would rather at this time not sign anything for it."

"Pedro, you know the Director himself approved the "Sign it out rule" and I can't release anything without a signature anymore."

"There's no way the Director will know, Jerry, I just want to study over it a while and get it right back to you."

"Pedro, you're one of my favorite people, but there are several that I esteem higher; my wife and daughter. If I got caught letting you have a file without having you sign for it, they would no longer have a husband and father. I'd get zipped out with no net. I'll ask permission from Tolson if you want me to, so I'm off the hook."

"That would defeat the purpose Jerry, then there would be a trail."

"Sorry Pedro but rules are rules, and we at the Bureau live by the Hoover rule: *Do unto others what Hoover tells you to do*. For an old friend like you though, I could do a little favor that isn't in writing not to do. I could let you come by my office and read the file, but even that's dangerous. I've got to have your word that you won't take any action against the individual without checking the file out first to clear me."

"Thanks, Jerry, you have my word. I'll be down in a moment."

"Who's the file on, Pedro? I'll have it ready for you."

"I'll be right down and let you know in your office."

Hannah laid the Maxwell House coffee and Merita bread on the table, threw the hamburger in the refrigerator, and hurried into Sonny's room. "Sonny, where are you? Sonny, are you here?" She ran around searching the house.

"I'm in here, Mama."

Hannah rushed back into Sonny's room. "Sonny, where are you?"

"I'm down here, Mama."

"Sonny, what are you doing under the bed? This is the happiest day of my life, and here you are hiding under the bed. What in the world is wrong with you?"

"I don't feel good. It's cooler under here."

"Well, we're going to see Dr. Holman right now, so get out from there and come on."

"I'll be all right, Mama, I just need to stay here and rest for a while."

"No! This has been going on for days, and now on this happy occasion it's still going on. We're heading to the doctor's office right now and find out what's the matter with you. Let me feel your forehead; you don't feel hot; in fact, you feel cool. Anyway, get out, and let's go."

Dr. Holman's office was above Mr. Geddings' shoe store, and as they went up the stairs Sonny lagged behind. "Sonny, if you don't get on up here I'm gonna tan your can. Now move."

Sonny not only was scared but he was physically drained. He felt like a balloon in a needle factory, but he managed to make the top step and enter the waiting room. Doc Holman's office was usually full but today there were just a few people waiting. Mrs. McKay was there with her two-year-old daughter, Molly. Mr. Ward was the only other patient there, but even those two, plus whoever was with Dr. Holman now, could take an hour at least. Sonny put two chairs together, curled up, and set in for the wait. Hannah went over to talk to Mrs. McKay and inquire about Molly.

"Molly's been listless lately, Hannah; I can't get her to eat, and she hasn't wanted to go out and play. I'm afraid she's coming down with something."

"Maybe she has whatever Sonny has, Thelma, because he's been acting the same way."

"Yeah, I hope we find out today. "Oh, Hannah, I know you're proud. When my Sally came home from school today she was as excited for Sonny as she would have been if she had won that award herself."

"Oh, I'm as proud as a six a.m. rooster, but I'm also quite worried about his sudden illness."

Dr. Holman's nurse, Nelda, came out of the examining room, and told Mrs. McKay that it would only be a few more minutes. "Doc's sewing the last stitch on Billy Truet's forehead now. Billy rode his bike under Johnny Clayton's store sign and didn't duck low enough. He'll have a headache for a while, but he'll be OK. Hey Molly, how you doing, Honey?" Molly just snuggled closer to her mother."

Nelda closed the door to the examining room and Doc Holmon had Billy sitting up. Mrs. Truet was finally coming back together from being summoned to Doc's office. Ankie Carter had pounded on her door and shouted that Billy had been injured and was at Dr. Holman's office. She had been in the middle of some serious bean shelling while she listened to Frank Sinatra sing in his one-on-one sounding manner. She was shelling and dreaming at the same time, and she got red in the face just thinking about it. She had been wishing that she could shell the coat and shirt off of Frank, like she was shelling those pole beans.

Mrs. Truet had rushed out of the house without even taking off her apron. Now that she knew Billy was going to be OK, she was embarrassed when she realized that she still had on the apron. She pulled herself together and said, "Thank you so much, Doc, this town couldn't do without you."

"Well, Mrs. Truet, I hope they never have to, because I need this town. I hope it doesn't sound egotistical, but I love being a doctor. The idea of making people well is something that I dreamed about when I was Billy's age. Now that I'm doing it, I'm afraid I'll wake up. Anyway, you make him rest until school tomorrow. If he doesn't have any fever he's free to do whatever he feels well enough to do. Of course, Johnny Clayton may be at your house tonight to complain about Billy knocking that heavy sign down with his head. If you promise me a slice of that famous blueberry pie of yours, I'll knock a dollar off the bill."

Mrs. Truet gave Doc Holman a big hug, and walked out holding Billy's hand.

Pedro dropped Joe off at Washington National Airport and Joe went straight to the loading gate. Pedro had assigned another agent to check Joe in at the ticket window so he wouldn't have to sit around and wait. Unfortunately, the weather was not being as cooperative as the Bureau was about Joe's waiting time. Once the passengers had boarded, the Captain announced that because of a thunderstorm in the area, they would have to wait a few minutes for clearance to take off. The few minutes turned into an hour. Mark had arranged the meeting so Joe could talk with the case agents as a group, so not only was Joe on hold but the Bureau personnel from Charlotte and Columbia were also waiting. Once the plane finally arrived Mark had Joe's bag sent directly to Mark's car on the edge of the flight line and he and Joe were on the way moments after the plane landed.

There was a slow drizzle as they left the Charlotte Airport. One of those rains that was heavy enough to require windshield wipers, but not heavy enough to keep them from making that squawking rubber on glass sound. Mark rolled the window down as they cruised along Trade Street and turned onto Tryon. Even though it would soon be fall, the Charlotte air was hot and humid. Joe had never lived in Charlotte, but he had spent two years in Raleigh, and many of the cases he worked there had ties to Charlotte, so he was familiar with the area.

After a short reunion with some of the agents that he hadn't seen for a while, Joe got right down to business. From the files it appeared that Jerry Hamby had the most direct firsthand information, so he set up a schedule time for the others to come back later. He got right into the sordid mess with Jerry. "Jerry, you've been following the activities of Antonio for several years now. How involved do you think he is in this hijacking?"

"Right up to the bald spot under that John Deere cap he always wears. Every truck that's gone down was either from Tony's terminal, or from Charleston where Tony's Longhauler's Union members could feed him information. We've lost four trucks, and all of them were taken somewhere on highway 76 in the Pee Dee area, or they were between Florence and Charleston. Antonio is not only a Longhauler's organizer, but he also schedules the drivers and the routes for Heavyhaul Trucking. Heavyhaul has a contract with the Navy for all of their hauling in the Southeast. To add to the intrigue, all of the drivers that have been hijacked gave pretty much the same details, and each one sounds like a memorized-in-advance story line. We've not had any luck breaking them down, but this last guy got whacked up pretty bad and his wife is feeding us some info. So far, nothing that'll get us a conviction, but I think a little more digging is going to pull it together. Speaking of digging, we've picked up rumors that the Navy CID agent, Ken Parnell, is buried behind a gambling joint in Timmonsville. The joint is owned by Antonio's pal, Gus Segars."

"Who else do you think is involved, Jerry?"

"We haven't been able to make it firm, but all of us are certain that Garland Webb, the police chief in Timmonsville, is a major player. Then, there's Gus Segars who owns the club that Ken Parnell was to visit with an out of town AMVETS card. We don't have any evidence that Ken actually made it to the club, but we've not heard from him lately and that's where our suspicions are. There's also Dalton Sellars, a low life hood that works at the club as a bouncer, and whatever else Gus tells him to do. He delivers the jukes and pinball machines for Gus's entertainment company. There's an ex-con named Cecil that doesn't seem to fit into all of the action but he's tied into at least a part of it. Then, this might be the shocker of the whole mess: we're pretty certain that the school superintendent, who is also the Sunday school superintendent at the First Baptist Church, is in the thickest part of the caper. To put that into proper prospective, you'd have to know that he's married to the daughter of Senator Tom Furman."

"How strong is your case on Furman's son-in-law, Jerry? Is there any reason to suspect that the Senator is involved?"

Dr. Holman's office was filled with all sorts of scary looking objects. Sharp knives, needles, and brown bottles of smelly medicine were on every table and counter. The alcohol smell alone was enough to make a kid throw up, but Sonny had to just sit there while Dr. Holman poked and probed. Dr. Holman looked down Sonny's throat, stuck a stick in his mouth, told him to say aah, and while the stick was in his mouth, asked, "Sonny, how long have you been feeling like this?"

Sonny sort of shrugged and tried to say, "I don't know", but the words just formed in his throat, and stuck there like a glob of peanut butter.

"Speak up, Sonny; Dr. Holman can't make you well unless you cooperate with him. Now tell him what he asked."

"I don't know, Dr. Holman, I guess about a couple of weeks."

"Well, lie down on this table, and let me check on a few things."

Sonny curled up on the table, and Doc Holman grabbed him by both ends and pulled him straight. He mashed on Sonny's back, pushed on his tummy, hit him on the knees, and listened to his heart with a stethoscope that felt like it had been in the freezer. He shined lights in Sonny's eyes and ears, put his hands in private places, and made Sonny cough.

Dr. Holman, gave Mrs. Sims a puzzled look, and said, "Hannah, I cannot find anything wrong with this boy. If he was a horse, he could run in the Kentucky Derby. His fever is below normal and his muscles seem to be very tense and tight, but otherwise he checks out good. It's probably just a touch of infection, or maybe his body is trying to adjust to growing up. Whatever it is, I think you can relax and not worry. He can do whatever he wants to do unless something changes." With that Doc patted Sonny on the shoulder and said, "Sonny, I heard about you winning that "Potential" award from Mr. McGloughlin. I'm very proud of you. Bring me back a big tuna from your fishing trip."

Sonny just humped over and didn't make eye contact or utter a sound.

Linwood Coker was not a large muscular man, but years of running a seed and feed store had kept him fit looking. Most of the feed came in one-hundred-pound bags, and plenty of times when there was a truck to be unloaded Linwood was the only one in the store. Most days he didn't really mind, and in fact, he enjoyed it. It was a way to relieve the anxieties of a busy storeowner, and the pressures of being Mayor of Timmonsville. This kind of day though, when the heat would boil a wet peanut, and the humidity was high enough to drown a flying sparrow, unloading a truckload of wheat seed was unpleasant.

The residue from the hundred pound sacks of wheat and rye seed stuck to Linwood's damp body and caused a skin irritation. Jimmy Wheeles hadn't been the best employee he'd ever had, but at least he was young, reasonably dependable, and strong enough to load seed bags on a truck and talk at the same time. Linwood remembered those days. Now, however, when he lifted a few bags of Purina Cow Chow, he was gasping for air. In spite of losing a needed helper, he was happy that Jimmy had gotten drafted. Linwood had served in the army and he felt that it helped him mature. He hoped the same would go for Jimmy. With all of the drafting going on though, he wasn't certain that he would be able to get the kind of help that he had in the old days. Back then he had able bodies like Buddy Waldrep, who not only lifted bags, but could also help with ordering stock and taking inventory. Linwood smiled at the thought that the servicemen would soon be returning and he could have his pick of able-bodied workers.

Linwood brushed the dust off, wiped sweat from his head, put a "Be back in thirty minutes" sign on the door, and walked the two blocks to city hall. He went first by his office, sat under the five-blade ceiling fan, and dried off. He contemplated what he was going to do about Garland now that he had evidence that Garland was drinking while on duty, he had perfect grounds to tell him to turn in his city Ford cruiser and get out. He could call the Florence Sheriff's Department to provide coverage until a new chief was hired. On the other hand, Garland was somehow strangely close to JT McGloughlin. If JT didn't agree with the firing, he could cause some problems with Linwood's anticipated run for the State Senate. He desperately needed JT's support. McGloughlin's support meant that he would also have Senator Furman's backing. With that backing, he was assured of winning the race and becoming a member of the State Legislature from the Pee Dee area.

Garland had one leg on his desk, the other looped over an empty Coca-Cola crate, and his head was hanging over the top edge of the chair. His overstuffed frame spilled out through the armrests and hung down toward the floor. He was semi-awake, but not far from dreamland when Linwood walked in. If Garland had fallen asleep, the lit Camel poking out of his mouth would have dropped on the mound of blubber just below his chest. Linwood wished he had waited a while to come in. At least long enough for Garland to burn off some fatty tissue.

Garland looked a little startled, and asked the mayor to have a seat. Linwood glanced at the available chair, checked out the ashes, doughnut crumbs, and spilled liquid and decided to stand. "Garland what have you learned about that whiskey bottle you found in the jail. Emily said you were going to send it to the lab."

"I haven't gotten the results back yet, Mayor."

Linwood moved over closer, stared him in the eyes, and said, "When did you send it, Garland? Which lab is analyzing it? Does the Florence Sheriff's Department have a lab?"

"Yeah, I took it over there yesterday, but it'll take several weeks to get an answer."

"Garland, I talked with Sheriff Sligh yesterday and he said they don't have a lab."

"Oh, I know that, they send it to the feds in Washington."

"Garland, I want you to look at me, and I want you to listen good. That bottle had better be in the lab, and you had better get me a report as to the contents and fingerprints. I'm trying hard not to interfere with your job, but as mayor of this town I have an obligation to make sure that this police department is run efficiently and effectively. I owe that to the citizens of this town that had confidence enough to elect me mayor. I am not pleased at this point with your performance, and I expect you to either move on to something else or develop a more professional attitude. I've tried to be as lenient as I can be, but from now on I plan to oversee your department much more in depth. I trust we have an understanding on this." With that Linwood stormed out of the building and headed back to his seed and feed store.

Garland put on his toughest facial expression and aimed it at the door. He shook his fist and yelled, "I'll show that SOB that bein' mayor of a small town don't make him big enough to mess with Garland Webb."   As much as Garland hated Linwood Coker, he loved the power of being a lawman even more. He knew if he had a tangle with Coker, the mayor had the necessary authority to fire him on the spot. Without a recommendation from town officials, finding another police job would be difficult.

Garland had once worked for the state highway patrol, and he loved that job. He had a neat uniform, a gun, a fast car, and the opportunity to catch speeders in the boondocks. He could either scare the hell out of 'em, whip up on 'em, confiscate their liquor, or all of the above; whichever he felt like doing at the time. Unfortunately for Garland he stole the wrong bottle of liquor from one of his "customers." He had pulled over a 1939 Pontiac on the Darlington highway, searched the car, and discovered a pint of Early Times bourbon. The driver, Mel McDaniel, did not make any attempt to stop Garland from taking the bottle of whiskey. Garland didn't beat up on him or give him a ticket. He just told him he was confiscating the illegal whiskey and would pour it out and let him go.

Well, Garland did pour it out, but his mouth was around the spout at the time. Turned out, that even though the whiskey was in a legal bottle, the contents were fresh from Burly Friar's still. The driver, Mel, had bought it from Burley in Sardis, drank some of it, and gotten very ill. He was on the way back to the bootleggers with one of the bottles he had bought. His intentions were to make Burley drink some of it himself. When Garland confiscated the bottle, knowing Garland's reputation, Mel was quite happy for him to take it. He would deal with the shiner another time.

Garland had told Mel, the "speeder," to "Get out of here." Once Mel was gone Garland chugalugged a large portion of the pint's contents. Several hours later a deputy sheriff found Garland in his wrecked patrol car, unconscious. When the hospital pumped out his stomach and found that he had been drinking while on duty, the head of the Highway Patrol, Doug Barden, breathed a sigh of relief. From the first day that he became head of the highway patrol, Barden had wanted to get rid of Garland. He had a festive feeling when he went to Garland's hospital room. Barden especially enjoyed the fact that one of the patients in the six-person ward had once complained about Garland roughing him up on a back road near Lamar.

"Garland, I suppose you already know what the hospital found in your stomach: moonshine corn whisky. Not only were you drinking on duty, but you also were drinking something that law officers are constantly fighting against. I'm here today to inform you, that as of right now, you are fired. Do you have anything that you wish to say to me?"

"Of course I have somethin to say. You've not even asked for my side, and you assume that I did such a thing. I stopped by Neilbert Watkins place to check out that stolen truck he reported last week, and he brought me a drink of what he told me was water. I was quite hot and thirsty and I took a huge drink before I realized that it was not water. He assured me he was sorry that he had mistakenly given me a glass of Four Roses whiskey. When he told me that it was whiskey, I made him get me some real water. It was time for me to be off duty, and I was on the way home when I blacked out."

Barden glared a while at Garland, shook his head, and left.

It took Garland two years to get back into law enforcement. Of course Garland was not really into "law enforcement" as the term is really meant to be. Garland was into enforcement of whatever Garland wanted to enforce at the time. Most Florence county citizens called it "Garlanforcement."

Once Garland heard of the opening in Timmonsville, he applied for the job. He went to the mayor and told him that he had been wrongfully fired from the highway patrol because he wouldn't let a certain politician get off without a ticket. Now, he wanted a chance to show that he could be a great chief for the Town of Timmonsville. There was a lot of discussion among the town citizens, but Garland was hired because there were no other applicants for the job. The job didn't pay much, and anyone with a little common sense and education could earn more clerking in a store. No way Garland would be a clerk though. He had to be the one in authority. In a retail store the customer is the one who is treated with respect. When Garland stopped a speeder, his "customer" had to treat him like royalty. Folks had to say "Yes Sir" and "No Sir" to him, not the other way around.

Joe Means had not formed an opinion as to whether or not Senator Furman was involved. He did know he was abnormally close to JT, and even though JT was his son-in-law, they seemed like an odd match. JT held a powerful job, but only because of Furman. Without the Senator's power, JT would have been booted out of town long ago. Even the honor of Sunday school Superintendent was bestowed upon him because of the perks he could get for the First Baptist members. Any member of the church that wanted a personalized birthday card from the Senator for a mother or father, or an anniversary card sent to one's grandparents, could be arranged through JT. He could even have cards sent from the President.

The first Baptist Missionaries might be continents away, but if they needed something that the U.S. Government could provide, all it took was a request to JT.

When Pastor Walker and his wife had a baby girl, the Senator came by the parsonage for a photo session with the parents of the newest Walker.

Pastor Walker's fondest memory is a trip to a Southern Baptist convention in Richmond, Virginia. After the conference, the Senator had a Secret Service agent pick up the Reverend in Richmond and take him to the Capitol. There, he had his picture taken with the Senator in the Capitol Rotunda, and the Senator's top aide, Jimmy Mann, treated him to a tour of the building. It was a heavy experience for Walker, and he gave some thought to leaving the ministry and going into politics. He enjoyed being a pastor, and he knew that was his calling, but there was a huge difference between his present office, the size of a walk-in closet, and the Senator's office, almost as big as his entire church.

Although Joe found nothing to directly tie Furman to any of the hijackings, the loss of a truck loaded with automatic rifles, grenades, and 45 caliber pistols was alarming. Standard procedure was for all weapons to be delivered by a military driver with armed escorts. Somehow, however, the orders for the high security transport had mysteriously disappeared. New paperwork, describing the load as routine was substituted, and the explosives were sent in the same manner as tooth paste and shoe polish. Joe noted that Senator Furman served on numerous Armed Services Committees that gave him access to purchase orders and delivery schedules for military weapons.

Joe had concluded that JT, Gus, Dalton, and Garland were involved with Antonio, and there was little doubt that Cecil Gaskins was involved as well. Cecil stayed in the background because he had done time in a federal prison for running moonshine whiskey in Spartanburg, and the gang knew that they should not be seen with him. Joe's problem was to come up with the evidence needed to put those away that were involved. He had to build a case that, even if the Senator were involved, would be airtight. Joe liked the idea of being on a case with the potential of snaring a powerful U. S. Senator. Working for Pedro was great, and he would share his last fig newton with him, but this could lead to getting the title of Assistant Director, Joe Means. "Boy, does that have a nice ring." Being an Assistant Director was the goal of every agent in the Bureau.

When the bell rang for recess, Miss Garner asked Sonny to stay. She stood by his desk, and looked at him a moment. "Sonny, ever since you won the award for having the most potential, you have slacked back on your studies, and you never participate in class. What in the world is wrong? You should be proud, and you should be applying yourself even more. What's going on? Is there something that I can help with?" Miss Garner wanted to say more, but she could tell nothing was reaching Sonny. He just sat there at his desk with a vacant look on his face.

"I'm just not feeling well, Miss Garner." Sonny slid down in his desk as far as he could and tried not to make eye contact with Miss Garner. She was exasperated, but decided to drop it for now and see if things cleared up soon. Maybe after his trip.

Just across the schoolyard, Garland was stretched out in an oversized, spring-back rocking chair in JT's plush office. He poured himself several fingers of imported Russian Vodka. With the size of Garland's fingers, that was pretty much a full glass. Garland enjoyed lying back in the regal office with all the celebrity pictures. JT had excused himself, and gone into another room to consult with Sam Hensley, the high school principal, about the behavior of one of Mr. Hensley's students.

Garland imagined one day that he would have this kind of office instead of the one with an ancient roll-top desk, a raggedy chair, and a coke crate for a table. Once he got his split for a few more hauls he could take his take and head for a new territory. He would leave his past record with the highway patrol in South Carolina and get a job with a real police agency, maybe New Orleans or Memphis.

JT came back in and closed the door. He too, poured himself a few fingers of vodka, but his few fingers made a small drink. "Garland, what have you heard about what the feds have found out at the sand pit? They're nosing around awfully hard, and I don't like all the attention they're giving this. Heck, in Newark and New York, they have this kind of stuff every day and the feds ignore it. Why are they giving it so much attention here?"

"JT, I've not been able to find out anything. I have a close contact on the Florence Sheriff's Department, but he hadn't been able to tell me much. The feds are bypassin' all the locals and workin' directly on it themselves. They're thinkin' they can come down here to the Pee Dee and find a bunch of dumb hicks that they can bust. They'll get frustrated after a while when they realize that we ain't the hillbillies they think we are. Just as long as no one gets hassled into talkin, we'll be OK. Problem is they're bad about offerin' one person a deal to get another one to squeal."

"Garland, do you think we've got anyone that would squeal on us?"

"Well, I worry about Cecil a lot. He done time in that federal prison in Atlanta several years ago. He swore he'd never go back. He said that pen was a livin' hell, and he would do whatever it takes not to go back. I just hope that 'whatever it takes' won't be talkin to the feds. Dalton wouldn't flinch about doin some time. He'd probably even run the place before he got out. He don't take orders from no one 'cept Gus. If those guards tried to push him, he'd take some of 'em out. Gus of course is no problem. He's got connections with the right people, and he could head up to the northern states, change his name, and have a new setup in no time. Besides, Gus being in that New York mob, he's got protection. They take some kind of oath, and once you get in, everybody stands up for each other. Somethin like we got here with them Masons and Shriners. If Gus got into a federal prison, there's enough of those guys to take care of him, so they wouldn't get nothing from him."

JT swirled his vodka around in the glass and stared at the clear liquid. "I hope they let it blow over soon and get back to hassling bank robbers. Anyway, Garland, we've got to be very careful. Some of the town folks would like to see you and me on the backside of the bars. Let me know if you pick up anything from your county deputy friend."

"I'll let you know what I find out JT, but for now nobody local don't know nothin. Anyway, I'll call you after a while."

Garland pulled the door open and looked back at JT, "By the way, JT, have you got ever thing ready for Saturday? I can't wait to see if that little pipstart knows anything. If he does, I'm gonna enjoy watchin' that big fish pull him overboard. I pity the poor sharks that eat his puny little butt, but they might consider him a good meal."

JT nodded his head and picked up the phone.

"Sonny, I'm almost ready to go take care of Phoebe, would you like me to drop you off at school? We can talk a few minutes on the way." Hannah was having second thoughts about going to Phoebes, but even if she didn't go, she knew of nothing she could do for Sonny anyway.

"No, Mama, I'm gonna walk today, I think it'll make me feel better."

"Come over here and let me see if you have a fever. I don't know what we're gonna do with you if you don't get over whatever it is you've got. You're going on that deep sea fishing trip Saturday morning and you don't even seem excited about it. Every kid in your class would love to have won that trip."

"I don't even want to go, Mama. I wish they would give it to someone else. I don't like JT, and I don't like Garland Webb, and there won't be anybody else there to talk with. I wish somebody else had won."

"Sonny, I can't believe you're saying that. You've earned this trip by having potential, and you should be proud that you were chosen. Now get ready for school and brighten up. You're gonna end up loving this trip, and you'll learn a lot from it."

"I might get seasick. I don't even like the idea of being out in the ocean, especially with two people I don't like."

"You know you shouldn't talk like that about adults, and especially those that are in authority.

George Malini slammed down the phone and used some words that his secretary, Susan Thomas, didn't like. George was usually pretty much of a gentleman and Susan loved working for him, but she despised his obscene outbursts. When he got off the phone with a client that was unwilling to compromise, George changed into a monster. Susan's desk was by the front door, and George's office was up a flight of stairs, but George's voice boomed all over the building. Susan suspected that even the Wingard and Evans Certified Public Accounting office next door was listening.

Susan marched up the stairs, got right in front of George's desk, and as she had done many times before, said "George, I have asked you over and over again, not to use that kind of devil's language. You are too wonderful a person to use those words. Please, I am begging you again to control that ugly temper tantrum, and be the gentleman that you are all of the other times."

"Oh, shoot, Susan, I'm terribly sorry. I know this offends you, but it's the only way I can vent my frustration after talking with a complete idiot like Gladys Segars. She wants to take everything Gus has and I just can't let her do that. She's due a fair settlement but she won't listen to any kind of reason. She keeps saying what we're offering is not enough, but she won't give a clue as to what she wants. Gus is trying to be fair with her and get it over with."

"Well, George, you know I don't interfere with your law business, but instead of trying to settle this issue with money, they should find a good pastor and keep the marriage together—Oh, I'm sorry, George, I know that isn't something you can control."

"No, Susan, but how I wish I could. Call Gus for me, and see if he can meet me at Jimbo's for lunch. Tell him it's bordering on urgent. And, Susan, I couldn't keep this practice going without you, so I'll eat a bar of Ivory soap for dessert today."

Sonny, Tommy, and Brian had been in the dark closet for over an hour but still could barely see the outline of one another. Even though Mrs. Buddin was at work, they were talking in low whispers. Tommy and Brian's mother, Marylou, worked long hours at the Telephone Company. She hated to spend so much time away from the boys, but she felt it was her patriotic duty to help families keep in touch with their servicemen sons, husbands, and fathers. She regretted that she could never patch a call through to Thomas. "Thomas?" Gosh, it had been so long since she had seen him, or even talked with him, the name seemed strange. Tommy and Brian missed their dad, but after a four-year absence, they learned to adjust. Now, though, the boys were acting strangely. She was angry with the military for taking her husband, and the father of her two sons, away for such a long time.

Thomas had enlisted in the army the day after Pearl Harbor. Except for one short stopover from Fort Hood, Texas, on the way to where ever he was now, they had not seen him, nor heard his voice. His letters were short and seldom, and even then, he was not allowed to discuss any details of where he was or what he was doing. He had trained to be a belly gunner on a B-29 and Marylou assumed that's what he was doing. Other than that she just knew he was somewhere in the Pacific. "The war has virtually ended, and other husbands and fathers are coming home. Why not

76

Thomas?"

"Tommy, I'm scared. If I go on that fishing trip Saturday with Garland and JT, I know they plan to kill me, but Mama won't even listen when I say I don't wanna go. What am I gonna do?" Even as dark as it was in the closet, Tommy and Sonny imagined they could see Brian's eyes popping out of his face when they talked about being killed. As long as they all three could remember they had enjoyed hiding in the dark closet, telling ghost stories, and teasing Brian about vampires and dragons. Now that it was real it wasn't fun anymore.

Tommy was usually sure of everything, so for him to say "I'm scared too" was terrifying. "If they throw you off that boat, they still don't know if we know about all of this or not, so then they'll come after us." Brian gave a sound like he was going to upchuck, but Tommy slapped him and said, "Shut up, or I'm putting a Band-Aid on your lip. Sonny, I'm scared they might have plans to torture you until you tell them that we were there at the warehouse too." Brian was chewing on his arm and moaning, and Tommy was so close to panic he just let Brian sob his heart out.

THE WIRETAP
Chapter Three

Joe Means and Jerry Hamby looked like army commandos. They were wearing camouflage fatigues, and each one had his shiny, 38 Colt Police Special tucked under his shirt. Each had on high-top hunting boots with a dull finish, as opposed to the spit-polished, conventional lace up shoes required by the Bureau. Jerry had on a small backpack filled with a variety of items that Jerry and Joe thought might either help them gain entry, or cover any tracks of the break-in.

Timmonsville at two a.m. was a pretty quiet place and tonight was no exception. As they drove by the Pepo 85 gas station the usual crowd was packed inside. The teen boys gathered around after dates to brag of conquests mostly imagined. After hashing out the details of how they did what to whom and how many times, the talk turned to top car speed and astounding gas mileage. Hardly ever was there a topic that didn't involve fast cars or faster women.

"Joe, what do you think of the information Mark picked up about Gus borrowing the "Junk yard-dogs" from Jimmy's Auto Salvage Yard?"

"I don't know, Jerry, but Mark's sources are usually pretty reliable. If so, we're gonna have a challenge getting in. I know that Gus and Garland are worried about the club being raided but I'm not sure if they have a suspicion that we might enter during the night. Anyway, we have to be ready for that, or any other booby trap that those two might have set up."

Jerry drove down a wooded lane that led to a place the

locals called the Millpond. It was used as a swimming area for those brave enough to ignore the leeches and water moccasins that were in the swampy stream. It hadn't rained in a while and the swamp had a vinegary smell, much like the salty brine odor of a pickle factory.

As they crossed the narrow wooden bridge Joe saw a car backed into a cleared area. His mind drifted back to his days of parking by the Wateree River off Highway 21. He didn't give much thought to the danger of parking in a deserted place back then, but years of taking fingerprints off of rape and murder victims had made him realize how lucky he was to have lived through those times. He hoped the occupants in the car they had passed would be as fortunate. Joe recalled an investigation of a serial rape-murder case on the swampy backwoods of Fort Benning, Georgia, when he was still a rookie agent. Although that had been many years ago, he still got the shudders as he recalled the sight and smell of the decomposing bodies.

Jerry was driving a 1937 Dodge pickup truck borrowed from his uncle. It was not the kind of vehicle that would look unusual in the woods and certainly it would not look like Government Issue wheels. He turned into a grassy lane that wasn't made for driving. It was bumpy and he had to ease along in low gear. He twisted and turned around pine trees big enough to hide a pregnant elephant.

"As soon as I find a place wide enough to turn around so we're headed out, we'll be an easy walk to the back of the club. That is, if a mile through a briar patch is an easy walk." It was four miles to town, and Joe hoped Jerry didn't get the truck wedged between two trees as he maneuvered around from low to reverse.

Joe pulled the canvas bag off the floor and checked to make sure the small phone bugs were still there. "I hope these things work, Jerry. They've never been used in a small town phone company but they've worked out well on the big city phones."

"I think they'll work, Joe, but I can't wait to get them in and find out for sure." They eased out of the truck and closed the doors as silently as possible. "Let's just stand here a moment and let our eyes adjust to the dark. I flew low over here yesterday with M.B Huggins and there's nothing but viney woods between here and there."

MB Huggins owned the local airport, and although it wasn't supposed to be known, most did know that MB worked on a contract for various federal law enforcement agencies. In addition to his work for the FBI, he scouted out moonshine stills from the air and then plotted the area on a map for the Alcohol and Tobacco Agency. MB had a knack for spotting the little puffs of smoke coming from a still, and many a shiner had been surprised that his backwoods operation had been found by the "Revernurs." MB was also a crop duster and it was a common sight to see his Stearman biplane flying several feet over a cotton field spewing out a steady stream of foul-smelling chemical powder.

"Yeah, Jerry, I'm glad I didn't go with you yesterday. I've flown with MB before, and he might be, and probably is, the best pilot on earth, but I like my pilot to stay in the sky. He has no fear at all of brushing the tops of trees to get a good view of what he's looking for."

"That's for sure. I probably was more terrified yesterday flying over this area with MB than I am now. That fool flies in between pine trees that I couldn't get that Dodge truck between."

Jerry flicked on his small flashlight and looked at his compass. Using maps and drawings, MB had plotted out a course for them to follow. They were to head almost due east. If they got a little off track, they would at least run into the road in front of the club and they could find the club from there. Getting his bearing was a little trickier than Jerry had expected but he had memorized all the details, and he edged along with Joe right behind. Thank goodness the clouds were not too thick so they had at least a pale light. Getting back to the truck would be even more of a challenge. If they missed the truck they would come out on the road that ran by the millpond. Finding the little clearing where the truck was parked could be difficult, so both knew that if they got lost they would have to hide out until daylight.

"God, Joe, I hope these genuine deer hunter snake boots are tough enough to work with leg size rattlesnakes." He was trying to lighten things up, but to Joe, the mention of giant snakes was not a pleasant subject. He was trying to concentrate on the giant briars that left marks all over his body. Each time a briar snagged him he just knew it was diamondback fangs.

"If the rattlers are as huge as I've been told they are what good would the snake boots do? They're probably big enough to reach up and bite my neck like a vampire." Joe was questioning his judgment about being on this caper. As the assessment agent on the case, he had no obligation to get involved in putting bugs in a building in the middle of the night. It sounded exciting when he first told Jerry he would go with him. Now, though, he found that three years in the home office in Washington had made him too soft for this kind of assignment. But, here he was, and he had to see it through.

"Stay still, Joe!" Joe froze, and stood still for what seemed an eternity.

Finally, he was able to talk and whispered, "What's wrong?"

"Joe, I don't want to sound panicky, but I think that noise I hear just a few yards left of us is something we want to avoid."

"You mean like a rattling sound?"

"Yep, Don't you hear it?"

"I was hoping it was my teeth clicking."

"Could be a cricket, Joe, but let's move over slowly to the right, OK?"

"My mind's already over there, Jerry. I'm just waiting for the flesh to follow."

Jerry stopped again, listened, and thanked God that the sound was now farther away.

"I think we're right behind the building now, Joe. That glow ahead is the club's Pabst Blue Ribbon beer clock."

Sonny clutched the envelope tightly in his hand. He ached all over to open it, reread the letter, and look at the pictures again. He didn't dare cut on a light though, because he had a panic attack when he thought someone might be outside looking in. At least in the dark he would have the upper hand if anyone broke in. Sonny's Mama, and sister, Jackie, were far away in dreamland, and he felt terribly alone. He had spent so much time either under his bed or between the bed and wall, that he didn't feel safe any place else. Not that he felt safe here, but at least he could get a feeling that he wasn't being watched. Tears tickled his face as they ran silently down to his chin, and some ran into his ears. He couldn't talk out loud but he begged silently for his daddy to come home. He had pictures of his daddy in his hand, along with a letter describing the army base he was on.

Sonny's daddy, John Sims, or Jack, as almost everyone called him, was not accepted in the army because of health problems. Sonny thought it was flat feet and a bad knee. His legs would swell when he walked. John Sims was a patriotic man and he wanted very badly to enlist in the army but he kept getting turned down. He went to Senator Furman, but even he, with all of his power, couldn't get John Sims into the army. But, as everyone knew, Tom Furman never took "no" for an answer. He told his aide, Tommy Mann, "Find a place for John Sims to use his talents in the transportation part of the military."

Sonny answered the phone the day the call came in. "Let me speak with your daddy, this is Senator Tom Furman."

"Daddy, Senator Furman is on the phone," Sonny had hollered to his dad. Little did Sonny know at the time that this call would take his daddy away for a long time.

"Hello, Tom, nice to hear from you."

"Jack, you'll be getting a letter from my office in the next few days about this, but I wanted to be the one to let you know. Your talents are too valuable to be wasted, even if you do have some ailments that keep you out of the military forces. The letter will explain in some detail what you'll be doing and where you'll report. You'll be heading up a team that will be responsible for getting some very important and extremely top secret equipment to our troops in the Pacific. You can go ahead and start making arrangements to leave; your train ticket will be in with the letter."

Sonny recalled how happy his dad was that he was finally going to be serving the cause of his country. Sonny had been happy for his Dad then, but now he surely needed his dad more than Uncle Sam did. After all a son is a closer relative than an uncle.

"How's it coming up there Jerry? You having any luck?"

"It's coming, but it's taking a lot of scraping." Jerry was on the AMVETS building trying to remove a skylight and Joe was standing watch on the ground. They had been there thirty minutes already, and still had not been able to penetrate the fortress-like building.

"You need me to come up and help?"

"There's a large chimney up here that blocks the view, and you can't see very well except in one direction. One of us needs to be on the ground watching, but if you don't mind, I'll trade places with you for a few minutes. My arms are so tired I can't scrape anymore."

"Sure, just standing here is getting spooky, maybe scraping a while is what I need."

"That's good, Joe, but how about coming up first so I can show you the side that I've already got worked a loose."

Joe had a little difficulty swinging from the large sycamore limb to the edge of the building. On his third attempt, he said, "Jerry, don't ever take a transfer to Washington and then go out on an assignment like this. Three years of working a telephone and pencil don't keep you in shape for climbing trees." Joe inched farther out on the limb, swung over, and Jerry grabbed his hand. He wondered how he was going to get down when that time came, but for now he went to scraping.

Jerry discovered he could sit on a limb in the huge sycamore tree and still see any cars coming. "if a car drives up we've got to get down and around back in a hurry while the engine is still running. Otherwise, we'll have to lay still up here until they leave. If they don't leave until the sun comes up, that tar on the roof will cook us. Get over here quickly if I holler."

"All right, Jerry, I think I've got this skylight loose enough for us to slide it off."

Jerry scrambled over from the tree like he was kin to Tarzan. "Now we're at the tricky part, if we get inside and someone drives up we'll have to get out fast. According to Mark this skylight is right above the kitchen and we should be only nine feet from the floor. I've already tied our rope to the chimney. You wanna go first or me? Either way we need to move, we've been almost an hour already and we haven't even touched the phones."

"I'll go." With that Joe gave the rope a tug and started shinnying slowly toward whatever he would land on.

"How's it going, Joe? You touched bottom yet?"

"I've got my foot on something but it doesn't feel solid." Just as he said that there was a cracking noise that sounded like a wakeup call from Gabriel. Joe shouted, "I've got my foot caught in something. Shine your light down here?" Joe hung on the rope with his foot attached to something—maybe a booby trap—while Jerry shined the light.

"Can you tell what it is? From up here it looks like some type of wooden box around your foot, can you shake it off?"

"I'm trying to push it off with my other foot, hold up for a minute." Joe kicked the box off of his foot and planted both feet on the solid concrete floor. "I'm loose, it was an orange crate that I guess just happened to be sitting there. Come on down."

With that Jerry slithered down the rope. There were no windows in the kitchen so Joe cut on a light in a storage room.

"Thank God. I don't hear any German Shepherds growling at us."

"Yeah, I'm happy about that too, but we have to get these phones wired and haul ourselves out of here. If we get caught, we won't get the pleasure of listening to these dipsticks plan their hijacking ventures."

"Joe, I'm gonna look around for the phones, how about you listening for any activity outside. They won't take long to wire but then we've gotta get back up the rope and replace the skylight."

Jerry was rewiring the last phone in the club, while Joe looked around. He made mental notes about what was there and where it was located so they could plan another trip soon and dig into the files. Knowing the layout of the place would enable the team to get in and out more quickly. "I think these are going to work, but I can't figure out why the taps the guys put on the pole down the road didn't work. What do you think?"

"I don't know, Jerry. The Bureau has a lot of experience with taps but most of it has been in large cities with a different type of phone system. We're sort of baking new bread here."

The club was located about 100 yards off a dirt road. It led to some farmhouses, and was also a short cut for many to the town of Olanta. Each time Joe heard a car on the dirt road he and Jerry had to get ready to hit the roof in a hurry. He would watch the car until it passed the driveway to the club and Jerry would get on the boxes they had put under the hole in the roof. "If we have to get out in a hurry and leave the rope hanging with the skylight off, it'll look like a robbery. They probably won't suspect us but then they'll increase security for the building, and the "junkyard-dog" rumor will come true. I hope and pray we can get out without anyone being the wiser about us being here."

"Joe, do you really think they would believe there was anybody in this town with enough guts to rob a place owned by Gus Segars, and watched over by Dalton Sellers?"

"Probably not, so hopefully, all of those cars on the dirt road will keep heading away from here. Where in the heck are all those people going at four a.m. anyway?"

"I don't know, but if any of them ever come to this place

and eat they have some tough tummies. If the fools that visit this club would ever look in this kitchen, they'd never eat any food here. It smells rotten, and some of it probably really is. They've got stuff sitting on counters that ought to be in the refrigerator. Every time I move my light in a dark place, I see roaches scatter and rats glaring at me."

"Yeah, I'll be glad to get out of this foul place. I'd rather deal with the rattlers on the way back to the truck, than stay here much longer. How you coming with that wire?"

"This one is being a little difficult; I can't seem to get it to make a connection. Go take a look out the windows, and if all is clear, I need you to hold one end of this wire until I can get them twisted together."

Joe checked the outside and all was quiet. "I had planned on you and me heading over to Jimbo's when we got back to the truck, but after an hour in this smelly place I may not be able to eat for a while."

"Hey, I've got an idea, after we get everything wired, we'll cook us up a nice breakfast right here in the kitchen."

"Jerry, there's a time for laughter; this ain't it. Hurry up."

They finished all the wiring, checked around to be sure that everything was like they found it, and crawled up the rope. "We've got to get that skylight resealed, or else when it rains, Gus will be suspicious. He's already spooked and if he thinks someone's been in here he'll start checking his phones."

"I agree, but I don't think this tube of caulk is going to be enough to give a perfect seal. The good part though is, it's the same color as the old, and if it does leak and they come up and look, they probably won't notice that it's ever been removed. I've cleaned up all of the old pieces that we took out, and in a building this age, I think they'll suspect that the seal just wore out. Anyway, it's the best we can do for now.

That is, unless you wanna go get another tube of caulk and come back."

"No thanks."

"You wanna go out on the limb first, or you want me to go first?"

"You go ahead, you're in a little better shape than I am and I'd rather have you down there to catch me if I fall."

OK, I'm down, come on."

"I am coming, but this limb is swinging more than I remember when we came up."

"I hate to tell you this while you're swinging on a limb, Joe, but I believe I heard a car turn into the driveway of this club"

"Is there a level spot under me? I'm gonna drop on down."

"Yeah, just come straight down. Your feet are only about four feet off of the ground."

He hit the ground and Jerry helped him balance himself. Then they crouched behind the tree to see who would be at the club at five a.m.

Novelene had once worked at the AMVETS club, so she knew her way around the kitchen. She had never really liked Dalton, but once in a while she would ride home with him from her new job at Jeff's Place on the Florence Highway. Dalton would often leave the AMVETS, and head for Jeff's Place. He could usually count on finding either a good fight or a woman, and on some lucky nights maybe even both. This night he had no takers in either category, at least not until Novelene's date didn't show up.

They drove up to the club, got out, and Dalton unlocked the door. Once inside, he told Novelene "Fix us up some hamburger steak and onions; I'll mix us a drink." Novelene didn't like being ordered around by Dalton; that was the reason she left the club and went to Jeff's in the first place. But tonight she was hungry, so she didn't mind fixing his steak while he fixed her a drink.

Dalton and Novelene had no idea they were being watched. Joe and Jerry were crouched by a window on the side of the building. There were heavy bars to prevent entry, but the frame around the window was loose, so they were able to hear what was being said inside. They listened to see if Dalton saw any signs of the entry. So far he had said nothing that would indicate that he had an inkling of an idea. They hoped he would make a phone call, then when they got back to town they could find out if the taps were working. Both agents knew Dalton well enough to know that he had two things on his mind- but eating was first. They reasoned it would take at least twenty minutes for Novelene to get the steaks ready and there was a chance that Dalton would think of someone to call. They reasoned correctly. It was only a matter of minutes before they heard him say, "Fred, this is Dalton, how goes it man?"

"OK, Dalton, but it's five a.m., what's so important?"

"I got me a feelin' about the game today, I wanna put ten big ones on the Cubbies."

"That's a pretty strong feelin' alright but I gotchu down. Now I'm goin back to sleep. Why don't you do the same."

"I got me more important things to do than sleep. I'll catch you later."

"Dalton, the burger steaks are ready, fix me another one of those Mexican drinks, while I get the fries out."

Joe punched Jerry and motioned it was time to leave. They moved quietly toward the truck until they were at least a football field away, then simultaneously they both shouted, "Oh Yeah!" They were ecstatic. Not only had they gotten the taps in place without leaving any trail, but they also had a precise time that a call was made on the newly wired phones.

Can you believe this? We not only got a time for the call, but he's calling his bookie. We might be able to start a whole new case while we're working on this one."

"Yeah, we'll probably work on this one until we retire. Whew, this fresh air feels great, I think we can go to Jimbo's and top this off with bacon, eggs, and coffee. We'll ask Bea to toss in a bottle of cranberry juice to help us celebrate."

The school bell rang, and Sonny and Tommy got in line to march into class. Mr. Mellette's rule was that no one entered the building until all students were lined up by grade, starting with grade one. Once he gave the OK, Sonny and Tommy filed in and went to Miss Garners' classroom. Brian was panicky. He was two grades behind Tommy and Sonny, and although he walked to class with the other kids, he felt like he was all-alone in the world.

Miss Garner usually started her class with some discussion about a science issue that the students could get into and enjoy. Today the topic was not one that the class could relate to. They had been over it with Miss Kennedy the year before, and Miss Kennedy had smacked Shady Young with her ruler to make him shut up about this being a silly theory.

"Now, class, I know that last year you had a discussion about certain aspects of the science of sound, but today we're going into it a little farther. Specifically, I want you to understand that what we will be discussing is a theory that scientists have been able to prove. I want you all to listen carefully with an open mind, because this is a scientific fact. Sonny Sims, tell me, if you were in the woods behind Lee State Park, and a giant pine tree fell, what would you hear?"

Sonny just sat and stared. "Sonny, I have asked you a question. Answer me."

"Uhh, I'd hear a tree fall." Sonny uttered the words, but his voice was so low, no one knew what he said.

"Sonny, give your answer again. This time, I do not want to hear a sound like a newborn puppy whimpering." The class snickered, but Miss Garner gave a steely stare and all got quite.

Sonny was perspiring; he had the look of a lightning bug trapped in a Mason jar. Finally, he was able to get out the words, "I'd hear a tree fall."

Miss Garner thanked Sonny for his answer, but she also scolded him for taking so long to get it out. "Now, class, raise your hand if you can tell me what sound that pine tree would make if it fell in the woods and no one was there to hear it fall?"

Kay Baker's hand was the first to go up. She held it high, and wanted to answer. Kay was the brightest kid in the class and Miss Garner knew she would give the correct answer.

"All right, Kay, tell us what sound it would make."

"If no one was there, it wouldn't make any sound."

"Correct, Kay, now class—" Miss Garner didn't get to finish her answer. Frank Wheeles had his hand in the air but started talking before Miss Garner could acknowledge him.

"Miss Garner, if these scientists aren't there when the tree falls, how do they know it doesn't make any sound?" All of the class except Sonny cackled out.

Miss Garner walked slowly over to Frank's desk, focused her face on his, and glared. "Frank if you ever speak out in class again without my OK, I not only will give you a lecture about noise that a pine tree does, or does not make, I will give you a demonstration. I will show you a product I have that is made from a pine tree, and I can assure you, you will not like the noise it makes, nor, will you like where that noise is coming from. Never, ever, talk in class again unless I ask you to. Just because you have your hand up does not give you the right to speak. Do you understand?"

"Yes Ma'am."

"Good. Now, I'm asking you to tell us why you think you know more about science than the scientists?" The class snickered loudly. Miss Garner didn't make a sound, she just held up her hand and stared. All quickly got quiet.

"Kay, please enlighten the class about how scientists develop such factual information."

Kay started to speak, but stopped when there was a knock on the door.

Miss Garner walked over, cracked the door, and six grade student Grady Wade was standing there. "Yes, Grady?"

"Miss Garner, Mr. Mellette sent me to tell you that he wants to see Sonny Sims in his office, now."

"Thank you, Grady, tell Mr. Mellette that Sonny will be there right away."

"Yes, Ma'am."

"Sonny, Mr. Mellette wants you to report to his office right away. When you get back, I want you to tell me your theory about how scientists get their information. OK?"

"Sonny tried to get up, but his legs were like warm butter. He tried to speak, but he felt as if he was in one body, and his voice was in another. Miss Garner looked at him with a puzzled expression and waited for him to get up and leave.

Jimbo's was the place of choice for business people in Florence to have a quiet lunch. The tables were arranged so there was enough space for a private conversation. "Well, don't I get a special treat today, two of the county's best looking guys at my table." Beatrice wasn't above pouring it on thick. She had learned as a waitress for over thirty years, that if you expect tips, you have to dish out more than food. "Bea" could ladle it out with the best, and it paid off. When she emptied her pockets into her tip jar, it made a clanging sound like someone pouring railroad rocks in a tin bucket.

One only had to glance at Bea to tell that she had not had an easy life. It was apparent that she had once been a beautiful woman, but that had been several husbands, and uncounted boyfriends ago. Her first husband was still in state prison in Columbia for stabbing her with a rusty ice pick. George Malini had been the state prosecutor at the time, and Bea had come to admire him deeply for the way he fought to have Kenneth put away for life. George had showed the rusty ice pick to the jury, and asked them repeatedly how they thought it would feel to, "Have a horrible item like this jammed into your rib cage!" Bea still remembers the look of horror on the faces of the twelve jurors as George violently thrust the ice pick into a stuffed teddy bear. The jury was out only twenty minutes. They found Kenneth guilty of, "The most violent of crimes that society can imagine." Five minutes later Judge Rodney Peoples sentenced Kenneth to thirty years in the state prison.

Bea's admiration increased when Kenneth was up for parole. By then, George was in his own practice and had no obligation to be involved in the hearing. He went, though, and implored the board to, "Keep this madman behind bars for all of his natural life." He reminded the board of several arrest documents that showed Kenneth had beaten Bea unconscious with his huge fists on prior occasions. She knew she shouldn't hate Ken so much, but her heart pounded so she almost didn't hear the Parole Board Chairman rap his gavel. He was trying to get the meeting back to order after the group had voted and made their decision.

"Mr. Starnes, it is the decision of this board that your parole be denied. We have seen no evidence that you have repented your grievous action. I request the warden, here and now, to show you the same degree of mercy that you showed your wife, Beatrice, when you tried to take her life in an unspeakable manner. Guards, please remove this excuse for a human being from my sight." With that he banged the gavel, and called the meeting adjourned.

Mr. Mellette met Sonny in his outer office, and again congratulated him on winning the award. He tried to get Sonny to talk about the trip, but Sonny's face was frozen. "I hope you have a good time, Sonny, and I'm expecting you to bring back enough tuna for the whole school to have a fish fry. Mr. McGloughlin wants to see you; you are excused from class until you leave his office."

Mr. McGloughlin's office was in a separate building on the outer edge of the school grounds. Sonny had to walk about a block and his legs were shaking. He wasn't sure he was going to make it. His mind was reeling, "I'm only three blocks from my house, I could just keep going past the superintendent's building and go home."

"Hi, Sonny, what brings you this far from school?" Sonny discovered his legs weren't that jelly-like after all. He hadn't noticed Mr. Tedder until he had passed by him, and when he spoke, Sonny sprang like a kangaroo on a hot stove. "Oh, hey, Mr. Tedder, I didn't even see you." Sonny was happy to know that Mr. Tedder was fixing a broken step on the side porch right off Mr. McGloughlin's office. Mr. Tedder was a big, burly, kind person, and Sonny got a little braver with him here.

"Where you headed, Sonny? Schools not out yet. You're not cutting class are you? If so, I'll cut work, and you and I'll go slide down the chute at the ice plant."

"No sir. Mr. McGloughlin sent a message that he wanted to see me." Sonny wanted to tell Mr. Tedder why he was there and what Mr. McGloughlin had done, but he knew Mr. McGloughlin could be standing close by and listening.

THE BOTTLE IN THE BAG
Chapter Four

Wilbert McMillan was only doing about thirty miles an hour but he was craning his head down toward the floorboard as far as he could lean. He had just left Carl Poston's house after he and Carl had put a new water pump on Wilbert's 1933 International pickup. Wilbert was straining his ears to see if the knocking noise was gone. Before he and Carl put on the new pump it had sounded like two billy goats buttin' heads. He was pleased that he didn't hear the knocking anymore, but he was startled to hear a horn beeping right behind him. When Wilbert raised up and looked in his mirror he was shocked to see Garland Webb motioning for him to pull over. "Oh, My God, what have I done now? I wasn't speeding. What's Garland stopping me for? I'm only two miles from Bay Branch, so I know I'm out of the Timmonsville town limit. I spent two weeks in Garland's jail last month. I sure as heck don't wanna go back there."

Wilbert found a wide spot beside the road, eased slowly onto the grass, turned off the ignition, and felt the blood drain from his veins. He sat still for a moment to compose himself, and to thank the Lord that he hadn't had anything to drink today. Wilbert was shaky from last night's case of beer and bottle of shine, but he calmed himself enough to get out of the truck. He walked back to Garland's car and stood there. Garland motioned toward the door, and said, "Get in."

Wilbert dragged his legs to the passenger side of Garland's Ford, pulled open the door that had the hand painted lettering on it "Town of Timmonsville Police" and slowly eased through the door. Wilbert tried to sit in such a way that he didn't put his weight down on the seat. Garland looked over at Wilbert and glared, but didn't say anything.

"You wanted to see me, Chief Webb? I was bending down to check out my truck. I just left Carl Poston's, and he helped me put a water pump on. I ain't had nothing to drink, Chief, I swear."

Garland lit a Camel, and offered one to Wilbert. "Have a smoke, Wilbert."

Wilbert didn't know how to interpret this situation. He had never heard of Garland Webb offering anybody anything except the back of his billy club or a slap across the face. Wilbert eased his hand over and pulled a Camel from the pack. It looked real, but—was it going to explode and kill him?" Garland flicked open his Zippo lighter and spun the spark wheel with his giant size thumb. The Zippo flame felt hot on Wilbert's face. He was afraid Garland was going to singe his nose. He was surprised when he sucked in a big drag of Camel and found that it was a real cigarette. Garland puffed on his and looked straight ahead. Neither said anything for several minutes. Wilbert's tummy was growling like two tomcats fighting over a fish head.

"Wilbert, you and me has had a few disagreemunts in the past, especially the last time you were in my jail, but I'm feeling real forgivin' today." Garland reached under the seat and pulled out a brown paper sack. Wilbert was afraid it was some type of thing in the bag that Garland was going to use to kill him with.

"Wilbert, to show you there ain't no hard feelings bout the past, I wanna offer you a drink." With that Garland pushed the bag over toward Wilbert. Garland squeezed on the bag, so the bottle was sticking out for Wilbert to grab, but

Garland was still holding the bag. Wilbert sat with the Seagram's VO pint bottle in his hand for a while. He was trying to think what the meanest police official short of Tombstone, Arizona was trying to pull. Was it poison, or some type of bad shine that would make him deathly ill?

"Go on, Wilbert, that's some of the smoothest whiskey you'll ever taste. I had a drink of it last night, and it flows down like water from a fresh dug well. I'd have one now with you, cept I'm on duty."

Wilbert put the bottle up to his mouth, hesitated just a little, took a small sip, and sure enough it did taste good. He looked over at Garland, and Garland gave a nod of the head that Wilbert took to mean, go ahead, drink the rest. Wilbert turned the bottle up, drained it dry, and gave a very soft, "Ahhh man, that's good."

Garland motioned for Wilbert to drop the bottle into the bag and Wilbert never noticed that Garland never touched the bottle.

"Well Sonny, how are you? I bet you're excited about your trip tomorrow." JT's secretary, Polly Askins, was always warm and friendly. In addition, she was an attractive lady. She was only nineteen, but Sonny thought she was old. He wondered how he could think he was in love with a woman that much older than he was. She was nice, and always had a peppermint patty ready when one of the kids went in to see Mr. McGloughlin. In the past, Sonny had come in every week to collect for the Florence Morning News. Polly paid for the paper and always asked about his mom and dad. He missed seeing his customers, like Polly, each week, and he hated that he had to turn his route over to Melvin Moore. No way, though Sonny was going to be pedaling around town at five a.m. and running the risk of being cornered by Garland.

Polly was pretty, Polly was nice, and Sonny liked her, but this was the last place in the world he wanted to be.

"Mr. McGloughlin is on the phone. He'll be with you in just a minute. You want to see some pictures Miss Kennedy sent from England while you wait?" She handed Sonny the stack of pictures. Right on top was Miss Kennedy, dressed in her Navy uniform. She had been his fourth grade teacher, but she felt the need to help with the war effort and enlisted in the Navy Ladies Corps. Sonny couldn't remember what they were called, Waves, or Spars, or something like that. He couldn't concentrate on the picture, but the small part of his mind that got through told him he still had a crush on her. She could be demanding, and she expected a student's best, but of all the teachers, she was his favorite. When Sonny had the mumps or chicken pox, Miss Kennedy always stopped by his house to help him keep up with his homework. "Here I am with Polly that makes my heart flutter, I'm looking at a picture of Miss Kennedy, the lady I use to dream about, and all I can do is think of a crooked school superintendent."

The intercom on Polly's desk made a buzzing noise and startled Sonny. Polly picked up the phone and said, "Yes, sir." She then said, "We'll be there right away." She hung up, looked at Sonny, and said, "Mr. McGloughlin is ready to see you now." She got up and walked to Mr. McGloughlin's office door with Sonny straggling behind.

Jack Sterling was despised by most of the people in Florence County, but he was the one everyone ran to when they had a serious legal problem. Sterling did not lose cases. He cared not what it took to win, and that's what he almost always did. He was totally oblivious to what folks thought of him, and if he could get a vicious killer set free—well that was his job. He wore expensive suits, some even said he ordered them from Italy, but he wore the same one for weeks at a time. Tense hours each day in a sweltering Pee Dee courtroom left their mark on his clothing. His white shirt was usually gray, and his suits had a slept-in look. The only reason he wore a tie was because Judge Peoples insisted that all officers of the court must wear them. Sterling complied, but his shoestring thin piece of loud colored cloth was always loosened so much that his coat hid the knot part. Many of his clients were wealthy farmers and Jack often walked out to the barn with a large landholder to discuss business. If his expensive moccasins got muddy, so what; that's what shoes were for, to keep mud from oozing between the toes. When he had several layers of mud on his shoes he tossed them in the trash and got another pair. That's why he did whatever it took to make big bucks, so he wouldn't have to give a damn what others had to say.

Benny Ballentine was reading a Look Magazine story about the life of General George Patton when Sterling walked into the Mecklinburg County jail in Charlotte. Benny laid the book aside, nodded, and mumbled a strained hello to the lawyer at the top of his hate list. Sterling signed the visitor registration log, and said, "I'm here to see my client, Gilbert Gaskins."

Benny pointed to the cup on the table that Sterling knew was for articles such as knives, nail clippers, and money. "I'm an attorney, I'm not required to give up my personal possessions."

Benny gave him a stare that was learned from years of dealing with every type of crook known to man, including crooked attorneys. "I'm a jailer, I'm not required to take crap from crooks, even if they do call themselves attorneys. Unless you place your personal articles on this table, the door you came in runs in two directions."

Benny lived almost 100 miles from Florence, and he wondered why he had to put up with an arrogant attorney from that far away.

Sterling tried to return Benny's stern stare, but as wicked looking as he was, he realized he had met his match. Sterling was used to dealing with crooks, but Benny was an honest public servant, and Sterling didn't know how to handle an honest person. Sterling emptied his pockets, glared at Benny, and waited to be taken to Gilbert Gaskins cell.

Garland drove to the rear of the Florence County Courthouse, found a just-vacated place in the shade, and eased his Ford into the spot. He was parked a little crooked, but no problem, "The car next to me ain't gonna hit no police car." The same courtesy didn't hold for Garland. While he shook and quivered his fat frame to get out, he shoved his car door into the car in the next parking space and scratched both cars.

Garland was a lot less than loved by Sheriff Strother Sligh, and most of his deputies. They had a tradition of honesty that Garland couldn't understand. "How can we live on the salaries they pay police, if we don't have some way to add to the meagerness of the money. Heck, if I'm gonna starve, I might as well sit on my front porch and rock myself to death."

Garland bounced into the Florence County Sheriff's Department lobby, and walked over to the Duty Sergeant. "Yes, Sir, may I help you?" Tommy Cobb, the one asking the polite question, knew Garland well, and he knew who he was there to see. He just wanted Garland to know the contempt he held for him, and he hoped that would make him come back less often. When Garland first joined the highway patrol in Florence, he and Tommy had worked several cases together. Tommy was one of those old-timey cops. He didn't understand Garland's philosophy: "When you arrest someone and search the car, you don't ever leave behind evidence that might be valuable in a poker game."

"Yeah, I'm looking for Olin Roberts."

"Hold on, Chief Webb, and I'll see if I can find him." Garland stood there and glared at Tommy while Tommy buzzed around to find Olin. Tommy never looked up, and he made sure he didn't encourage any conversation with Garland. Once Garland finally got the message that Tommy didn't want to talk with him, he went over to a bench by the wall and spread out his big frame. He had to shift and squirm around a lot to get his peace machine onto the bench so it wouldn't be hanging off. He was aware that all the deputies coming and going made an effort to avoid him. He was too vain, though, to notice that they gathered, pointed at him, and snickered about his doorman uniform, and the "Rifle" he had in his holster.

Sgt. Cobb walked a few feet toward Garland and said, "Mr. Webb, Olin is interviewing someone about a stolen car and will be a few minutes. He asked for you to wait."

"Any idea how long he'll be?"

"No, I don't, but he'll be with you as quickly as he can."

Garland did not like having to wait. Since he was a chief, he thought that should give him more respect. "Heck," Garland thought, "If Sheriff Strother Sligh had any balls, he'd come ask me to wait in his office. I shouldn't be sittin' out here like some lowlife tryin' to visit a prisoner."

Olin and Garland had a lot in common. Olin wanted to talk with Garland, but he wished he wouldn't have come to the office. Olin walked into the lobby, waved, and said, "Hey

Garland, I'm on the way to check out a stolen car report I just took. Can I get with you later?"

"No. I've got some evidence here that I need analyzed." Garland handed him the bag with the whiskey bottle that he knew to have the fingerprints of Wilbert McMillian.

"Garland, Quentin Metts handles all the evidence that we send to Washington; hold on and let me see if he's in." Olin took the bag and started toward the back.

"Wait a minute Olin, I need to tell you what the bag contains, and where it came from. It has a suspect's fingerprints, and it shouldn't be touched."

"Well, keep it in the bag, Garland, but I need Quentin to come out and get you to sign a statement." Olin handed the bag back to Garland and walked off, wishing he could show Garland a little more personal treatment, but he needed his job. Showing friendship with Garland Webb didn't buy points in Sheriff Sligh's headquarters.

Sonny shuffled into Superintendent McGloughlin's spacious office and stood by the huge desk. His heart felt like someone had cranked a chain saw inside his chest when he heard Polly close the door.

"Sonny Boy, come right on in, young man. It's good to see my student with the potential of a first class performer. How've you been doing? I haven't seen you since you won the award. If my memory serves me right, you were a little excited that day. Have a seat." Sonny just stood there wondering if he should run out the side door and yell for Mr. Tedder.

"I sent for you, Sonny, to discuss our fishing trip tomorrow. The weather reports are calling for rain, but we can work around that. If it rains too much to take the boat out, I have a first cousin who operates a drawbridge over near Sullivan's Island. We'll go there and fish off of the bridge. How does that sound?"

Sonny didn't have anything to say. All he could think about was, either he would be with two criminals on a boat, or on some backwoods drawbridge over a flooded river. Either way, he didn't have much chance of making it back.

"Sonny, are you too excited to speak? Come on, boy, loosen up, this is going to be the trip of a lifetime."

Those were not the words Sonny wanted to hear. This could very well be the end of a lifetime. He just shook his head, and mumbled something like, "Yes, Sir."

"Just look at these pictures on the wall. Many of them are shots of some big fish that I caught. That mounted one over the door was caught in the same waters that we'll be going to tomorrow. We'll no doubt catch some bigger than that."
Sonny just stood there in some sort of shock.

"I know this is a lot of excitement to take in, so I understand your quietness. You just tell your mama that we'll be by your house at five a.m. Tell her we'll take good care of you, and she needn't worry at all about you. Now, you get on back to class and show that crowd in there what a fella with your potential can do."

"Yes, Sir." Sonny was so happy to get out of there he wanted to run and shout, but his system was shut down. He couldn't make a shouting noise, and his legs were too jelly-like to run. He told Polly bye and headed for the outside fresh air.

Quentin Metts walked over to Garland and said, "Olin said you needed to see me about this bag, Garland. What's on your mind?"

Garland pointed at the bag and explained "I've got a bottle of what I spect is whiskey that I found in a jail cell. I wanna have the contents checked to see if it is whiskey, and I need to have fingerprints taken. I wanna know how it got into one of the cells in my jail. I search every prisoner before I lock 'em up, so somebody had to sneak it in. I wanna find out who it was."

Quentin had a hard time keeping the laughter that was in his head from spilling out through his face. Quentin was thinking, "This is the funniest thing I've ever heard. Everybody knows that if Garland Webb found a bottle of whiskey, he wouldn't care where it came from. All he would want to know would be where can I get more?" Quentin would like to have said that to Garland, but he opted to be more professional. "When did you find it, and where, Garland? Did you touch the bottle?"

"Well, of course I touched the bottle; I was startled to find it there. When I picked it up, I put my hand on just a small corner and eased it into this bag. After that I opened the cap with a rag and smelled the contents. It smells like whiskey. I need to know as soon as possible what we're dealing with. I don't allow no contraband in my jail."

I'll send it to the lab, Garland, but it'll take several weeks at least. Wait right here while I get a form typed up for you to sign." Quentin took the bag to his office and typed out a short statement:

> *I, Garland Webb found the attached Seagram's VO pint bottle in one of my jail cells. I am releasing it to the Florence County Sheriff's Department to have it examined for contents, and for fingerprints.*

Quentin then typed Garland's name, and drew a line underneath for his signature.

Quentin came back to the lobby and said, "OK Garland, I

need you to sign this. I'll let you know as soon as we get a report from the Bureau." Garland signed, and Quentin wheeled around and disappeared into his office.

Garland was angry. "Here I am the head of the Timmonsville Police Department, and some county deputy wouldn't even give me the courtesy to invite me back to his office. Well, these rat turds are on my list. They may be rude now, but somehow I'll get 'em back. Big time."

"Bucky Harris brings me to this place every time I visit Florence. It has the best food in South Carolina, probably North Carolina and Georgia as well." Joe and Jerry settled into a smooth, vinyl-covered booth near the back of the L shaped dining room.

"That explains why Bucky doesn't want to visit Washington any more. He's afraid J Edgar will see his fat paunch and make him go back through the obstacle course."

"I'm gonna call Bucky now and let him come over and celebrate with us. He just lives a few miles from here. When I tell him the country fried ham is cooking, he'll be here in minutes."

I'm so excited, I can't wait to talk with Bob Johnson and see if the taps are working. I haven't been able to get through to him, but I hope that's because Dalton is still popping calls on that phone."

"One thing about our boy Dalton, he spews as much out of his mouth as he puts in. With him there at the club, Bob will have a hot headset. I'm gonna volunteer to help him; I can't wait to get evidence about what happened to Ken Parnell."

"You guys are up mighty early. I thought you police was nighttime workers. Is somebody gonna get busted today, or have you two been to a late night party?" Bea had coffee in one hand and silverware and napkins in the other.

"Actually, we've doing a little celebration. By the way, Bea, this is Joe Means. He's never had any of your pan-baked biscuits. In fact, he's been living in DC for three years, and I think he's good-food deprived. Give him a reminder."

"Well, Honey, you came to the right place to learn about good food. We got the best this side of Paris, and you don't have to get on no boat to get to it. What can I bring you?"

"I'm hungry enough to eat a horse, Bea, but I hope that's not what you serve here."

"Nah, but we can give you enough to fill one up."

"Just give me whatever Jerry is having. He's been here with Bucky Harris, so he knows the secret order."

"By the way Bea, Bucky is on the way over here now, so you can go ahead and fix his special, and give us the same. We're celebrating, so bring us a few glasses of juice. We're gonna have a toast."

"Speaking of the devil, I see your buddy Bucky parking now, I'll be right back with your cranberry wine."

Garland dogged his Ford to Timmonsville and called Dalton. They were talking when Mayor Coker knocked on the chief's door, then pushed it open without taking time to be invited in. After all, he was the mayor; he didn't have to wait for acknowledgement to enter.

Garland told Dalton he would get back with him later and hung up the phone. "Mayor, can I help you with somethin?"

"You sure can. I just got a call from, Melvin Grubbs, an attorney in Florence that says he's representing Joe Sharpe. Sharpe is in the hospital and he claims you beat him for no reason, and now he has internal bleeding. What do you have to say about that?"

"I've got plenty to say. He was speeding down Keith Street and when I pulled him over he cussed me. I smelled liquor on his breath and told him to get out of the car. When he refused, I did what any good police officer would do: I pulled him out of the car. When he resisted the handcuffs, I had to smack him a few times. I placed him under arrest and took him to jail. He brought it all on his self."

"His attorney says he was not speeding, he was not drinking, and he has witnesses that say you roughed him up for no reason at all. He also says that he is missing a set of Craftsman tools that were in his car when you drug him out of it."

"Well, he's a damn liar."

"I hope you can back up that claim, because his attorney is filing a complaint. He plans to sue you and the town. As Mayor, I cannot have town officials acting in an unprofessional manner. I'll hold off until I see the lawsuit, but if you cannot prove that you acted in a proper manner, I will have to take action against you. I have to protect our town."

Garland clinched his fists, bit his tongue and did everything possible to not say anything to the mayor that would sound disrespectful. His time would come, but right now, he needed to be police chief. That made loosening the loads on those big wheelers easier. "I understand, Mayor, and there probably won't even be a law suit. You know how them lawyers do, they try to intimidate you, and hope you'll cave in. I ain't done nothin wrong, and they'll soon back down and apologize to us."

"We'll know soon. Now, what have you learned about that whiskey bottle you found inside the jail. Has Sheriff Sligh's Office given you the results yet?"

"I was over there yesterday, Mayor. I talked with Olin Roberts, and Quentin Metts, but they ain't heard nothin yet."   "Garland, let me be sure we understand each other.

You have taken the bottle to the sheriff's office to be tested. Is that correct? We must find out right away how that bottle got into your jail." Mayor Coker wanted so badly to tell this huge lump of blubber to get out of his town, but he fought the urge and held back. He reminded himself how close Garland was to JT. He was also thinking, "As soon as I get the evidence that Garland is drinking on duty, then I'll be able to explain to JT why I had to fire his friend, the Chief. JT will understand, and I'll still have the goodwill of Senator Furman."

"That is affirmative, Mayor."

"OK, but if we've not heard anything by next Monday, you and I will have to visit Sheriff Sligh and determine just why this is taking so long. Is that clear?"

"No problem, Mayor."

Mayor Coker rushed out of the Chief's office and almost bumped into Mrs. McKay. "Well, Linwood, you certainly seem to be in a hurry. Is the town on fire, or do you have seeds in your store starting to sprout?"

"Good morning, Mrs. McKay, I guess it's a little of both. Sometimes I wonder why I don't just settle back in the feed store and forget all of this bureaucratic mess. Every time I find a good worker that has promise at the store, they get drafted. There's hardly anybody left in town that's old enough to be out of school. The ones that haven't been drafted are too feeble to lift a sack full of seeds."

"You need to slow back, Linwood. You're working too hard. Your face *is redder'n* Mr. Fogle's fire truck."

"I'm gonna cut back soon, Mrs. McKay. Give my best to Archie."

Garland went back to his secret place in the jail bathroom, reached behind the loose tiles, pulled out his new pint of

Jim Beam and sucked in about half of the contents. Then he bruised his knuckles hitting the concrete wall. Holding back wasn't his style, but in this case the big haul was worth it. Garland replaced the bottle and called Dalton back. By then, Gus had sent Dalton to Florence to pick up some new pin ball machines that had come in on Overland Freight Express. Garland left word he would call back later.

"Joe, how about trying Bob again. I can't wait any longer to find out if the wires are working."
Joe could hardly wait either, but he had tried for hours to reach Bob's private number in the recording booth. Joe made sure no one was around the pay phone and dialed Bob's number."

"Hello?" Only a few agents had the number of the taping room, so Bob felt confident that the call would either be Joe, Mark, or Pedro.

"Bob, this is Joe, I've been trying to get you for hours. What's going on? Have you had any calls?"

"Joe, you wouldn't believe some of the stuff we've gotten already. The first day on the wire, and not only have we got Dalton Sellers placing bets with a bookie, but also talking about a connection with Garland Webb and the big kicker— they discussed a connection with Tom Furman's son-in-law, JT McGloughlin. Man, that wire is hot, Joe. Did you and Jerry have any trouble getting it in place"

"Not really, Bob, but we have some concerns about the rain that's supposed to be on the way. We didn't have enough caulk to get the skylight sealed back as well as we would like."

"Joe, it looks like this is going to be a prize wire with some fantastic information, it's definitely worth going back and making a reseal."

"Yeah, Bob, we're planning on that. The good part is that while we were inside we made impressions of the locks and we're having keys made. We can go in the door, look through the files and then go up and re-caulk the skylight."

"I don't want to tell you what to do Joe, but I really think that would be worth doing tonight."

"Jerry and I'll start on a plan for tonight right now. Don't blush from some of the language you're gonna hear on that line."

"My headset's ringing now Joe, see you later."

THE CHASE
Chapter Five

Garland flicked on his red light, hit the siren, and swirled his plug of Brown Mule around in his mouth. The occupant of the 1936 Chevy pickup was no stranger to Garland. Chief Webb had arrested Calvin Key numerous times. Usually, Garland didn't even have to take him to jail. Calvin paid his "fine" on the spot, in cash, and always turned over several bottles of bonded whiskey that Garland would use for "evidence." Calvin was a "white collar" bootlegger; he dealt only in bonded, store-bought liquor. After Sundown during the week, and all day on Sunday, liquor is not sold in South Carolina. Thirsty town folks would come to Calvin's house and pick out a bottle of their favorite brand that they otherwise would have to do without until morning. Garland liked stopping Calvin because he usually was anxious to slip Garland his fine and a few bottles of evidence, and get on his way.

Why this day Calvin chose to run is unknown, but as soon as Calvin heard the siren he shoved down on the throttle towards Lamar. Garland slammed his Ford into second gear, and stomped the foot feed. Garland's police special was a wreck to look at, full of coffee cups, doughnut boxes, and empty Camel packages, but it was a hot car. It was equipped with one of the same powerful engines used by the pursuit cars of the state highway patrol. When Garland shoved down on the accelerator the tires burned rubber. Man, oh, man, how Garland loved that sound. He could even imagine the fresh rubber smell he was leaving behind. Garland was right on Calvin's bumper when they hit the town limits.

Calvin wound up his truck but Garland stuck right on his tailgate. Several miles out on the paved road, Calvin took a left fork that became a dirt road. When Calvin spun onto the dirt road, he kicked up so much dust that Garland couldn't see beyond the windshield. Garland went into a spin before he could slow down, zoomed between two trees, hit a third, and rolled over. Calvin was long gone.

"Peewee" Lee was checking on his tobacco plants when he heard Calvin roar by; moments later he heard an awful crash. Peewee ran over to the crumpled Ford police car and heard Garland moaning. The car was resting on the passenger side, and Garland had slid down and was lying on the passenger door, with his feet turned toward the back.

Pee Wee climbed up on the driver's side and peered in. "Garland, this is Peewee Lee, are you OK?"

"Get me out of here."

"Hold on Garland, I'm trying to get the door open."

"Hurry up, I think I've got a broken arm, I can't move it."

"Garland, I can't get the door open, I'm gonna hafta run to Burl Windham's store and get some help."

"Get me out of here!" Garland yelled, panic in his voice, but Peewee was already on his way. He started toward Windham's, which was only several blocks. He ran over to the paved road, turned left toward the store, spotted Wib Weatherly in his 41 Plymouth, and flagged him down.

"Garland Webb's hit a tree over by my barn, I need you to help me get him out."

Peewee jumped into Wib's Plymouth, and pointed toward Garland's car. Several other cars had already stopped, and George Denham and Carl Poston were trying to open the door. Like most everyone in Timmonsville, Wib had had his share of run-ins with Garland. He was less than excited about hurrying to his aid, but he was a compassionate person, and he joined in the effort. The entire crowd in the rescue effort disliked Garland, but each realized that Garland was a human being, although a despicable one. It was eerie hearing Garland moan for help. He was always the one making others moan. He kept crying out, "I can't get out. Get me out of here!"

Wib jumped onto the side of the car that was on top, the driver side door, and hollered for Peewee to get a lug wrench out of his car. Carl had already gotten one and handed it up to Wib. Wib pushed the bar into the doorjamb as far as it would go and pulled with all of his might. The metal would bend, but so far the lock had not sprung. Wib toyed with the idea of smashing the window but he knew that would spray Garland with glass. Tommy Suggs drove up, and before he could get out of his car, Peewee yelled for him to go to Windham's store and call for an ambulance.

Sonny was in his second home: Tommy and Brian's dark closet. His first home was under his own bed. "Sonny, what are you going to do? Are you goin to Charleston with those murderers tomorrow? Maybe it's time to call the FBI."

"I don't know, Tommy, I'm scared, but nothing seems to be the right way. Right now, I'm thinking of going, and then when we get to the dock in Charleston, I'll jump out, run, and find a boat to hide in. No matter where the boat goes, I'll be better off than I am here." Brian just sat with the side of his arm in his mouth, his eyes wide open, obviously terrified.

"Whatever happens, if I don't come back, you tell your mom and my mom. Then they'll call the FBI, and that will start an investigation. If I leave with them and don't come back, they'll have to look for me—Senator Tom Furman or not."

"But what if they try to do something to you on the way?"

"I've thought about that but I don't think they plan to attempt anything until they get me far out to sea. That way, they know I won't have any chance of gettin away, or calling for help. When I was in McGloughlin's office, he was sugar nice, and tryin' to be friends. That's the way I think they'll be until they get me on the boat, or think they'll get me on, cause there ain't no way they're gonna get me aboard."

"How bout as soon as you leave we go ahead and tell Mama. That way when they report that you've run away, Mama'll realize that those two are criminals."

"I want you to tell her, but wait till later in the day. I wanna be sure I've gotten away before they start lookin for me. You know now that I have a plan, I'm startin' to get excited about all of this. It sounds like an adventure. I'm actually lookin forward to hoppin' out and runnin. They'll be the scared ones then. How about you two comin' with me and sharin' the excitement?"

Before Tommy could answer Brian gave out such a whimper they all just sat there.

Wib finally pried the door loose on Garland's capsized car, pushed it back, and sprung the hinge. "Hold on, Garland, I'm gonna ease down beside you. We'll have you out in a little while."

"Hurry up, I'm layin' on somethin that's jammed into my back, and I can't move. I need to get to the hospital."

"We're working on that, and we'll have you outa here soon. Just lay still while I unlock the back door. I'm gonna get several other guys in here to help hold you in place while the others right the car."

Peewee, Carl, and a number of others that had crowded around were set to gently put the car back on its wheels.

Wib Weatherly, Tommy Suggs, and Frank Davenport, the ambulance driver, were inside bracing Garland for the jarring bump. Frank gave Garland a shot of morphine and yelled for the group outside to right the car as gently as possible.

Peewee repeated Frank's plea, "Ease it down gently folks." Peewee was sharing as much of the load as anyone, but he was still acting as the leader. After all, he was the one who first found, and reported the accident.

"Sonny, you don't know how happy I am to see you eating for a change. This is the first time you've been at the table in a week. I don't know how you've survived lying under your bed just eating peanut butter."

"This stew beef and rice tastes great, Mama. You know this is one of my favorite meals."

"I'm glad, too, that you finally are excited about the trip tomorrow, I was afraid you weren't going to go. After winning the most exciting prize the school has ever offered, I would have been heartbroken."

"Actually, Mama, that's the reason I'm going. I don't like Garland and Mr. McGloughlin, but I know you would be disappointed if I didn't go, so I'm gonna go, just for you, Mama."

"You're gonna enjoy this trip, and, Oh, how I'd like to be there when you catch that first big tuna. Mr. McGloughlin told me he knew a spot that was always swarming with fish that are as fat as footballs, just waiting to be pulled in. Mr. McGloughlin said he was carrying the school camera and he would be taking a lot of pictures for the school yearbook. He's gonna have me a set made, but just to be sure I've got a camera packed in your bag for some special pictures."

Word spread fast in Timmonsville. It wasn't long until JT knew that his sidekick had been injured. He shut his office door, picked up the phone, and dialed the club. "Lacy, let me speak with Gus."

"He's not here. You wanna talk with Dalton?"

"Yeah."

"I'll call him. JT, Honey, how you been doing?"

"Fine, Lacy, but right now I need to talk with Dalton in a hurry."

"Dalton, you got a call, its JT, pick up the phone."

"Yeah, what's up, JT?"

"Dalton, have you heard about Garland? He's been in an accident."

"No, I just got back, JT, what happened?"

"From what I hear, he hit a tree while he was chasing someone. They think it was Calvin Key. He's been taken to McLeod's Infirmary, but we don't know how serious it is. I need him to be with me tomorrow to take care of our little peeping tom."

"Don't worry about a thing, JT, I'm dyin' to go. Once I get my pig sticker out, his eyes'll pop off the boat, and he'll dive in after 'em. I never did like that little smart butt anyway."

"I thought about that, Dalton, but if he falls overboard and you're on the boat, it'll look suspicious. You know as well as I, that your reputation as a bouncer and barroom brawler are wide spread. Garland doesn't have any better reputation, but at least he has the badge to give it a little respectability."

"JT, whatchu gonna do? That little pimple head has to be taken care of."

"I don't know yet, Dalton. I'm going over to the hospital and find out if they can patch Garland up so that we can still go. I'll let you know."

"Right, but if Garland don't get to go, I can carve my

initials on the inside of little peepin' eye's tummy. He won't do no talkin after I finish with him."

"I'll get back with you, Dalton. Find Gus, and let him know."

"Sonny! Have you heard about Garland? He's been in a wreck, and he's over at the hospital." Tommy was so excited he could hardly get the words out.

Sonny jammed the phone against his ear; he couldn't believe what he was hearing. "What happened?"

"He was chasing Calvin Key towards Lamar and ran off the road and hit a tree."

"I wonder if JT will cancel our trip now that he doesn't have blubber belly to throw me off of the boat."

"He'll either have to cancel or get someone else, Sonny. That boat is too big for one person to handle. What if he gets Dalton or that person called Cecil?"

"I'd rather have Garland, at least that hunk of lumpy fat can't run. I'd have an easy time getting away from him. In fact, I've started to look forward to this trip, Tommy. Meet me down at the drugstore, and let's see what we can find out."

"Dr. McLeod, this is JT McGloughlin, how is Garland?"

"It looks like he's pretty lucky, JT. He's got a broken left elbow, a sprained right wrist, and a lot of cuts and bruises. Nothing life threatening but he'll need to wear a cast for a month and work out the stiffness, otherwise he'll be OK."

"He's supposed to be my deck hand on a school trip tomorrow, Doc. Will he be able to go?"

"He can go as far as I'm concerned, but I suspect that he'll be so sore he won't be able to climb onto the boat. He certainly wouldn't be able to fish, he'll only have one working arm, and that one is swollen and painful. The only other thing wrong with Garland now is an upset tummy. He swallowed a plug of tobacco when he hit that tree. Even as tough as Garland is, a plug of raw tobacco down your windpipe takes its toll. So, to answer your question, he can medically go, but physically, I doubt he'll be up to the trip."

'Thanks, Doc, how long will he be in the hospital?"

"As soon as he wakes up I'll give him some tests, but I think today or tomorrow at the latest. Even if he is up and out tomorrow, he won't be doing much moving around. You can call me in an hour, and I'll let you know."

"Doc, when you give him the tests, will you ask him if he's up to working on the boat? If not, I've got to make some other arrangements. Can you let me know as soon as you find out?"

"I'll have Donna call you right after we check him out, JT."

"As soon as JT put the phone down, it rang again. "JT, this is Gus, Dalton just filled me in on Garland. What are you gonna do about the trip tomorrow?"

"I don't know yet, Gus. Doc McLeod is going to call me as soon as he determines if Garland can go or not."

"What are you gonna do otherwise? Do you need me to get in touch with some of my guys and let 'em put muscle on the kid?"

"Let me see first what Doc says, Gus. It may be that Garland can go, if so, that'll be our safest route."

"OK, JT, but I'm gonna get in touch with Tony and fill him in. We've gotta do somethin about that little onlooker."

"Yeah, Gus, that's a good idea, but I'm still hoping we can go with this plan. It's safer than any other that we've discussed."

"OK, JT, but you keep me posted. I don't wanna get blindsided because of some little punkass kid. You got me?"

"I'll let you know today, Gus."

"Garland, can you remember what happened to you?" Doc McLeod was leaning over Garland's bed, shining a light into his eye, and probing around.

"Get that light out of my eye, it burns."

"Hold still, Garland, I've got to make sure you didn't get a concussion. Now, I need you to tell me everything you remember about what happened to you."

"What do you mean, me tell you? You're the doc, you tell me what's wrong with me."

"Garland, I'm not asking you what's wrong with you, I'm asking you what you remember about the accident. I've got other patients to tend to, so tell me now what you remember. It'll have a bearing on whether or not I release you."

"What day is it?"

"Friday. Now, what do you remember?"

"I was chasin' somebody, and all of a sudden I couldn't see the road. I hit somethin, I think it was a tree."

"Do you remember who you were chasing?"

"Right now, I can't remember, but I'm sure it'll come to me later. I'm ready to get outa here, I got a fishing trip tomorrow I gotta go on."

"I haven't decided yet whether or not you can leave the hospital, Chief Webb. You may have a concussion, so tell me what you remember about the chase?"

"I was in pursuit of a truck. Right now it's a little hazy, but when I do remember, the driver will be in some serious trouble."

"Sheriff Sligh's office will take care of that, Garland, you're going to have to take a few days off and rest. If you can get up and walk around the hospital, I'll release you to go on the fishing trip but you'll have to sit back and relax."

"OK, Doc, I wanna get out of here, now. You got me in this room with somebody I've had to arrest more times than I can count. I don't wanna be in the same buildin' with him. Get my clothes and let me get out of here."

"I'll tell Donna to have an aide help you dress. Then you walk down to my office. If you feel dizzy, you'll have to stay here for a while."

"Right."

"Tony, this is JT, how're things in Charlotte?"

"JT, they're OK but the *fedies* are pushing hard. They haven't found anything so far that they can prove, but we've got some bullheads over there that won't quit digging. We've got to be very careful for a while."

"What do you think they do know, Tony?"

"I've got some contacts that have been letting me know most of what they're comin' up with, but my information seems to be harder to come up with all the time. I don't know if my contacts are being shut out or not. Also, I've got to consider that any info now could be designed to make us do somethin rash."

"Tony, we've had some experience with undercover spies. Are you checking out the people you hire?"

"WHAT? Who the hell you think you're talkin to? You're a small time Sunday school and county school superintendent; I run a union operated truck-loading dock. Unless you want me leanin' on your school teachers, you stay the hell away from how I run my docks. We're on a good thing, and you've got a helpful contact, but you keep your damn tongue out of my phone. You got me, McGloughlin?"

"I got you Tony. I didn't mean to pry into your affairs."

"Well you were, and I don't want to hear it again. From

now on you get to me through Gus. Understood?"

"Yes, Sir." JT thought of himself as cool, but his hands were shaking and his edges were rumpled. He had imagined himself on friendly terms with Tony, but now he realized Tony is not the kind to be friendly with. He had a rough exterior and JT found out that underneath was even rougher.

Gus drove into the club parking lot and Lacy met him outside. "Gus, you've got some urgent calls. I don't know which is the most important, but Dalton is trying to find you, JT is looking for you, Tony needs you, and George Malini says it's urgent that you call him right away. You're an important person."

"How long ago did they call?"

"Gus, they've been calling since you left."

"OK, thanks, Lacy, I'll get started now, bring me a double and a cheeseburger"

"Right away, boss."

Gus lit a small Cuban cigar, pulled his chair over so the oscillating fan could dry off the sweat, and stared at the phone. His mind was racing around and he had no clue which one to call first. All of these calls had the potential to be trouble. He decided on George Malini. Gladys can be a real knife in the heart if she chooses to be. "Susan, this is Gus, let me speak to George."

"Oh, Gus, I'm so glad you called, George needs to talk with you right away. He's having a chocolate shake across the street at the Palace Grill but he said he would be facing this way, so hold on; I'll go on the porch and wave him over."

George saw Susan's signal and came running. He ran by Susan's desk, bounded up the stairs, and grabbed the phone. "Gus, I'm glad I've got you. I don't know what you've done that Gladys knows about, but whatever it is she thinks it's something big. She's already made an appointment for Monday morning with Ambrose Hampton at the State-Record Newspaper. Whatever she knows she plans to tell him unless you give in to her demands. She says either you come through or you'll be sorry. She sounds so serious I'm concerned. Any idea what she might be telling them? On second thought, maybe I shouldn't know."

"George, I just don't want her talking to any reporters and making my personal life public. Did she give you any idea how we could resolve this?"

"Well, she was definite on one thing: that you must admit to adultery in the divorce proceedings so it can go through swiftly. In addition, she says that you must give her the kind of settlement that she deserves for putting up with your antics for 22 years."

"Did she give any idea, George, as to what she might be looking for? Or any idea what she might say?"

"Only that you have to call her. She will speak to no one else about the matter. She says she'll give you until Monday morning, but she told me to tell you that the longer you wait, the more irritable she will be."

"Thanks, George, I'll call the bitch this afternoon and let you know what we work out."

Donna, this is Linwood Coker, how's Garland Webb doing?" Linwood was perched on a bag of oats, leaning his head on a sack of corn. He was holding the phone with one hand and a tall mug of sweet ice tea with the other.

"Hi, Linwood, Doctor McLeod just checked Chief Webb over, and he's having him walk down to his office. If he makes it downstairs OK without getting too dizzy, he's gonna let him go home. I don't think he'll be able to do any speed chases for a while; he's got a cast on his right arm."

"How long will he be there, Donna? I need to talk with him; also, Sheriff Sligh's deputy, Clyde Moody, has to get a statement from him. I think Tommy Moore, with the highway patrol will also need a statement."

"I can't say for sure, Linwood, he could be weaker than he thinks. He may have to stay, or he may be able to walk out of here. If he gets out though, he'll need a ride. You want me to tell him you're coming over to get him?"

"Yeah, Donna, tell him I'll be there in about twenty minutes. Don't let him leave until I get there."

"I'll tell Dr. McLeod to detain him until you arrive."

"Thanks, Donna."

"Pedro, how are things in DC city?"

"Kinda quiet at the moment Joe, but I'm glad you called, you're on the hottest case we've got going. Bob is picking up some unbelievable stuff on your wire. We've got a lot of suspicions confirmed, but no mention yet of Navy CID Agent Ken Parnell. Gus Segars' wife is pushing him hard to pay her off, or she's threatening to talk with the newspaper in Columbia. He plans to call her back today, so maybe we'll find out what she knows. We're gonna be busy for the next year on all the trails this bunch is leading us."

"Jerry and I are going back over tonight and look around the club. I saw some bank statements and loan papers on a desk last night; I wanna shuffle through them while Jerry re-caulks the roof."

Joe, are you sure you're up to going? After all, you've had a cushy job the last few years."

"Pedro, I had forgotten what fun it is working in the field, and I do mean field. I do have to get back in a little better shape though. I had to struggle to get up and down the tree limb to the roof of the club. Tonight, I'm gonna let Jerry do that while I go inside."

"Just be careful, Joe. Other than that I have some exciting news for you. All of the agents working on this case, including you and me, have to be in the Charlotte office tomorrow morning at eight a.m. The Director wants to address the group on the phone-patch office intercom. I've got a suspicion that it's about mollycoddling Tom Furman, but we'll have to find out together in the morning. I bet you can't wait.

"Ugh."

"I knew you would be elated."

"Yeah I am, Pedro, it'll take several hours to get to Charlotte, so Jerry and I'll have to go to the club earlier than we had planned. We'll have to be outta there by five or so. Bucky Harris has an eating place here that's out of sight. I was looking forward to feasting out again after our trek through the woods."

"Who knows, Joe, you might get lucky and have a doughnut in the office tomorrow."

"Thanks for your cheerful news."

"Gus got off the phone with George Malini, and yelled for Lacy to bring him a straight Scotch double. After talking with George about Gladys and her demands, he pounded on the booth table for a while, and then returned McGloughlin's call. "JT, what's up?"

"I'm glad you called, Gus. Have you heard about Garland's accident?"

"No, I just got back and had to get on the phone with George Mallini. What happened?"

"He was chasing Calvin Key, ran off the road, and ended upside down between two trees. I'm not sure he's going to be up to making the trip with the kid tomorrow."

"JT, I've got more irons in the fire than I've got flame. What in the hell are you calling me about this for? This assignment has already been doled out to you, and you damn well better get it taken care of. I don't want to hear no more about it until that little bastard is buried at sea!"

"I'll take care of it, Gus."

"You'd better! Else you'll wind up in his place."

Miss Rose was at her desk grading papers, deep in concentration. She was startled when she looked up and saw Sonny. "Sonny, I'm so happy you have a smile on your face today. You've looked like death itself lately."

"I'm feeling much better, Miss Rose. I guess that fishing trip tomorrow will do me good. I'm looking forward to it. By the way, you have a lot of maps; do you have one that would show Charleston?"

"Not only that, Sonny, but I was born in Summerville. I know Charleston quite well. What do you want to know?"

"I'd just like the route we'll probably take, and about how long a drive it is."

"You'll take highway 56, and it'll take about two hours. By the way, Sonny, now that Garland is in the hospital, who is going to net the fish? Mr. McGloughlin said he would have someone do that, and now it doesn't look like it will be Garland."

"I'm not sure, Miss Rose. Mama called the hospital and her friend Donna says he may very well be able go. He just won't be able to drive."

"He won't be able to help bring the fish in either. You may be the only kid in the world that will have a school superintendent bait your hook and help you haul in the catch."

"Yes, Ma'am, I'm looking forward to that part. Miss Rose, when we get into Charleston, will we go right thorough town, and will there be a lot of red lights and stop signs?"

"Oh yes. You'll have to go to the Battery to get there, so you'll go through a lot of the city."

"Can you draw on the map how you think we'll get to the boat."

"Sure. I've never been on his boat, but my family once had a small sailboat we kept in the Charleston Marina. I can tell you almost exactly how you'll get there and what you'll see. I'm so glad you're finally excited about this trip."

"Thanks, Miss Rose, I'll bring you a porpoise back."

Joe grabbed the phone on the first ring and spit out a quick hello. "Hi, Joe, you and Jerry still got your trip planned for tonight and tomorrow."

"Yeah, Mark, I'm looking forward to tonight, but tomorrow sounds like a cliff drop."

"Tomorrow may not be so bad after all, Joe; you might get relieved of the meeting. Bob sent me some tapes off your wires, and although we don't have much info, they're talking about doing away with a kid. It sounds like they plan to throw him off of a boat. Trouble is we don't know who, where, or when. Whoever it is, he must have seen something, because they called him a snitcher."

"Have you called, Pedro? You know I can't miss Uncle J Ed's meeting unless I'm either dead or plan to be within 24 hours."

"I just got off of the phone with him, Joe; he's in Tolson's office right now. I'm sure Tolson will take him to the Director's office."

"You think the Chief'll cancel one of his meetings just to keep a kid from getting killed, Mark?"

"It'll be interesting to find out, won't it? Just stay in touch Joe, but plan on looking through the club very thoroughly tonight. Maybe you can find something there that will tell us who the kid is."

"Jerry and I'll go early and wait behind the club until it closes. We'll go in as soon as it's clear."

"Be careful in that club Joe, we're not dealing with kind and gentle folks here."

"Mark, those folks we can handle. Right now, I'm meeting MB Huggins to fly over the club. Going up with MB is more frightening than the thought of the bad guys, but I've got to find a closer parking place for tonight. The spot we had before is a mile through the woods, and we have to find a place near enough to be on the road shortly after we get out of the club. If the Charlotte meeting isn't cancelled we're gonna be racing the clock.

Gus squirmed around in his chair, clenched his teeth, wiped the sweat with his red bandanna, and pleaded, "Gladys be reasonable. I've agreed to admit to adultery so the divorce can go quickly, but you've got to understand that if I pay the kind of money you're asking I'll have to sell the club and my amusement company as well."

"So! Is that supposed to interest me? I don't care if you have to sell your last pair of drawers. I just want my settlement, and I want it right away. That means an agreement before Monday morning if you don't want me to talk with Ambrose. Once we agree, I'll give you a little time to raise the cash. You're involved with the kind of people who have shoeboxes filled with big bills. Get it from them."

"Exactly what do you plan to tell Ambrose if I don't?"

"I don't think you want to find that out, Gus. I don't have proof of some of the things I'll be telling him, but I have enough facts that he can piece together quite a story. I think from there the federal people will start looking around. By the way, the information that I'll be giving him is stored in a lockbox, and I have instructions about it if something happens to me. I've learned to be prepared for anything with you Gus. Actually, as much as I've learned to hate your guts, I hope and pray that what I'll be telling isn't really true. Then again, I guess we'll find out unless you come through. Now, I'm tired of talking. Don't you even call me back. I want George Malini to call me and tell me exactly when I can expect the money. Otherwise, you can read the Columbia Record Monday afternoon and see what I know."

"Gladys"

"Goodbye Gus."

Gus banged on the wall and yelled, "Lacy, bring me a double. Now!" He had one Lucky Strike burning in the ashtray and he lit another. There was a real decision to make. "Do I give in to blackmail from Gladys, or do I have Dalton take her out? If I go with the Dalton plan what about the info in the lockbox? What'll I do if I give her all of that money? Heck, I'll have to sell everything to give her what she wants. Damn, everything looked rosy peach last week and now it's turned to cow crap."

Sonny had finally gotten up the nerve to ride his bike to Tommy's house without trying to hide. He pedaled casually through town and felt ten feet tall. Man, this is great; I'm gonna string those butts along a dead end trail. The only thing I'll miss is the look on their faces when I jump out of the car and run. I'm gonna "Yes Sir", and "No Sir" 'em to death on the way down and they'll be thinking how easy it's gonna be. When I run, they're gonna have some kind of heart fits.

"Sonny, what the heck are you doing coming to the front door?" Tommy hadn't seen Sonny outside of a dark closet for days. "I almost didn't recognize you. What are you smiling about?"

"I told you yesterday I was getting braver now that I have a plan. Well, now I'm so excited I can't wait for tomorrow to get here."

"Have you picked a jump-out place yet? Where will you go then?"

"Miss Rose told me some things about the route we'll take. There are a number of places we'll have to stop, so I'll have plenty of opportunities to jump out. When we get to a place with some people around, I'm gonna hop out and holler that I've been kidnapped. Even then I'm gonna keep running and hide out for most of the day.

"Do you think Garland will be able to go? What if he can't and somebody like Dalton goes. He wouldn't wait all the way to Charleston to start waving his switchblade."

"I thought of that. If it looks scary in the morning when they pick me up, I'll jump out when we slow down at the corner. Either direction we go from my house, we'll have to get to a place to slow down and turn. I'll jump and run then. I'd rather get out of town, so it'll be harder for them to explain, but I'm gonna play it safe. Hey, you sure you don't wanna go with me?"

"I'm sure."

MB banked the J3 Piper Cub and pointed down, "OK, Joe, right down below is the club, and in just a minute we'll be over the millpond area. I'll circle several times so you can get your bearings, and then we'll see if there's a better place to park." MB skimmed the treetops, and when he circled the small J3, Joe felt like they were getting hit with tree limbs.

"MB, is there a chance you could pull the plane up a little, I think my feet are dragging the ground."

"Sorry, Joe, I forget you guys have never been crop dusters. I'll go up a few more feet, but by staying low we can get a better look at how thick the underbrush is. I'm gonna make a sharp left now and show you a place probably no more than a quarter mile from the joint. If it looks clear enough to get the truck into, this'll be the place to stop."

"We need to park as close as possible, MB. When we leave there tonight we have to head for Charlotte unless we can get a meeting cancelled."

"See that place right there, Joe. It's on your side, the area with the pine tree kind of all alone. I think that's your spot; map it out while I circle again."

"I've already reached out and put a ribbon on it, MB. I'm ready to put my feet on still ground. Besides, we don't want them to see us flying this close to the club, they might get suspicious."

"We don't have to worry about that, Joe. We're just a mile or so from the airport, so there's a dozen different planes over here every day." MB circled the J3, aimed at the runway, gently sat her down, and taxied to the hanger.

Joe got out the side door and wobbled around a while. "Thanks, MB, we'll be able to get in and out a lot faster tonight if I can walk straight by then. At least we won't be so far from the club. Last night we had to stroll through rattle country for several miles."

Linwood glared at Garland and almost felt a little pity. The man that everyone feared was all bruised and battered looking. "Garland, I need a full statement about what happened. Who were you chasing, and why?" Linwood had never seen the chief looking so vulnerable. He usually was apprehensive when talking with Garland; he never knew when Garland might freak out and start swinging. Although Garland had on a cast he could swing, he didn't look like he had the energy or strength right now.

"Mayor, my head is spinnin' and my arm is hurtin'. Can't we wait on this for a while?"

"No. We cannot." A town vehicle has been totaled, and the town is without a chief. As mayor, I have to determine what we will do to provide law-enforcement coverage until we get a new police car. Tommy Moore with the Highway Patrol is on the way over here now. He needs a statement from you right away. The doctor said that it was OK for you to give a statement. If you are not able, he said he would need to keep you here. Now, tell me, who were you chasing, and why?"

"Damn, a fellow almost gets killed tryin' to make your town a better place, and all you do is come over here to the hospital and harass me. Anyway, I was chasin' a pickup truck; I remember that. I'm pretty sure he ran a stop sign and was speedin' down Byrd Street. It'll come to me soon, I can pretty much see the truck but that stuff doc gave me has me a little woozy. Mayor, I need to go over and see JT. We have to get the details of our school trip planned out for tomorrow. You did agree, you know, that this fishin' trip for the school would be good PR for the town."

"I remember that, Garland. I'm still OK with you going, but JT will understand that we must conduct an investigation of this accident. I'll call him and tell him that you will be delayed. Now once again, what else can you tell me about this? Who were you chasing and why?"

PEDRO'S REPRIMAND
Chapter Six

Nadine ushered Pedro into the spacious office of the second most powerful person in the Bureau. As usual, there was no small talk. Clyde Tolson sat straight up in his chair with his hands holding on to the soft leather padded arms. Pedro knew to move right down to business. "Mr. Tolson, we need to get the Director to postpone the meeting with my agents working the Felici case in North and South Carolina. We've picked up information on the AMVETS Club tap in Timmonsville that they're planning a hit on a kid. We're still trying to find out who the kid is and where they plan to carry out the murder. It sounds like it's going to happen tomorrow, so our guys need to put all their effort into finding this kid.

"Pedro, you know as well as I, that when the Director plans a meeting, there has to be some very direct evidence to have him call it off."

"With all due respect, Sir, we're talking about a kid's life here. Surely he will delay the meeting for that?"

"I cannot make any guarantee of that, but I will discuss it with him at lunch."

"Mr. Tolson, we have to go in and see him now. Please at least get him on the phone."

"Agent Stokes, I am still your superior. I told you, I will discuss it with the Director at lunch. You know very well the Director does not want to be disturbed in the morning hours."

"Pedro realized that when Tolson called him Agent Stokes that things were getting serious. But so was a kid's life serious."

"Mr. Tolson, we must have all of the case agents in North and South Carolina working leads to see who this child could be. We can't go to a routine meeting and then find that a kid has been killed while we were listening to some oration."

"Mr. Stokes, consider yourself on report for insubordination. I will discuss the punitive action this afternoon. Report back here at three p.m. This discussion is terminated as of now."

"Sir, I'm trying to prevent a child from being murdered. That is precisely what the Bureau is supposed to be about. I've been a loyal person for all these years, but I can't just stand by while a child is killed if I can prevent that from happening."

"Agent Stokes, you are excused as of now. Report back here at three p.m." With that Tolson got up, opened the door, and motioned for Pedro to leave. Pedro sat and stared for a moment, his mind racing. Finally, he regained control of himself. He realized that if he got taken out of his position, he would not be able to do anything. Tolson stood by the door and held it as Pedro left and went back to his office.

"Donna, this is JT McGloughlin, I need to speak to Garland."

Donna White, as usual was running from one room to another, taking blood pressures, temperatures, handing out aspirin, trying to console family members, and checking IV machines. In spite of all the patients' needs she had to juggle, she never was caught without a calm attitude and a pleasant smile. "Hi, Mr. McGloughlin, I'll go and get a phone to him, he's in an examining room talking with the Mayor."

"Is he going to be able to leave? He's my deck hand on a school fishing project tomorrow."

"I don't know, Mr. McGloughlin, but I'll get him, and you and he can decide if he'll be able to make that kind of movement."

Donna brought a phone in, plugged it into the wall and handed it to Garland. Garland shuffled around, picked up the receiver, and moaned "Hullo."

"Garland, this is JT, how are you doing? Will you be able to make the trip tomorrow?"

"I don't know right now, JT. The Mayor is here and he's wantin' all the facts of the chase. I've been through an ordeal, and I hadn't quite got myself back together. If he would let me go on the trip, I think my head would be clear and we could do this investigating Monday."

"Let me speak with Linwood." Garland handed the phone to the Mayor.

"Hello JT, this is Linwood."

"Linwood, I need very badly to have Garland on that trip tomorrow. I have promised the Sims kid, and the entire school body, that the police chief will be using the net to pull in the catches. Because of that, the other students are already competing to go on next year's trip. Having the chief as the deck hand is one of the prime incentives. I would appreciate it if you would let him come over to my office so we can discuss the trip. It'll be a favor to me."

Linwood's mind jumped on that thought. "A favor to JT is a favor to Senator Furman. I need this investigation, but I also need the good will of the school superintendent, and most certainly, the good will of the Senator." Linwood didn't hesitate long. "Of course, JT, after all, this is a school function. I think the town can wait until Monday to find out what caused the accident."

"Thanks, Linwood, I won't forget this. Now let me speak a moment to Garland."

Linwood, trying to act nonchalant about having to back down, handed the phone to Garland. JT waited until he knew no one was listening and said, "Garland, don't gloat at the mayor now, you can do that later. Just get him to bring you by here, now. OK? I'll see you shortly."

Pedro had to have some quick action if he was to get the meeting canceled. He picked up the phone and buzzed Connie. Connie was half way through typing a lengthy investigative report, and she was exasperated. The type on the page had started looking uneven and light, and she was in the middle of changing the ribbon. Connie hated changing ribbons, it was so messy; but that was part of the job. She wiped ink off of her fingers, grabbed the phone, and said, "Yes sir."

"I need you to find Mark Hughley and Joe Means, right away. This is a first priority."

"Of course, but I do need to let you know that the report I'm typing is supposed to be on Mr. Tolson's desk no later than four p.m."

"Get back on that as quickly as you can, but first get me Mark and Joe."

"Yes sir, I'll let you know in just a few minutes."

George Malini was drawing up a will for one of his clients, Ira Rainwater, when the phone buzzer rang. Susan never buzzed George when he had a client in his office unless it was an emergency. "Excuse me, Ira, I don't normally get a buzz when I'm with a client." George looked at Ira as he said, "Yes, Susan."

"George, I hate to interrupt, but Gus Segars is on the line

hyperventilating. He says he absolutely must talk with you right now."

"Tell him to stay on the line, I'll be with him in three or four minutes."

"Yes, Sir."

"Ira, I have a client that has an emergency. Can we get back together tomorrow morning?"

Ira Rainwater was an even-tempered and reasonable person, but he was not used to having his business interrupted. "George, tomorrow will be fine; as long as you guarantee that I won't die before we get this will changed."

George was perplexed. He was a well-organized person, and never interrupted an appointment, but from Susan's voice it sounded urgent. "Ira, I do apologize. You're one of my most treasured friends as well as a valuable client. I would not even consider asking this if it wasn't an emergency. I would do the same for you."

"I understand George. How about 10:00 tomorrow in my office? It'll be quiet there."

"Thanks, Ira, I'll be at your place in the morning at ten."

"Pedro, I have Mark on the line; I'm putting him through."

"Thanks, Connie."

"Hi, Mark. How are things in the Carolinas?"

"They're pretty much OK here Pedro, but Bob is picking up some hot and heavy stuff from the club in Timmonsville. This is the best wire we've ever had, but we still have not been able to determine who the kid is. There's so many things going on with those guys, killing a kid seems to be pretty uneventful."

"Then you don't have any clues as to who it is, Mark? No name, or reasons?"

"Not yet, but with the communication that's going on, I

feel like we'll have something soon. We have everyone on alert. Also, Joe and Jerry are going back into the club tonight after closing. Hopefully, if we don't get anything off the wire, then maybe something will be in the files there."

"OK, Mark, now the next hurdle is the meeting tomorrow. I have to be back in Clyde's office at three p.m. I have not been able to get a cancellation thus far, but I'm not going to let a kid get killed just so I can listen to a Bureau political speech. Therefore, I am ordering you to have all agents under your supervision continue around-the-clock efforts to find the child. I know I don't have to order you, but I'm doing so to avoid any repercussions on anyone but me if it backfires."

"Pedro, surely you're not going to disobey the Director? You know that's sudden death in slow motion?"

"I understand that, Mark, but this is what I've decided. If I have to end my career over this, I can live with that. If I don't take this action and a child is harmed, I can't live with that. So, don't discuss this conversation with your guys, except for Joe. You can let him know, but have him call me so that I can order him to comply also. I don't want to be responsible for anyone being drummed out of the corps except myself."

"OK, Pedro, you're doing the right thing in a moral sense, but otherwise, you're facing a firing squad without a blindfold. Hell, Pedro, you won't even get a last cigarette."

"I don't smoke. Now get out and find that kid. Now!"

"Pedro, we'll make every human effort to find him today."

Mark was finally able to get in touch with Joe. "Joe, you can't repeat this to anyone, but our boss, Pedro, has put his neck in a noose."

"What'd you mean, Mark? What's happened?"

"Nothing yet, but Tolson has ordered Pedro to his office this afternoon. Pedro wouldn't give me all of the details, but he may be planning to ignore the demand to attend the Director's meeting tomorrow."

"He can't do that Mark, that's certain suicide."

"I tried to tell him that, Joe, but he said, and rightly so, this kid's life is more important than the meeting."

"What can we do, Mark?"

"You are to call him but I don't think there's anything we can do except find the kid before tomorrow. You know Pedro, he doesn't change his mind when it's made up. He's ordered me to have all of my agents work this case and ignore the meeting. He plans to order you also, so you won't be responsible for what happens."

"Ahg, Mark, we've gotta find this child, right away. We can't let Pedro do this."

"I'm having my guys stay in touch at all times. If you and Jerry can find any clues at the club tonight, maybe we can track down the kid and still make the meeting."

"Jerry and I'll turn the club topside down, but since we already know that Webb and McGloughlin are involved, did Pedro give us permission to lean on them?"

"No. He doesn't think we have enough information to push them yet, but we are watching all of the ones that we know to be involved. By the way, Bucky Harris called in and said Garland had an accident, and is in the hospital. He's finding out the details now, but he should be checking in with me soon. The police car was totaled so Garland may be out of action for a while. Of the others, the only one that I think would take an active part in a killing would be Dalton Sellars. He'd cut his Grandmother's throat if she put the wrong kind of jelly on his toast."

"Yeah, he's the one that would enjoy killing a kid. I'll call

Pedro now and see if there's anything more pro-active he'll let us do."

On the ten-mile trip to JT's office, Linwood and Garland spoke only a few words. Garland had a little difficulty getting out of the car, but Linwood just sat and glared while Garland struggled out. He finally was able to hobble into the superintendent's office. Once inside, Garland mumbled and moaned as he eased down into one of the plush overstuffed chairs. Finally, he got settled enough to talk. "JT, you shoulda seen the look on Linwood's face when he was on the phone with you. He was all torn up. He wanted to hassle me, but he didn't wanna refuse you. He looked like somebody had squeezed Texas Pete on his ulcers. Thanks, you made my day."

"We'll jump on his case more later, but right now I want to know if you're up to going tomorrow."

"I feel wobbly, that's a fact, but I can make it; It's somethin that has to be done. Actually, I'll enjoy it once we get out to sea."

"Well, it will still be a long and tiring day, so I'll take you home so you can get some rest." It was only a few minutes to Garland's house, but JT had to wake him when they got there. "I'll be here at five a.m. Garland, so be ready."

The Mayflower Restaurant, one of the better places in Washington, was usually filled at lunchtime with high profile attorneys and department heads of various federal agencies. Attorneys sipped martinis and discussed arguments they would be presenting later that day in court. Heads of federal agencies made decisions that would affect every US citizen for generations to come.

Director Hoover and his close associate, Clyde Tolson, ate in the Mayflower Restaurant every day. They always came late so that it was not crowded, and they always sat at the same table. The table was placed, at Hoover's request, far enough away from other tables to offer privacy. The waiters never had to linger at the table: Clyde's secretary, Nadine, telephoned the Maître'd each morning and ordered the daily fare for both Hoover and Tolson. Hoover required the head chef to personally prepare the meal each day.

Hoover sat with his back to the wall and Clyde was directly across, facing Hoover. Both men were finicky eaters, both ate slowly, and neither ever talked with food in the mouth. This day, Clyde picked at his meal and left most of his food untouched, except for his salad with tomatoes, onions and spinach. Clyde always had spinach instead of lettuce in his salad. As soon as the bus staff cleared the table and brought coffee, Clyde told Hoover about his meeting with Pedro.

"Edgar, I had a rather strained discussion with Assistant Director Stokes today. He does not want to have his agents attend the meeting tomorrow."

"Why not?" Hoover raised his eyebrows and wrinkled his long, tall forehead.

"Seems the Antonio Felici case is producing a lot of conversations on the wire, and they have talked of making a hit on a kid. He thinks it will be very soon and he wants the agents to continue on the case and find the kid. He says it will look bad if a child is killed while the agents are at a meeting."

"What did you tell him, Clyde?"

"I told him he would have to attend the meeting, unless he

is excused. He is to be in my office at three p.m. I had to put him on report. I've never seen him like that."

"Does he realize that I'm the one that called the meeting?"

"Yes, he is aware of that, Edgar, but he is adamant that his agents need to be out finding the people that are trying to kill that child. He says the hit is planned for tomorrow."

"Clyde, I must either have this meeting or find some other way to get the message across. If this investigation rattles the bones of Tom Furman, the Bureau will suffer. I need to address the agents about the sensitive political issues in this case. However, he may have a point. If a child is harmed, and he told the press that it could have been prevented, it would be bad PR for us."

Clyde had a hangdog look. He had told Pedro he was on report. If the director let him get by with insubordination he would have a problem with Pedro from then on. "What do you want me to do, Edgar? He was insubordinate."

"Tell him that he is on probation. Tell him that I'll deal with his insubordination later, but for now, tell him to find that kid. Advise him that he is forbidden to take any action that would make Tom Furman unhappy. We'll reschedule the meeting as soon as the child is found."

"I'll tell him at 3:00 p.m. Edgar"

Pedro, sat in Tolson's outer office, and thought back over his twenty-five years with the Bureau. There had been a lot of good times and a few bad ones, but this seemed much worse than the rest of the bad totaled. Pedro wasn't ready to hang up his career, but he couldn't keep it going if it meant that he had to ignore what the Bureau stood for. "Hoover himself has emphasized that the 'I' in FBI stands for integrity. How could I have integrity and let a serious crime happen that I might prevent. No way am I calling off my order for the agents to keep working on this case, unless I'm stripped of my official duties. Then it'll be out of my hands. If that happens, and Clyde Tolson wants to order them to the meeting, he'll be responsible for the outcome. I'll have the satisfaction of ending my career with my integrity intact."

Nadine was busily typing reports and taking numerous phone calls. Finally, the intercom buzzed. It was 3:25 p.m., and Pedro had been waiting in Nadine's office for thirty minutes. Pedro and Nadine were on reasonably good terms, but she was not one that you could ever feel close to, so Pedro had waited silently.

"Pedro, Mr. Tolson is ready to see you now."

Pedro walked in, and Tolson, as always, was seated behind his massive mahogany desk. As usual there was one piece of paper precisely in the center of the highly-polished desk-top finish. Pedro could only imagine that the paper was about him. Tolson didn't say anything, he just sat and looked puzzled, like he had not decided what action to take or else, the director had allowed Pedro to miss the meeting. Finally, Tolson picked up the piece of paper and handed it to Pedro. "Agent Stokes, I have discussed your reprimand with the Director. You are on probation, and the Director will deal with you personally, but as of now he has permitted you and your agents to work on the case around the clock. The meeting will be rescheduled as soon as the child is safe. You still must be held accountable for your action, but it will be postponed. You have not been forgiven for your unprofessional conduct. Do you understand that?"

Pedro nodded, and read the memo entitled:

OFFICIAL NOTICE OF CORRECTIVE ACTION.

This memo is to certify that Assistant Director P.R Stokes was insubordinate to a superior on September 7, 1945. Corrective action will be taken by the Director as soon as all facts are determined.

I understand that I am on probation until further notice.
Peter R Stokes _____Date_____
Clyde Tolson_____
Assistant Bureau Director
cc: Director J Edgar Hoover

Pedro stared at the paper, looked at Tolson, picked up a pen, and signed. "Am I excused?"

"Yes, but I want to be kept apprised of every effort made in this case. In addition, you are to take no action that might cause concern to Senator Tom Furman. Do you understand?" Pedro nodded, mumbled a weak, "Yes sir" and left.

"Joe It's almost 2 a.m., I wish the heck those folks would get out of there." They had found a large oak tree that they could lean against and still have a good view of the front of the club. Mosquitoes were buzzing and biting, and they both were sweating heavily in the humid air. "I do too, but surely they won't stay much longer. Some of that crowd must need to sleep sometimes."

Joe and Jerry had been waiting over an hour for the club to close so they could reseal the skylight and look around the club. "I don't like at all sitting motionless in these woods, I can still feel the vibration of that last rattle."

"Yeah, just sitting here is worse than moving. You figure a

rattler will get out of your way when you're moving, but when you're sitting still, they might be attracted to the warmth of our bodies. They're cold natured, and would no doubt like to snuggle up to us."

"Change the subject, I don't like that thought."

"There are only three cars there now, Joe. One is Dalton's; do you recognize the other two?"

"I'm not sure, but I think the 39 Ford belongs to the bartender, Lacy. I've seen the DeSoto, but I can't be sure. Gus Segars is not there, or at least his Lincoln isn't. Wonder where he is this time of night?"

"Oh, there comes one of them, can you tell who it is?"

Actually, there come two, Jerry. One is Lacy, and the other I don't recognize. That means Dalton is still in there, but we don't know if he's alone or not. God, I hope he gets out soon, I'm anxious to get in and see what we can find. How long do you think it'll take for you to re-caulk the roof?"

"I think that I can do that in ten or fifteen minutes, then I'll come down and help you look around. Hey, the lights went out. Dalton is finally leaving. As soon as he clears the driveway, let's go."

Sonny lay back on his bed and listened to one of his favorite radio programs: "The Squeaking Door." It was late, and the program usually came on earlier, but tonight it was some type of repeat special. Sonny, had heard it the first time, and was frightened by it, but this time he had been through so much he was oblivious to fear. His Mom was asleep, but she had promised to get him up at four a.m. to see him off for his trip. He read and reread the worn handwritten letter and looked at the pictures of his dad and one of his buddies on the war project. He wanted so badly to be able to talk in person with his daddy, but some type of war rules prohibited him from talking right now. What he really couldn't understand was, the war had been over more than several weeks and his Daddy was still on a secret mission. Some big project was in the works and his daddy was right in the midst of it. The letter Sonny received was two pages, but his Dad had written a long letter and then went back over and censored out the restricted parts. There were just a few lines left; those few lines were like a fairy tale.

> *"Dearest Sonny, I wish you could be here. You would not believe the xxxxxxxxx I can't give you any details, but I can assure you that this war will soon be over. You and I are going to spend a lot of time together. Maybe we'll even come back here to xxxxxxxxxxx on a trip, and I can show you the xxxxxxxxx I love you very much, and I miss you. Stay good and sweet, and keep up your grades at school. I'll have some very important follow up duties, even after the war is officially over, but I'll finish it up as quickly as possible. I'll at least be able to xxxxxxxxxxx*
> *Love you lots, Dad."*

Sonny had read the letter, and cried on it so often, the few words left were unreadable. Sonny held the letter and prayed, "God, please let my daddy come home. I need him now more than ever. If I knew where he was, I'd go there as soon as I get out of JT's car tomorrow. Well, maybe when I'm reported kidnapped they'll let my Daddy come home. This trip may accomplish more things than getting back at Garland and JT."

Margie was frightened. She had never seen Gus like this; he was a madman. She and Gus had been seeing each other privately for over a year before Gladys caught them together at a nightclub in Darlington. Margie was glad that Gladys had found out about them so they could get their relationship in the open. But now, Gus was banging the walls of her Lake City apartment. The landlord lived just two units over and would surely call the cops if Gus didn't quit raging and breaking things.

"That damn bitch. I gave her a life of leisure for 22 years, now she's tryin to take every damn thing I've got. Well, she ain't gonna find me bowing to her. She don't know nothin' bout my business affairs. Let her talk."

"Gus, please settle down, Mr. Phipps will call the police. That'll make Gladys that much happier, and also that much easier for her in the divorce proceedings."

"I'll settle down when I'm damn good and ready. Fix me another Scotch and soda, and shut up."

The phone rang and Margie ran to the kitchen to answer. "Margie, this is Jim Phipps, what's going on over there. Do I need to call the police?"

"Please don't, Mr. Phipps. Gus got some bad news today and he's upset, but he'll be OK in just a few minutes."

"Margie, I'll give it five more minutes and then I'm calling. I'm sorry, but I have other tenants that need to sleep."

"I'll quiet him down, Mr. Phipps. Thanks for the few minutes."

Marge walked over and handed Gus the Scotch and soda, and also a cheeseburger that she had fixed earlier. "Please eat this, Gus."

Gus stared at Margie for a moment, then at the burger. "I'll eat when I'm damn good and ready. You understand that?" With that, Gus flung the burger against the wall.

Cheese, hamburger grease, onions, mayo, catsup and bits of lettuce stuck on the faded wallpaper momentarily, then slowly oozed down to the floor.

Margie knew now she'd have to find another place to live. That is, if she lived thorough Gus's rage storm tonight. "Please, Gus, Mr. Phipps just called and he's gonna call the cops in five minutes if we don't settle down."

"HE'S WHAT? I'll go over and whip his ass. Nobody threatens Gus Segars!" Gus whirled toward the door, ran into a lamp, knocked it over, and spilled his Scotch and soda on the sofa. The lamp hit him in the face and the hot bulb took a patch of skin off of his cheek. Gus picked up the lamp and slammed it on the coffee table. With that the lights went out. "Cut those lights back on. Now!"

"I'm trying to find another light, Gus. Just sit tight." Margie put her hand on the switch, but delayed cutting it on. "Lord, please help him go to sleep."

It wasn't unusual for Antonio to be at the loading dock in the wee hours of the morning. He had a sleeper sofa, and often didn't go home for days. Tonight he was gathering papers to take home and burn. He was always careful about leaving a trail, but now that things were hot, he felt better if nothing could possibly be in any of his files. He grabbed the phone on first ring. "Yeah."

"Tony, this is Gilbert; I got a message to call you."

"Where are you calling from?"

"I'm not at home, don't worry. Nell has been so pushy about me talkin more to the feds that I've tried to stay away. I'm at a phone booth in the Charlotte Inn."

"I've not heard from you lately, Gil, what the hell's going on? Sterling got you out of jail several days ago. Have the feds been leanin' on you again? What have you told them?"

"Tony, I've not told 'em nothin. You know I wouldn't do that. They've almost stopped askin'. The last thing they wanted to know was why I wasn't drivin' no more. I told 'em that I still hadn't gotten over the shock of bein hijacked."

"What else did they ask?"

"They wanted to know where I was gettin money from to live on. I told 'em the union was takin care of me 'til I get over the shakes."

"Gilbert, you know they've not given up. You hafta watch what you say and where you go. Stay in touch with me, but don't call from your house. If Nell hears you talkin with me she'd probably report it to the G's."

"Right, Tony. Look, I'm feelin better now. I think I'm ready to get back to driving. I miss the heck out of it. This is the first time in ten years I've not been at the wheel of my semi. In fact, what do you think of me back next week?"

"If you're ready I think it would be good. If you stay out too long those G-boys will try to make somethin out of the union supportin' you while you get back your health. Why don't you plan on a trip Monday? I'll line up somethin. I got several Baltimore and some Florida trips comin' up that don't have any military supplies. I'm keepin' you off government trips for a while, else you might get some extra scrutiny from the Quartermasters."

"Right, Tony, I'll be there Monday Mornin."

"Joe, I've got the skylight sealed pretty well. It's a good thing, too, because there are some dark clouds coming up. Hopefully, I've got it leak proof. Have you found anything down here?"

"I found some things that might interest the IRS, and we'll get them on it, but there's nothing here that would tell who the kid is they plan to whack. This is interesting though.

Look back in this storeroom; they have an awful lot of premium brand whiskey in there: Seagram's VO, Crown Royal, Jack Daniels and Cutty Sark Scotch. Those are the exact brands that were taken off the truck that was going to Charleston Navy Base. You and I know that Gus and Dalton don't serve anything that good in this place. I'm sure this is from the haul that was stolen last month. We'll report it to the Navy and their investigators can let us know what to look for on a return trip. I've got a couple of sample bottles to see if they can verify if they were part of the shipment."

"Great, we can celebrate on the way to the truck." "I don't think we can these aren't filled with cranberry juice. Right now, though, we need to get out of here and call Pedro. He's standing by the phone."

As soon as Gus passed out, Margie had called Dalton. There was a knock on the door and Margie came running. "Dalton, thank God you're here. I don't know what got into Gus, but as you can see he went wild. My landlord had just called to say he was calling the police when Gus hit the lamp and passed out. I'm scared. If he wakes up and makes any more ruckus, Jimmy will have him arrested. Can you get him to your house and let him sleep it off?"

"Hell, Margie, Gus *couldn't* have been too drunk. Look at how perfectly he hit the center of that wall with—what is that a hamburger? I'm hungry, you got another one of those?"

"Dalton, please just get him out, I'm afraid. What's wrong with him? Why is he so angry at Gladys? I know he hates her, but I've never seen him like this."

"That bitch has been givin' him some grief. I've begged him to let me go and see her, and she won't be pushin him no more. He had'n give me the OK yet, but now that she's pushin so hard, maybe he will. Anyway, I'll take him to my house. We got some business to check on tomorrow mornin anyway. Open up the door, I'll carry him to my car."

Joe and Jerry stopped at an all-night diner on the outskirts of Florence, and Joe tracked Pedro down. "Pedro, Jerry and I just got back from the club, but unfortunately we didn't find any clues about the kid. We found some stuff that will be interesting to pursue later, but what do you want us to do now?"

"I've spent the evening going over the transcripts that Bob has picked up, Joe, and I'm pretty sure that Garland and JT McGloughlin are involved with the kid. There's no mention of them by name, but there are some discussions about the Senator's boy and chief taking care of the "problem." I want you and Jerry to stay right behind those two and see what they're up to. Mark has several of his guys on the way to cover Gus and Dalton. Whatever they have planned is going down soon, so we'll just have to watch them. Mark also has someone on the way to observe Antonio's place, but the problem there is, he has so many goons that he can use we can't watch them all. We do have an agent in Birmingham, though, that's married to a Charlotte girl and believe it or not he can horse around a semi. He's gotten his new ID and will start driving next week out of Antonio's dock. If whatever they plan hasn't happened before then, we'll at least have someone to watch the store there."

"Pedro, what about putting wires in Garland and JT's offices?"

"We're gonna consider that, Joe, but, even though I don't like to back off of anything for political reasons, that's a hot issue. If we're wrong about JT's involvement and he finds we've bugged his office Senator Furman could cause budget problems for the Bureau. I'm under orders to handle Furman with baby diapers, but if we pick up any further evidence that they're involved, then we'll do it."

"OK, meanwhile we'll stick on 'em like a squashed fly on a wall. I just hope we can prevent the kid-whacking."

SONNY HEADS FOR CHARLESTON
Chapter Seven

Hannah shut off the alarm at four a.m., got up and went into Sonny's room; "Sonny, You're up and dressed, I thought I'd have to shake you awhile. You really are excited. I can't wait to eat some of those fish tomorrow."

"I am excited, Mama. This is going to be a big day for me."

"I'm so happy that you realize now how special this trip is. It's such an honor."

"Right, Mama, I finally realized how important it is and I can't wait to get started."

"What's all that stuff you're carrying? I didn't know you would need your Cub Scout camping gear. Why do you have so many peanut butter and jelly sandwiches? You know JT will have lunch on the boat."

"He'll probably have some dried beans or something, Mama, and you know how I like 'P jelly's.' I've just got a few things: my compass, my Boy Scout knife and I thought it would be nice to carry a few of the C rations that Daddy sent me. It'll be like a camping trip."

"Well, you sure do have enough food. Anyway, for now, how about some bacon and eggs, and even coffee if you like."

Sonny was surprised that his mama had offered him coffee. One of her rules was, "You can't drink coffee until you're twelve.

"Coffee, Mama? Are you sure? That would be great."

"Well, finish getting ready, and I'll have us some breakfast in just a few minutes. Garland and JT will be here soon."

Miriam Webb shook Garland, "Get up and shut off that

alarm." Garland just mumbled and moaned. Miriam got up, pushed the alarm button and pulled the covers off of Garland. Flab was spread everywhere. "What an awful sight" Miriam thought, "Why in hell did I marry such a miserable excuse for a human being? Get up, Garland, or I'm gonna roll you out on the floor." Miriam didn't really care one way of the other about the trip he was going on, she just knew that if he stayed at the house he would be a nuisance. He'd be wanting this and hollering for that. "Now get up Garland. Now!"

Garland winced in pain, but managed to push to a sit-up position on the bed. The pills that Dr. McLeod had given him were making him dizzy. He put his feet on the floor but couldn't stand up. Miriam tried to help, but he screamed for her to let him sit there for a few moments.

"Garland, JT will be here soon. Now get up, I'll fix some coffee." She left him there and went into the kitchen. While she was making the coffee she felt the house shake. "Old blubber butt's finally up, I'll be rid of him for the day. Let JT babysit with him."

JT was anxious. He got up before the alarm went off and started getting dressed. He never even thought about what he would wear. Even on a fishing trip he wore a suit and tie. If only he knew what a joke it was with the other boaters he might think twice, but JT never went anywhere without that dress up outfit.

JT turned the burner on the gas stove and lit the fumes with a kitchen match. Once he got the pot on the flame, he stropped his straight razor and mowed off the little pieces of stubble that he called whiskers. "I hope those pills that Doc McLeod gave to Garland don't prevent him from going, it just is no way to cancel this trip, even if I have to call Dalton to go and be the deckhand. No way can I do it alone." JT hated the little Sims brat, and he sure as hell didn't want him to tell what they had been up to, but no way could he be the one to shove him over to the sharks.

Joe and Jerry rode by JT's house and then by Garland's house. All was quite. "Joe, I'm starving, you think maybe we could scoot over to Jimbo's and get a couple of eggs before we stake out Webb and McGloughlin. Surely they won't be up to anything this early."

"I think you're right, my tummy's growling too. It won't take us long to run over to Florence and get back. There won't even be a station in this town with coffee going until seven or so."

"Yeah, we'll get Jimbo's short order guy to fix us a couple of takeout plates. On the way, I'm gonna take Julian's truck back and pick up our car. I'll feel more ready for action if we have red lights and whistles."

"Right. Not to mention the shotguns in the trunk."

Garland was as kooky as JT. He never went anywhere without his gold braided uniform. Problem right now though, how could he get it on? The cast was too big to go into the sleeve holes. Garland put his left arm in, shook the other sleeve over his shoulder and with a lot of effort got a couple of buttons hooked. Now, how in the heck do I do the pants? He wasn't used to this one arm stuff, and he could tell Miriam was in no mood to help him with that. He thought about asking JT to come in and support him while he pulled up his pants, but that didn't conjure up a pleasant notion either.

It took a lot of effort but Garland sat on the edge of the bed, got one leg in, then the other, and gradually shifted until the waist band was around his layer of "Protective fat." "Any law enforcement officer needs that layer of protection," he reasoned. "It's good against fists, ice picks, knives, and will even slow down a 38 slug." After a little straining he was able to get the button in place. Actually, he had trouble with that even when he had two good arms. He shuffled to the kitchen and Miriam poured his coffee. "Damn. How does anybody learn to hold a coffee cup with the left hand?" Then he wondered how he would handle his peace machine. He never went anywhere without that, but could he use it with his left arm?

Joe and Jerry drove the ten miles to Florence in less than eight minutes and quickly exchanged the Dodge pickup truck for the government Plymouth. A short time later they had two boxes of scrumptious smelling food, two extra-large containers of coffee, and were on the way back to Timmonsville. Jerry pushed it to 85, and the Bureau Plymouth felt comfortable with that. Five a.m. on a Saturday morning in this county and there were only a few cars on the road. Getting stopped by the highway patrol wasn't a problem. Not only was there no patrol on the road this time of morning, but they had the G-man ID if the unlikely event of a speeding stop should happen.

JT drove in front of Garland's house and decided to go up and knock. Miriam came to the door and told JT that Garland was ready but he needed a little steadying to get to the car. JT went inside and balanced JT and they stumbled out. JT stayed an arm's length away. He wanted to steady Garland, but no way would he even attempt to catch him if he started falling. "Heck, it would take a crane to hold him up." JT finally got him into the car and headed for Sonny

Sims' house. "Garland, you sure you're up to going? You seem a little shaky."

"I don't feel good JT, that's a fact, but I still can't wait to get my hands on little sneaky nose's neck. I never even liked him before all that snoopin' he did. I really do think he shot out some street lights and then lied to me. Anybody that'll lie to a police officer deserves to be thrown to the sharks."

"Garland, remember, we're gonna question him first and see if he saw anything, then we'll find out if any kids were with him. I still think he wasn't there alone."

"I know he wadn't, and him not comin back from the trip will serve as a reminder to any others that was snoopin' with him. I'm sure it was them Buddin boys."

"Garland, before we get to the Sims house I want you to promise to let me handle everything until I tell you it's up to you. You understand and agree to that? We can't go off halfcocked on this. We've got to find out what he knows, and then decide what action we have to take."

"I'm OK with that, JT, but I can tell you now, you may as well get the notion out of your head that we won't have to carry this thing through. You're not gettin soft on me are you? If so, take me back home. Damned if I wanna spend the day baitin' fish hooks for one of the little rascals."

"Garland, I'm not getting soft on the idea, if we have to do it. I'm simply saying that we may have to change the course. If we determine that he doesn't know anything we'll tell him the weather report doesn't look good and pack up and go home. Actually, the weather doesn't look good; it's cloudy over toward Charleston. We may not be able to go out as far as I had anticipated, but even if the weather is bad we can get far enough out for our chore. Actually, the stormy weather will help us. If it's storming, and he falls overboard, there will be fewer questions asked. Bad weather may be a blessing."

JT pulled in front of Sonny's house and no sooner had he stopped the car than Sonny and Hannah came out. "Good morning JT, good morning Garland. I'm glad to see you're OK, I heard that was a pretty bad smash up you were in."

"Yes Ma'am, it was, but I'm pretty tuff. Takes more'n an oak tree to do me in."

"Well you better be well enough to take care of my boy, Garland. He's excited now, but he was afraid earlier, and when he sees the ocean he might get scared. You watch him good now, you hear?"

"Mrs. Sims, I'm gonna take good care of your little boy. Now hop in Sonny Boy, we gotta get out to the tuna runs before they get full of food. If they eat too much before we get there they won't bite our bait."

Sonny climbed into the back of JT's 1941 Packard Clipper. It was roomy, and Sonny thought, "Thank God it has four doors. I can make my exit when the time comes."

Jerry pulled up in front of JT's house and parked. "I don't see any activity in there, Joe. Hand me one of those plates, I'm starving."

"Yeah, I guess JT is snoozing, but I don't see his Packard, Jerry. Wasn't it here when we drove by earlier?"

"Oh, my God, Joe, you're right. His car was on the side of the house. Where in heck could he have gone this early in the morning?"

"I don't know, Jerry, but we've gotta find out. I've finished my eggs, move over here and eat while I cruise around town. He can't be very far away."

"Drive by Garland's and see if there's any activity there." Joe cruised slowly while watching for JT's car. He pulled over across from Garland's.

"There's a light on in Garlands, Joe."

"Yeah, but he might be up taking some pain pills. His car's over at Redfern Ford, so we can't tell if he's home or not."

"Do you suppose that JT could have come over and picked him up?"

"I don't know, I'm gonna ride around some more and see if we see any other activity."

"Most of the houses are dark, but there's one that has a light on. Wonder who lives there?

"I don't know, but I don't like JT's car being gone. I've got an edgy feeling about that. Let's ride over to Clyde Moody's house and get him up. He lives not far away on Keith Street. Maybe he can give us a clue as to whether a kid lives in that house. Even if so, it could be a paper carrier, but we've got to try something."

Sonny sat close to the door. He knew the route they would take to Charleston, and he had a spot in mind to make his escape. When they stopped at one of the lights on Bay Street, he would jump. If no red lights or stop signs caught them he would make his jump at the dock. The dock was his last choice because he didn't know if there would be any people around at that time of morning. The one thing for sure, no way they could catch him once he got out. The only concern he had was what if they pulled off on a dirt road in a wooded area? It could happen. One of them could say he needed to use the bathroom and all of a sudden Sonny would be in the woods with them. It wasn't a thought he liked, but he was still confident he could be out of sight before they even realized that he was running. Sonny even toyed with the idea of telling them that he had to use the bathroom and then making a run from there. He discarded that idea. He could be miles from any town and might get lost in the woods. The Charleston plan was better.

Sonny was about to throw up; Garland was smoking one Camel after another and JT was sucking on a Cuban cigar. Even with the windows down it still smelled like a burning trash dump. Sonny was sitting directly behind Garland. He knew that with the cast on Garland's arm he couldn't move fast, but once when Garland shifted in his seat and looked back, Sonny felt the hairs on his neck rise up and his heart started pounding. He put his hand on the door handle and got ready to make his move; no way would they put their hands on him even if the car was moving sixty miles an hour. He would jump before he would let them get him cornered. Finally, Chief said "Sonny, there's a pack of food back there on the floor, get me one of them honey buns out. You can have one if you like."

"Yes, sir, if you don't mind I believe I will have one, I'm already hungry."

JT and Chief relaxed a little. Now that Sonny was talking and eating, they convinced themselves that he was totally unaware of what was in store for him.

"Who is it?" Clyde Moody was wiping the sleep from his eyes. It was after midnight when he got off duty, and it was only two hours since he had gotten into bed. Whoever was there had better have a good reason.

"Clyde, it's Jerry Hamby and Joe Means, with the FBI. We need your help."

Clyde cut the porch light on, opened the door, and Jerry and Joe stepped inside. Jerry had worked some cases in Florence County and he and Clyde knew each other. He introduced Joe, and then got right to the point.

"Clyde, we have reason to believe that a young boy is in danger. There's a light on at 504 Warren Street. Does a child live there?"

"You mean the gray house next to Pee Dee State Bank?"

"Yes, that's it."

"As a matter of fact Sonny Sim's lives there. He's about ten or eleven years old. Why would anyone wanna hurt him?"

"We'll give you more details later; he may not even be the one. What can you tell us about him and do you know why they would be up so early? Is he a paper carrier?"

"He was a paper carrier until last week, and then he just quit. I didn't get a paper for several days, and when I called the office in Florence they said Sonny just didn't show up. Tom Boland, a district supervisor, is training Melvin Moore to take over the route."

"Do you have any idea why he may have just quit? Have you seen him since?"

"No, I don't know why, but he was always on time and the paper was never in my bushes. He's a pretty typical kid; his folks are good friends of mine. His Dad is somewhere working on a secret project as a civilian transportation expert."

"Does his mother get up early, and could he be carrying the paper again?"

"No, on both counts. His mother takes care of a sister-in-law in Florence, but she leaves late. I'm quite sure Sonny is not on the route, I saw Tom Boland yesterday, and he's still training Melvin Moore as Sonny's replacement. Is there anything that I can do? Oh, heck, I forgot. I know where Sonny is today, he's gone on a fishing trip with the school superintendent and the local police chief."

Joe and Jerry flinched. "Do you know where they're going, Clyde?"

"No, but JT has a cabin cruiser that he keeps in

Charleston Harbor, they may be going there. I've never seen it, but I've heard JT's been to Cuba in it, so I guess it's a pretty large boat."

"Thanks, Clyde, sorry to wake you, but now that you're awake, we need another favor."

"Of course, Mr. Means, whatever I can do."

"Since you know Sonny's mother, and we know that she's up, how about calling over there and see if she has any information about where they're going. Just tell her that you're trying to get in touch with Garland about his accident."

Garland asked JT to stop if he saw an open filling station. He was about out of Camels. Sonny decided this would be his jump out place. He would tell them he was using the bathroom and then take off. JT pulled into a dilapidated Shell station, and JT and Garland went inside. Sonny looked around the area and there was nothing but woods. It looked like a spooky place. He wasn't going to go to anybody's house, but he wanted to be somewhere with people around. If he made his move here, and they caught him, he would have no help. The station had only one person working, a man that looked to be in his eighties, at least. Sonny opted to go on to Charleston and jump out there. It seemed unlikely that they would try anything before they got there, so he could relax a little. Anyway, it wasn't far.

"Mrs. Sims, this is Clyde Moody, how are you this morning?"

"I'm fine, Clyde, but something must be wrong for you to be calling this early. Nothing has happened to Sonny has it? You don't have any bad news about Jack do you?"

"No, nothing's wrong that I know of Hannah. I'm trying to

get in touch with Garland about his accident yesterday, and I heard that he was going fishing with JT and Sonny."

"Yes, they left here about an hour or so ago, Clyde. Garland has a cast on, and looked like he had already been out to sea. He was as pale as a ghost. It's so cloudy I still wonder if they'll be able to go out and fish, and I'm concerned about that. If you talk with Garland tell him not to go out unless the weather is OK."

"I'll tell him Mrs. Sims; I'm sure Sonny will be fine." Clyde hung up the phone. "Fellows, Garland and JT picked up Sonny about an hour ago. They're going to JT's boat in Charleston."

"Thanks Clyde, we may need you some more today, what time do you go on duty?"

"I'm set to go in at four this afternoon, but it doesn't matter if I'm on or off duty. I'll do whatever I can."

We appreciate your help Clyde, and we may need you later. We don't want anyone to panic, so keep quiet about this. If you hear anything suspicious call this number and have them get in touch with us."

"No problem, you just holler if you need me."

Joe and Jerry went back to the car and Joe called Pedro. "Pedro, Jerry and I just found out that there's a kid named Sonny Sims that's on a fishing trip with JT and Garland and they're on the way now to Charleston. They've been gone about an hour already."

"Sonny Sims? Do you know anything about him, or why he's on the trip?"

"Some kind of school trip, Pedro, but he's the only student going with them so that seems a little strange."

"With all of the info we have, this must be the kid that's in danger. I want you two to high tail it to Charleston. Meanwhile, I'll call the Coast Guard and get them to find out where the McGloughlin boat is stored."

"We're headed out right now, Pedro. By the way, they're in JT's black, four-door, 1941 Packard Clipper, license number A-55-321."

"Right, Joe. Also, I'm gonna call MB Huggins and have him get down to Charleston. If they're already in the water when you get there he can assist the Coast Guard in finding the boat. Get going."

Jerry gunned the 41 Plymouth and the tires screeched and the engine roared. Bureau cars weren't especially hot cars, but by the time Jerry hit high gear they were above the legal limit. "Jerry, I sure would like to know what this is all about. Evidently though, that Sims boy saw something, or found something out, and they're gonna throw him off the ship. I wonder why he went with them if he knows they know, and if he doesn't know they know, how do they know he knows?"

"Joe, speak English. I'm doing ninety miles an hour, and I can't decipher all that gibberish."

"Jerry, I'm just trying to fit a few things together, but right now it doesn't make sense. Could he have seen something while he was delivering papers? Surely, if so, he would know they saw him and he wouldn't be going with them voluntarily"

"Yeah Joe, I hope when we hear from Pedro he'll have some new information."

"This is Commander Ogden; how can I help you?" Coast Guard Commander Mac Ogden had been on duty almost 24 hours. He constantly held a coffee cup in his hand filled with Coast Guard coffee, which as the legend goes, makes Navy coffee seem like weak chicken broth.

"Commander, this is Inspector Pete Stokes with the FBI in Washington, I need to know right away where a Florence county resident, JT McGloughlin, keeps his boat. I don't know any numbers or anything about the boat, but it's an urgent matter."

"We have every boat in the harbor listed by the name of the owner, Inspector. I should be able to get that information to you right away."

"As soon as you determine where it's kept, I need you to get a patrol boat over to it. Don't let anyone leave until my guys get there. Call me back at FR4014 in Charlotte as soon as you find it. Meanwhile, have all of your craft that are cruising the harbor stop any boats that are leaving. If you stop one that belongs to McGloughlin, don't let them leave. I have agents on the way to Charleston now."

"Right, Inspector. We shouldn't have any trouble finding them today because there isn't much activity on the water. We've got a storm on the way, so already we're advising any boats we see leaving to go back to shore. I'll be back with you in a short while."

"JT, those honey buns are not stoppin' my tummy growls. I don't think I had anything to eat yesterday with all that doctor stuff I was doin. Why don't we head over to one of those diners Charleston's so famous for and get some breakfast fore we go out."

"I guess that's not a bad idea, what about you Sonny, you hungry?"

"No sir, I ate breakfast at home, but I sure would like a glass of orange juice and maybe a donut."

"Well, we'll stop in a minute. You eat up good, boy, this'll be your last meal, before we go out to sea that is." JT and Garland chuckled at that, and Sonny bristled in his seat.

"They think I'm too dumb to know what they're up to, but I'll show 'em soon. I just wish I could see their faces when they discover me gone."

"Garland, this place is famous for grits and cat fish. Ever have any of that?"

"I don't think so, JT, but right now it sounds better'n a honey bun."

"It's only a little after seven and the place is crowded, so you know they have good food. God, I can smell it already. Let's get in and get some of that stuff."

"What'll it be gentlemen?" The name tag said Ruby, and she was one of the typical early morning waitresses in an all-night diner. She looked tired and worn, her hair was in a tight bun on top, and she licked her pencil before she took an order. The Toddle House was typical too, a few vinyl-covered stools at the counter and wooden booths around the inside by the windows. The jukebox was situated right by the door leading to the rest rooms, and the flashing lights beckoned the crowd to ante up a nickel. Each booth had a small chrome box on the table with a listing of songs, a slot to insert money, and numbered buttons to make a selection. Diners could pick out a song and play it right from the table. The Andrews Sisters were belting out: Drinking Rum and Coca-Cola. Several of the customers looked as if they had done that the night before.

The short order cook was flipping eggs and mixing waffles right behind the cash register. There was enough waffle batter and egg yolk on his once-white uniform to feed a Boy Scout troop. Garland was trying to hold the large plastic covered menu with his left hand and balance it with the cast on his right arm.

"Bring me some coffee while I look at all of this stuff on the menu." Garland pointed at JT, "He recommends the catfish and grits but all this other stuff looks good too."

"Well, take your time, Honey, I'll be right back with your

coffee."

Dalton pulled his 37 Chevy half-ton pickup in front of his trailer and looked over at Gus. "Gus you wake?"

"Who wants to know?"

"Gus, it's Dalton, we're at my house. Can you make it in OK or do you need some help?"

"What the hell are we doing here? Where's Margie?"

"She got sick and had to go to the doctor. I came over to get you."

"Well, damn it, you can take me back. I don't need for Margie to be home, I got all my stuff there. I don't member tellin' you to pick me up so get the hell back and wake me when we get there."

"OK, Gus, you're the boss."

"You damn well better believe I am."

Dalton pushed on the starter and Gus was snoring as soon as the engine roared.

Dalton drove around, but he was thinking, "No way I'm gonna take him back there now. He'll cause a ruckus and get his self-arrested, we got too many other things goin on now for that. The place to settle a grudge with somebody is not on his property. We can handle this smartass Phipps guy later."

Dalton drove around Timmonsville for a few minutes and decided to ride over to Florence. If Gus woke up, he would just tell him they were headed back to Lake City. On the way he changed his mind again and decided to ride by the club. Maybe he could get Gus to go in and sleep on the sofa for a while. That way JT could get in touch if he needed them.

Clyde Moody hadn't had much sleep but no way he could go back to bed with whatever was going on. He shaved and dressed and decided to cruise around town and see if he spotted anything unusual. "Why would somebody wanna harm a nice kid like Sonny? For the FBI to be involved it has to be somethin serious. I think I'll see if I can find Leon Lott, he came on duty at midnight and should be still cruising round. Maybe he's heard somethin or seen somethin suspicious."

Clyde drove over to Jimbo's. It was about breakfast time, and if things were quiet he more than likely would find Leon there. When he pulled in he noticed Leon's cruiser, as well as Ben King's Highway Patrol car. Clyde knew if anything is going on, those two are bound to know about it. Clyde eased in by Leon's cruiser, parked, stuck a nickel in the slot and pulled a copy of the Florence Morning News out of the rack. He went inside and slid into the booth by Leon.

"Clyde, what the heck are you doing here? You're supposed to be home soaking in some sack time."

"I couldn't sleep and decided to ride over and have some coffee with my friends. How you doing?"

"Pretty good, Clyde, but you're more than welcome to take over my shift; I wouldn't have any trouble sleepin' now."

"What kind of night's it been Leon? Everything pretty quiet?"

"For a Friday night, it was unusually so. I've stopped my quota of speeders, chased a few kids, and answered a couple of domestics, otherwise nothin goin on. We were just sittin' here marvelin' that no one has got shot or killed as far as we know. I didn't even get a bar cuttin call all night."

"I hope it'll be that way tonight when I go back on duty. I'll no doubt be quite sleepy then, and wish I were home in bed."

"Well I won't pity you, you're missing a good chance this morning, it'll be rainin' soon and that's always the best time to sleep."

"Inspector Stokes, this is Commander Ogburn. I think we have your craft located. It's at the Charleston Marina. I have a crew over there now, but so far all around the harbor is quiet. The wind is getting up and we no doubt are in for a pretty serious storm. You still have some guys on the way over here?"

"I do. I told them to head for the Battery and I'd let them know where to go from there."

"It's pretty easy, Inspector, just tell them to head down East Bay Street; when they get to the curve on the Battery I'll have a seaman posted there with a jeep. Just follow him to the Coast Guard Station. Meanwhile, don't worry, that boat is going nowhere until I hear from you."

"Thanks Commander, Agents Means and Hamby will be in to see you very soon. How long will you be there?"

"I'll stick around until you get this resolved. If need be I can get some cruisers out of our other stations. Are you sure they're heading for that vessel?"

"Nothing now is certain, so I appreciate your offer of help. Do you have any boats farther out?"

"Yes, I've got one over at Fort Sumter. That's not far out, but I've already checked with them and they haven't seen any activity at all. They're watching now, and I've given instructions to intercept any craft and ask for identification."

"Thanks, I'll be back in touch soon. By the way, I have a pilot on the way. He's not a Bureau employee but he contracts for us and has ID and clearance for access to any information he needs. I'm gonna have him call you when he gets over the area. You can direct him to any place that you think might have other ships that are being boarded. His name is MB Huggins, and he'll be in a J3 Piper Cub."

"I do have some places that he could sail over and look. Our boats usually can pick up activity, but he can get a larger view. I'll have to keep him informed on the weather though; he may have to put down soon. There's a low ceiling now and it could close in."

"Keep him informed, Commander, but don't worry too much about MB he's an old crop duster and I'm told he can fly under water if need be."

As soon as JT stopped in the Toddle House parking lot Sonny opened his door. Before Garland and JT had a chance to get out he took his bag and slid it under the car. That way, if they locked the car it wouldn't matter. After they got inside Sonny got his orange juice and said "I'm too excited to sit here, I'm gonna go outside and stretch my legs a few minutes."

"Yeah, you do that." Garland waved him toward the door. Once outside, Sonny inhaled his orange juice, grabbed his bag, and took off down Meeting Street. It was daylight now and he could see enough activity to feel safe. He turned off on Columbus Street and slowed down; he didn't want to create any attention. He looked at the maps Miss Rose had given him and decided to walk to the huge bridge over the Cooper River. Shrimp boats were close by and there were lots of places to hide. Sonny was euphoric. He had gotten away so smoothly they probably had not yet discovered that he was gone. He was glad that he waited to get to Charleston. Not only were there more places to get lost here, but they had gotten more confident, and would now be even more surprised to find that he had vamoosed.

Sonny found a small Texaco station and bought a Pepsi Cola with money he had saved from his paper route. He could drink that, eat his P-Jelly sandwich, and have a full tummy to start out on. Later he would call home, but now he wanted JT and Garland to sweat a while. He took a winding trail and in fifteen minutes he was more than a mile away. No way could they track him down. They were probably just now noticing that he was gone. He had thought about hiding where he could see them looking for him but he decided against that. With Garland in uniform, they may have caught him and convinced the bystanders that he was under arrest and they were transporting him to jail.

"There's our swabby Joe, just ahead."

"Hey there, sailor, we're agents Means and Hamby and we're looking for the boat harbor."

"Yes, Sir. I'm Seaman Robinson, Commander Ogden requested that I go with you to the dock."

"Great. Hop in, Seaman."

Seaman Robinson motioned for the driver of the jeep to head for the Harbor dock and then he got into the back seat of the Bureau Plymouth. "It's only five or six blocks, but there are several twists and turns to get to the boat, even after you're in the harbor parking lot. Actually, though, you can see the lights on the cutter from here."

"Your guys have the boat surrounded, Sailor. No way the folks we're looking for have gone anywhere in that rig."

"I'll take you over and introduce you to Ensign Taylor, he'll be providing any assistance that you need."

"Thanks, Sailor, you've been a big help."

"Ensign Taylor, these are the FBI agents you're expecting."

"Hi, nice to meet you." He shook hands with Joe and Jerry and pointed toward the harbor, "No one has been anywhere near this boat, and there's been no activity anywhere in this marina. With the weather like it is, most folks are not gonna go out today. It'll make it easy for us to find them if they try to go out in another craft."

"Ensign, can you keep a few men here in case our suspects show up. More than likely there will be two adults and one young boy."

"Yes, sir, we'll keep the rig guarded, and we'll detain anyone that tries to board."

"Thanks, that will be a big help. Now, how do we get back to Commander Ogden's office?"

"Seaman Robinson will lead you there."

"Thanks, Ensign Taylor, you'll call his office if you see anything suspicious here?"

"Yes sir."

"I'm stuffed, JT, those catfish and grits are some of the best things I've had in a while, I'm gonna hafta come down here more often." Garland caught the eye of most of the patrons in the diner; He picked his teeth with his fingernails, made gruesome sounding burps, and moaned and groaned every time he moved.

"Well, it won't be long before you can afford your own boat, Garland, then you can come over every day if you like."

"I can't wait to get my hands on that money, JT."

"Yeah, me too, Garland, but first we have a very unpleasant chore to take care of."

"Not unpleasant for me, JT, I'm gonna enjoy watching snoopy snitch swim with the sharks."

"Well, let's get him and get out, the weather's not looking good at all. We need to get our work done and get back in. The storm'll be a good thing, we can say that a huge wave came over the ship and when we were able to get our footing we noticed that Sonny was not on deck. In addition to that, with your cast and sprained wrist, it will be obvious that you couldn't help much with pulling him back into the boat."

"Soon as that happens I'm ready to get back to shore, JT, I still feel a little woozy from yesterday. Hey! Where is that little fart? He's not out here, and I don't see him in the car."

"Maybe he's lying down in the back seat. Check and see."

"JT, he ain't here. Not only that, his bag's gone and all them honey buns. That little bastard has skipped on us. Quick, get in, let's cruise around and look."

Sonny found a peaceful spot near the bridge. It was close to the road, nice and shady, and no way JT and Garland would ever find it. He could spend some time here. The only thing bothering Sonny was how worried his mother would be when they told her that he was missing. He was going to have to call her soon, but for now he was pretty sure that Garland and JT would be scouting the area looking for him. He was full of excitement and he patted himself on the back for being cool enough to carry out this plan. Truth be known though, there were a lot of times when he thought it was a bad idea. "Now, though, when I talk to the police, I'll have a little more believability. They'll have to investigate the matter and I'll show 'em where the stashed stuff is located. There'll be a trial and I'll get to be the star witness. Man, this is working out marvelously."

Sonny leaned back against a huge Cyprus tree, sipped on his Pepsi, and scanned the area. He spotted a grapevine just a short distance away in the reedy woods and started making his way over. He was under the grape filled vine when he heard a sound nearby. He froze in his tracks, and there, less than thirty yards away, were two men that had walked over to the edge of the marsh. They looked like they were just walking in the woods, but Sonny wasn't taking any chances with strangers. Problem was, they were between Sonny and the road. They had not spotted him yet, but the only direction he could get away would be right by them. He hid behind a large clump of marshy reeds and prayed. Now, he needed his bed to hide under. If they came near him, he was going to have to try and get the jump on them and run by before they saw him. "Oh my God. My bag's over there and they've spotted it."

Garland wiped the sweat off of his head with a dirty bandana. He was puffing a Camel and looking out the foggy Packard window. "Damn, Garland, he couldn't just disappear, where in the hell can he be?"

"I don't know, JT, but what are we gonna do if we don't find him?"

"He has to be out here somewhere, but I've circled the area several times. We may as well head for the boat, I've got a radiophone on there and we can have Gus call Tony. Tony has hundreds of dock loaders down here that he knows. They can help us look."

JT, this weather is gettin nasty. Are we bout at the harbor?"

"There's the boat right over there, Garland. But wait a minute! Who are all those people around the boat? My God, there are sailors on the boat. They look like the Coast Guard, what the hell are they doing there?"

"I don't know, JT, but I don't like it, get the hell outta here."

JT backed around, and drove South on Lockwood Blvd.

"Commander, this is Ensign Taylor, are the federal guys still in your office? We just witnessed a large, black, four-door car speed away from the dock and we thought it looked suspicious."

"Yes, they're right here, Ensign."

Commander Ogden handed the phone to Joe. This is Ensign Taylor on the line, he may have seen a car near the boat."

"This is Agent Means; what type of car was it?"

"Sir, we're not sure of the make, but a four-door, black, late-model car with at least two males in it just drove into the parking lot. When they saw us they took a hasty exit."

"Could the car have been a Packard Clipper?"

"I can't be positive, Sir, but it was a black four-door luxury sedan. They backed away in a hurry, and we couldn't get a good look. We didn't have a land vehicle here, so we couldn't stop them."

"Well, this is a big help, Ensign Taylor, we already have an APB out on them, but now I'll call in and get the search intensified in that area."

"Look what I just stumbled over Meggs, some kind of knapsack. Wonder what's in it?"

"I don't know, Ritchie, open it up and see."

Richburg reached down and picked up the backpack. He looked at the ground where it had been lying and said, "Ain't been lyin here more than a day, Meggs; look at how green the grass is where it was. Look at this, there's some camp items in here. And, man, oh man, some *sammiches*. They still feel fresh and soft, so it don't seem to have been here long at all. Look around and see if you see anybody watchin us."

Sonny crouched behind the bushes and crawled over behind a large palm tree. He hoped the two men would go back toward the road, but they headed straight in his direction. His only chance was to try and race past them and get to the little station on the road. As soon as he heard them on the other side of the tree, Sonny sprang up and ran. The one with the bag in his hand hollered, and the other one reached out and grabbed Sonny.

"What's your hurry little feller, why you tryin to run? We

ain't gonna hurtcha. Is this here your bag?"

Sonny was frozen in fear and didn't say anything, just kind of whimpered.

"I told you boy, we wadn't gonna hurt you, but I *ast* you a question. Is this here yo' bag?"

"Yes, sir."

"Who else is with you? You alone? You runnin away from home, boy? "Whatchu doing here?"

Sonny sniffled a little and said, "My daddy and I were coming here to go fishing and we ran out of gas. Some men took him to a station."

"Ran out of gas? Where?"

"Right up there on the road, he'll be back here any minute."

"Boy, we can see all the way to the bridge and a mile in the other direction. You lyin to us; ain't no car in sight."

"No, sir, I ain't lyin. A man in a truck stopped, and they're pushin my Daddy to the ESSO station down the road. I told him this place was so pretty that I would wait for him here. He and that man in the truck will be back any minute."

"You know what? We might let you join up with us. You as good a liar as we are."

"You just sit tight right here. We ain't had nothin to eat since we broke the Moncks Corner chain gang. They had us on work detail at some kind of museum on Tradd Street two days ago. Our guard ate too much and dozed off, and here we are, free as two blue jays in a shade tree. These *sammiches* and cookies look mighty good."

Joe sat in Commander Ogden's roomy office and dialed the operator while he sipped Coast Guard coffee. "Pedro, I don't know what's going on here, but we think they may have driven up and been spooked by the Coast Guard. They should have been here over an hour ago if they were going out to sea."

"Joe, we're going to have to treat this like an official kidnapping and expand the APB. Mark and I are leaving for Florence as soon as I hang up. Have you heard from MB?"

"He and Commander Ogden have talked, Pedro, he's probably over the area now."

"Well, get the Commander to have him look for the car instead of a boat. Get out and start looking, and stay in touch with the commander so you and MB can connect up. He may need one of you in the air to spot for him. Is there much traffic?"

"No, fortunately the weather is looking nasty, so most people are not getting out. There's no activity on the water, and not much on the roads. We'll stay in touch and start riding the area."

"Mark and I will have to go and talk with Sims' mother. I hate to do that, because it's going to upset her and we don't have enough information to give her any explanation. We have to have a picture, though, and we need to know what he was wearing. Then, we'll go by McGloughlin's house and Garland's place and see if we can get any information from their families. What's the name of that deputy who knows Mrs. Sims? I'm going to find him and have him go with us. Hopefully, that will lessen the shock for the mother."

"I think it will help, Pedro. He and the Sims are pretty close. His name is Clyde Moody, and he lives only a couple of blocks from the Sims house.

"Commander Ogden, this is MB Huggins, I'm approaching North Charleston, and I'll be over the Battery area in about five minutes. Have you heard any further instructions from Inspector Stokes or Agent Means?"

"Yes, I have Mr. Huggins. Inspector Stokes has asked that you start a search for a black 1941 Packard Clipper, license number A-55-321. It should be somewhere in the Battery area. He also said that if you needed some help in spotting, you could get agent Means or Hamby to ride with you."

"That would be good, Commander, the cloud cover is thick and visibility is exceptionally poor. It'll speed things up if someone uses binoculars while I take it low."

"Right, Mr. Huggins, there's a small airport on the Navy Yard that's large enough to land a Piper Cub. I'll get clearance from the Base Commander for you to set down there. Meanwhile, I'll inform Agents Means and Hamby that you are heading to the landing strip."

"Roger, Commander, I'll circle the Navy Yard until I hear from you."

"You can use a wide circle and be looking for the car if you like. It'll take me a few minutes to get clearance from the Navy to allow you to land."

Ten-four, Commander, what's the latest on the weather?"

"We still have a major storm possibility, MB. We may have a few hours before it hits, but it's definitely coming. I'll have my weather folks keep you up to date on what's happening. The only problem right now is the low cloud cover."

"Roger, I can see that. I'm over the Charleston area now, and thank goodness there isn't much traffic, so each car will be easy to check out."

"I'm told the Commander of the Navy base is on the line, I'll be back with you soon, MB."

"Roger, Commander."

"Commander Owens, this is Commander Ogden, how are you today?"

"I'm fine, Mac, I'm told you have an emergency. What's

up?"

"Ray, we have a request from the FBI in Washington to allow a Piper Cub to land on your strip and pick up two agents. They're on the way to your base now. Can you call the gate and have them escorted to the strip? One of them is to get into the plane, and one may want to stay there by your radio. There's been a child kidnapped and they're searching for the car."

"No problem, Mac, is there any other way I can help?"

"When the agents get there you might ask them. They may want to have some of your Navy police help with the search."

"I'll call the gate now, then I'll authorize the landing on the strip. I'll stick around a while so check back with me soon, OK, Mac?"

"Right, Ray, I'll talk with you in a short while."

"How come you runnin way from home, boy? What's your name anyway?" The two men were wolfing down Sonny's P-jelly's and questioning him between bites.

"I ain't running away. I've been kidnapped, and the police are searching for the people that kidnapped me. They'll be looking here soon."

"Boy, you could pass for one of our friends on the gang. You lie with the best. You have that look about you that you're tellin' the truth. Me and Meggs is gonna let you join in with us. I can think of a dozen good ideas for makin' money with you along. You can go ahead of us and check out a place, and nobody'll spect you. We'll cut you in a share, and me and Meggs will take the place of that family you runnin way from. Now tell me, what's yo' name? You in with us now, and you need to know that I'm Richburg, and that there is Meggs."

"I ain't running away from home; I'm running away from

kidnappers. The police chief of Timmonsville and the school superintendent were taking me to the ocean to feed me to the sharks, but I got away. They're looking for me now, and the police are looking for them."

"I'm a patient man, and I like a good lie as well as the next guy, but I done asked you three times what yo' name is. I ain't no mean and violent person, but if you don't tell me yo' name right now I'm gonna give you a man to man whoppin'."

"My name is Sonny Sims, but I ain't lyin to you about the police and the kidnappin'."

"Well you keep on b'levin that. You see that road out there? It ain't had but a few cars since we been here, and none of 'em's been a police car. So hush up that story."

"You see that plane circlin' over, I betcha they're lookin for me."

"Right, kid."

Joe and Jerry pulled up to the Navy Yard guard gate and Joe flipped his ID toward the sentry, "We're agents Means and Hamby."

The sentry snapped to and said, "Just follow me, Sir." With that the sentry jumped into a waiting jeep and motioned for Joe and Jerry to follow. On the way they could see MB circling for a landing.

The commander came out to meet them, offered his hand, and said, "I'm Commander Ray Owens."

"Glad to see you, Sir, I'm Joe Means, and this is Jerry Hamby." They shook hands and Commander Owens asked, "is there anything I can do to assist with your search?"

"We could use some extra manpower, we're on a short time table. We don't know what's happened to the young boy, and so far we haven't found the ones that have him. If you could get some of your SP's to scout the area, it would be helpful. Our Assistant Director will be here later with pictures of the kid, and pictures of the suspects. We do know that the car is a 1941 black, four-door Packard Clipper, license number A-55-321. Have your guys begin searching for the vehicle, and when we get more info on the ID of the others we'll let you know. Meantime, if one of them sees a fat guy with an odd looking police uniform, a skinny guy with a suit and tie on, and a ten-year-old boy, have them get in touch with us. Also, Commander, if I can use an office with a phone, I'll make some calls and see what the latest is."

"You can use my office, Joe, and I can surely get you some manpower. We have a Shore Patrol training class going on this month, so we have some experienced sailors and marines ready to put that training to use."

Clyde Moody's two buddies were officially on duty and had to head back on patrol. Clyde finished his third cup of coffee and decided he would ride around for a few minutes and then head for the house. Maybe try and get a few hours of sleep before he went back on duty. He'd better get some sleep, Saturday Night after a quiet Friday was going to be an ordeal. He didn't see any activity, but when he got home, his wife met him at the door, "Clyde, I'm glad you're back, I have a number for you to call. Some federal person that says he needs your help."

Thelma handed Clyde the phone and read him the number. Clyde repeated the number to the long distance operator, and soon someone answered "Hello."

"This is Clyde Moody, I had a message to call Assistant Director Stokes or Mark Hughley at this number."

"This is Mark Hughley, hold on; Mr. Stokes wants to talk

with you."

"Officer Moody, we need your help. I've talked with Joe Means and Jerry Hamby and they feel we can trust you. Can you meet us somewhere so I can go over something with you?"

"I'll meet you wherever you say, but my house here will be fine if we need privacy."

"We're in Florence now, and we'll be there in about fifteen minutes, how do we find your house?"

"It's not hard to find but I'll meet you part way and you can follow me here. When you get into town just go to the caution light, look on your right, and I'll be sitting there in a 38 Ford."

"Thanks, Clyde, we'll see you in a few minutes."

Clyde told his wife where he was going and asked her to make some coffee for the two visitors. "Then, I'd like for you to stay back, they tell me it's a very hush-hush investigation and they need my help."

"Sonny Sims, huh, where you live boy?" Richburg was not threatening Sonny, but he did not believe Sonny's story. He had been asking over and over what he was really doing there and where he lived.

"In Timmonsville."

"Timmonsville? That's probably a hundred miles from here. Whatchu really doin way over here?"

"I'm telling the truth. I witnessed a crime, and the police chief and the school superintendent were involved. They were trying to get me onto a boat to throw me overboard. We stopped for breakfast at a Toddle House and I got away."

"Alright, Kid, Let's say for a moment that's true. How you happen to have a survival kit with plenty of eats? Did they tell you yesterday they were gonna come for you, and then give you time to prepare to get away? Meggs, what you think of that? Maybe we oughta get in the kidnapping business, don't seem like you need to be very smart to be in that business."

"Right, we could start by kidnappin' this kid, but we already promised him he could throw in with us. It wud'n be right to go back on our word, now would it?"

"I'm really telling the truth. Maybe you heard about all the hijacking of military supplies that's been going on. Well, I know the people that are doin it and I know by now they're lookin for me, if they haven't already been caught."

Richburg reached over, gave Sonny a tender pat on the head, and sounded genuinely disappointed. "OK, I guess you don't wanna level with us and be part of our gang. Too bad, I'm sure you could be real helpful."

"We can't just let him go, Ritchie, he'll have to stay with us. Maybe he'll change his mind and join up."

"Yeah, Meggs, you right. Son, we're makin' our way to a friend's house in Mt. Pleasant, and we gonna have to cross this river. It ain't no way we cud get across that bridge on foot, and not get caught. We gonna make our way down and find a place that's got a bend in the river. We may have to find a log to float across, but we gonna take good care of you. Don't you worry none, we gonna go slow, and make sure you're safe. We don't want nothin to happen to you. You're either a kid that'll decide to join up with us, or you're tellin' the truth and you done been through a lot. Either way, me and Meggs don't hurt nobody. Even when we escaped the gang, we waited till we could break without havin' to hurt no guards. Although, I would like to beat up on that damn Wendell Gaskins. He didn't give us no break at all. We had to dig ditches and pull corn from sunup to sundown, and then we would have to wash his car, and cut the grass at his house. All the while we were doin' all this, he sat there sippin' ice tea, and fannin' his fat fanny. If he hadn'a had that shotgun, I would a cracked his skull. If we meet up again, I might. Anyway if we can get across this marsh, we'll be able to get to a place we can eat and rest. So let's get at it."

"I won't tell on you, Mr. Richburg, I swear. Just leave me here so I can go back home."

"Now, Kid, you know we can't do that. You done tole us so many fibs now we wouldn't stand a chance with you in a lyin contest and we been on the gang for three years. We 'spose to have 'sperience and you lie better'n us. You ain't afraid to go cross this marsh, are you?"

"Yes sir. I can't swim very good, and I'm sure it's over my head. Besides, I know there are alligators and snakes out there."

"I'll tell you, boy, my heart goes out to you. I wish you hadn'a seen us when we found your bag, but now that you have, we ain't got no choice; which means you ain't got no choice. So get behind me and step where I step. Meggs'll be right behind you."

Commander Owens handed MB coffee, and told him to help himself with the box of sugar coated doughnuts. "Thanks, Commander, I needed that. I didn't have any breakfast this morning. I put my wings up as soon as Pedro called and told me a kid was missing. Just as quick as I finish off these doughboys we'll hit the air. Joe, have you two drawn straws to see who misses out on the opportunity to look for a car."

"MB, Jerry is the lucky one and I know he can't wait. With these clouds as low as they are, and thunder off in the background, I bet he's gonna be one thrilled guy to be in the air today. Isn't that right Jerry?"

"Right."

MB added a little sugar in his coffee and took a big bite of donut. The fluffy donuts had just come out of the Officer's Mess Hall oven, and the sugar coating was almost juicy. MB had flakes of the powdery looking concoction on his chin and it made him look like he had a partially gray beard. The chin coating, plus MB's twinkle like smile, and his few extra pounds in the belt area, gave him a Santa Claus look. "Well, Jerry, I've got good news for you. You don't have to wear a chute today. With this cloud cover we're gonna have to fly very low. If something happens to the plane you just grab yourself a tree limb, and climb down."

"Thanks, MB, you really know how to make a man feel secure."

"Clyde pulled his Sheriff's Department Ford into the vacant lot close to the caution light, lit up a Chesterfield, and waited. Clyde was thinking "Being a deputy with a small county sheriff's department is usually pretty dull, but now I'm on a federal case. Maybe I'll be able to do somethin meaningful." It wasn't often that a car passed, but when one did the passengers waved at Clyde. He'd been a deputy for twenty years and there weren't many people in the county that didn't know him.

"There's the caution light, Mark, and I see a Ford over there. That must be Clyde."

Mark pulled over by the Ford and asked, "Is that you Clyde?"

"Yeah, it's me."

"Well, Clyde, we appreciate you meeting with us. Where can we go and talk?"

"Follow me to my house, we can talk there. It's just a few

blocks." Clyde pulled into his front yard, and left room for Mark to park right behind him. "Come on in fellows, my wife has made coffee, and then she's goin over to her sister's house. Honey, bring us some coffee before you leave."

Mrs. Moody hollered from the kitchen, "Does anyone want sugar and cream?"

Pedro said, "Yes, I would like a touch of both, Mrs. Moody."

Mark waved his hand and gestured, "No cream for me, just a little sugar."

Thelma brought the coffee, poured for Pedro, Mark, and Clyde, and set the cream and sugar on a table nearby. "Nice to meet you folks. I'm leaving now, Clyde, I'll be at Marie's."

Clyde saw her out the door, came back in, sat on the edge of an overstuffed chair, and said, "Now fellows, how can I help?"

"We have a situation that's pretty confidential right now, Clyde. We need your word that you will keep everything between us for now. I know this is difficult for you, but we prefer that you don't even tell any other law enforcement person, including your sheriff."

"I'll do whatever you say, but it's gonna be awkward not telling Strother. He and I 've worked together for twenty years. We go back even before he was elected sheriff, but I'll do whatever it takes to help."

"Clyde, we have reason to suspect that the Sims boy has been kidnapped. The really confidential part is that our suspects are the Chief of Police, Garland Webb, and School Superintendent, JT McGloughlin. We think they're involved in something that Sonny Sims may have seen. Now, we don't have any proof at this point, that's why it is so urgent that you keep this to yourself."

"I can keep it to myself, you don't have to worry about

that. As for Garland Webb, I wouldn't put anything past him. He may be chief of police, but as far as I'm concerned he's the chief criminal in the county. You don't have to worry about him being in cahoots with our sheriff, either. Strother hates Garland's guts. As for JT McGloughlin, I wouldn't trust him with my pet water moccasin. Anybody that hangs around with Garland Webb has to be a crook. He also has some contact with a club owner here named Gus Segars and his bouncer, Dalton Sellers. Those two are really bad news, so whatever you tell me about them won't be no surprise. We have a lot of rumors about them at the sheriff's department, but like you said, we've never been able to prove anything. There's only one officer at the department that will hardly ever speak to Garland. When he comes over to get somethin from us he's treated like the criminal he is. In fact, that wreck he had was suspicious. Our witnesses tell us that the truck he tried to pull over was going within the limit and did not run a stop sign. Our suspicion is that Garland was trying to roust him for some personal reason."

"Clyde, we need for you to go with us to the Sims boy's house. We've got to get some pictures, what he was wearing, and any other information we can find. It's going to be hard telling his mom because we don't know exactly what's happening. We do know they have never gotten to the boat."

"Mr. Stokes, Hannah Sims goes to Florence every day to take care of her sister-in-law. We probably better go soon, or we might miss her."

"Call her and tell her we're coming, Clyde, and we'll go on over. Then we've got to go by Garland's and McGloughlin's and see what we can find out there."

"MB, is there any way you can pull up a few inches. That last flower bed you flew over tickled my toes."

"You federal agents are supposed to be brave, and you're a fraidy-cat, but really, you can look and see why we have to stay low, Jerry, because of the clouds. Even this low, they're closing down on us. I don't think we'll be able to keep looking much longer so quit worrying about us hitting something. Let me worry about that, you train those glasses on any car that looks like a long Packard."

"MB, I don't need to use the spy glasses, I can reach out and feel the license plate from here."

"Jerry, put your binoculars on those people walking in the marsh over there, it looks like two men and a boy.

"It is two men and a boy, MB, but they're not dressed like Garland and McGloughlin."

"Well, there's no other activity here, so I'm gonna make another pass over near the boat, then it looks like we're gonna be socked in for a while. It's starting to rain over on this side, you can see the sheets of it out in the ocean, so it's just a matter of time. That lightening is getting closer too. I'm a crop duster and I feel comfortable in a plane almost any time, but when it starts storming and you can't see, it's best to land for a while." "Whenever you want to land, you'll get no guff from me."

Roger Dill eyed the two suspiciously. He wondered why a fat policeman and a skinny guy in a suit were checking into his inn on a Saturday morning. "How many nights, gentlemen?"

JT glanced around the room, looked out the window, and said, "Just for today. We're on a fishing trip and the weather is too bad to go out. We're gonna hang around a while, call some of the others, and let them know we can't go. We'll need a room with a phone."

"No problem, all our rooms have a phone, but there's only

one bed. You sure you don't need two rooms?" Roger was eyeing the big bunch of blubber, and pitying the skinny guy if they tried to sleep in the same bed. "If that guy rolled over on him, he'd look like one of them cardboard movie statues. But that's their problem. The room is four dollars in advance."

"OK, where can we get ice? I got in a wreck yesterday, and the doctor told me I needed to put ice packs on the sore spots."

"I'll give you a bucket now, and if you need more, just come back here. You're in room 19, that's right over near the end." Roger Dill pointed a bony finger toward the window, "See that yellow electric company truck? It's right beyond that."

"Thanks, we'll be back for more ice later."

JT moved the car to the room while Garland waddled over. He decided that it was easier to walk than to try and get in and out of the car. Garland plopped down on the bed as soon as they entered the room. "Fix me a drink, JT, I can't do it myself with this damn cast on my arm."

"No problem, I'm gonna have one too, then we gotta decide what to do."

"I thought you was gonna call Tony, JT, and have him get some of his union guys looking for the kid."

"I'm gonna call Gus and have him get Tony. I don't have Tony's number." JT didn't mention that Tony had threatened his life if he ever called him again. "Anyway, Gus can call him and get some guys on the lookout."

JT picked up the receiver and Roger Dill came on the line. "Yes, this is the front desk."

"How do I call out? I've got several calls to make."

"Just give me the number and put the phone back down. When I get 'em on the line, I'll ring your room and you can pick up."

"Thanks, I'll find the number and call back."

"Damn, Garland. To make a call from here, we have to give him Gus's number and he makes the call and gets him on the phone. I don't like him knowing my business and I know Gus won't like that either. I'm gonna drive down and find a pay phone. Why don't you take a nap? And stay out of that bottle too heavy, we've got some serious work to do."

"Yeah, I'll just sip on this drink and try and clear my head. Them pills I got from Doc McLeod make me woozy."

Captain Jody Hopkins was the Assistant Provost Marshall at Paris Island Marine Base in Beaufort, but he was temporarily assigned to the Charleston Navy Base to conduct Shore Patrol training classes for Navy Seamen. He had brought ten of his best Military Police officers from Paris Island to give on-the-job experience to the class of trainees. Captain Hopkins heard there was a child missing and asked for volunteers. Not only did he get some of his MP's, but he got a lot of the trainees and some experienced shore patrol as well. He explained to the group: "You'll be looking for a ten-year-old kid that has been kidnapped. I know some of you worked late last night, and some will be working again tonight, but according to the FBI it is urgent that we find these kidnappers. I want you to search the city for a black, four-door 1941 Packard Clipper, license number A-55-321. Check out parking lots at hotels, cafes, and any other places you can think of.

"Sergeant Miller will be your contact; if you find the car, or, if you see suspects that fit the description, call in immediately. There's a skinny guy in a suit, a fat guy in a police uniform and a ten-year-old kid. That shouldn't be hard for seasoned guys like yourselves to spot." That sent a teeter of laughter through the room. "All right men hit the street and find that car."

"You suppose you could give me something to eat, I had all those peanut butter and jelly sandwiches and honey buns in my knapsack." Sonny was not only hungry, but he was scared. When he got scared, his tummy growled, and the only way to stop it was to eat something.

"We bout out of 'em, boy, but I guess you can have one of them honey buns. Eat it slow though, cause we don't get nothin else to eat till we get cross this river and get down to Amers house."

"Mr. Richburg, you sure you can't just let me go, I still promise I won't tell anyone. I just want to go home. The only ones I want to tell on are that pair that was gonna throw me off a boat."

"Son, b'lieve it or not, but I got kids. I wish I could let you go home, but I just can't do that. Now keep at it till we get to Amers house and you can eat and rest. Then we'll decide what to do bout you. Don't be afraid though, me and Meggs ain't no people hurters."

"Hey, look, Ritchie, there's a loose boat floatin' over there. Help me grab it."

"Man, look at this, Meggs, it even has the paddles in there. Now we gonna get out of this marsh mess. Hop in and let's get this thing movin'."

"Yeah, it probably just broke loose from somebody's dock. What a stroke a luck. I wad'n hankerin' at all to try and get cross floatin' on no log."

"Yeah, me too. It looks like just ahead there's a bend in the water. If we go downstream from there, we can get to that small island out there; then we can make the other side by just anglin' over."

"Yeah Meggs, let's take it to that bend, and head for the island."

Once Meggs, Richburg, and Sonny got to the bend they hopped in and started paddling. Before long Meggs hollered and started pointing. "Ritchie, we sprung a leak; look at the water that's now in the bottom. It must be a leak on the side of the boat cause till we put our weight in here it was dry inside."

"Well it ain't comin in very fast, and it won't take us long to reach the other side, so just bail out what you can. You, boy, cup your hands together and get out some of that water. Oh, I know, you got one of them foldup aluminum cups in your back sack. Get it out and start bailing with that. Me and Meggs got rowin' to do."

"It's starting to rain, Mr. Richburg, and the lightning is getting closer. My Cub Scout master said we shouldn't be near water when a lightening storm's overhead."

"Well your cub master ain't never been on no chain gang, boy. If he had a, he *wuda knowed* that on the gang you work, storm or no storm. They don't even care if you get hit. Just one less body to watch and one less mouth to feed. So, we either gotta take a chance now, or we gotta go back to the sure thing on the gang. I don't plan to go back without some desperate effort."

Sonny started a frantic attempt to get the water bailed out. The middle of the Cooper River looked mighty deep, and he was scared. "Daggumit. How many times am I gonna get the wits scared out of me. Every time I turn around something is happening to me. I gotta figure some way to get over there and then get away." Sonny decided that he would not tell on the two runaways. Even though they were technically kidnapping him by keeping him against his will, his heart went out to them. They seemed like decent people, and they were treating him nice. He tried to imagine what they had done to be put on the gang.

Meggs and Richburg were pushing the paddles as furiously as they could, but the little boat was still going down the river and not heading for land on the other side. Not either side. The current had pushed them out to the middle and it didn't appear they were going to be able to get to the edge. They had walked all that way upstream from the bridge and now it was looming right ahead.

"Where does this river go, Mr. Meggs?"

"I don't know, kid."

"I do, Meggs, and you don't want to think about it. It goes into the ocean."

"Oh, God, please get me home to Mama."

"Yeah, I'd like that too, kid. We'll figger somthin out."

"Mrs. Sims, this is Clyde Moody again, I hate to bother you but I need to come by your house."

"Clyde, something is wrong. What is it?"

"Can I come down now, Mrs. Sims?"

"Please hurry Clyde, something has happened to Sonny or Jack and I want to know what's going on."

"I'll be right there, Mrs. Sims."

Hannah was waiting in the front yard. Clyde got out of the car, hugged her, and said, "Hannah, this is Assistant Director Stokes, and Special Agent Hughley. They're from the FBI."

"OH, MY GOD! NO!" Hannah started crying and wailing and screaming for them to tell her what was wrong, but she couldn't stop her fit long enough for anyone to explain the problem. Finally, she got herself together. Although she was sniffling, she sat down, took several deep breaths, and calmed down enough to talk."

Pedro took Hannah's hand and sat beside her on the couch. "Mrs. Sims, I wish I had some news for you, but frankly we don't know what's going on either. We've been trying to locate McGloughlin's car and so far we've had no luck. We have all of our agents in the area as well as other law enforcement out looking, so we'll find them soon."

"Well, I want to know why you're looking for them. Where are they? They were supposed to be on a fishing trip."

"I know, Mrs. Sims, but we have found the boat, and it's still in the Charleston harbor. It may well be something simple like they pulled off on a back road to use the bathroom, and got bogged down or had car trouble."

"I've got to get in touch with my husband. He's somewhere out West on a secret government project. I don't have any number that I can call, and he seldom is allowed to call me. Can you get in touch with him? You're the FBI."

"I'll do my best, Mrs. Sims, but as you know, even though the war is over, there are a lot of highly classified operations still going on. Sometimes it's difficult, even for us, but I do promise to have my office work on it."

"What can I do? I want my boy."

"You can help us a lot, Mrs. Sims. We need to know exactly what Sonny was wearing when he left home this morning. We also need a recent picture and a list of things that he may have taken with him."

"He had on short pants, they're brown khaki, and he had on a blue and white pull-over shirt with a picture of a US Marine in dress uniform. He was wearing a pair of tennis shoes, and he never goes anywhere without his Brooklyn Dodgers baseball cap. Here's his grammar school class picture from last year; I think that's the most recent photo. You can take that with you if it will help."

"It'll help a lot. Now do you know if he took anything with

him?"

"He took his scout knapsack. It's a red Cub Scout pack that the cubs wear on campouts. He usually has his canteen and his Boy Scout knife, and he had a small Kodak camera. He also carried some sandwiches, and he even had some C rations that his Dad sent him. I still don't understand what's going on. Why did you start looking for him unless something has already happened? Surely the FBI would not be involved unless something was already wrong."

I wish I knew more and I would love to tell you, Mrs. Sims, but I don't know. It is one of those things that we'll just have to learn about as we go along. We have the license number of the car they're in, and we're going now to Webb's house and McGloughlin's. We'll be in touch. I'm going to call the local sheriff and have him release Clyde to us. He'll stay in close contact with you. We'll let him know when something develops, and he can let you know. We have to leave now, Mrs. Sims, but we're gonna do everything we can to find Sonny right away."

"Thanks, Mr. Stokes, I'll call a friend to take care of my sister-in-law today. I'm gonna wait to hear from you. If it's long, I'll be calling you, so you let me know what's going on. Is that a promise?"

"Yes Ma'am, that's a promise. Now we have to go."

Hannah leaned against the bed in Sonny's room and cried until she was dry. The crying helped, but she still needed to get in touch with Jack. "I don't think that Inspector is going to have time to get in touch with Jack. I'm going to call Senator Furman."

Petty Officer Andy Blackwell had been in the Navy for fifteen years. Andy had served a number of assignments as a

Shore Patrol officer, and had handled every kind of call imaginable, in all kinds of port towns, but this one was unusual. Now, he was looking for a kid, a policeman, and a school superintendent. Most of his previous suspects had been AWOL sailors. He had worked the night shift on Friday night and had just gotten off duty at seven a.m., but when he heard a kid was in trouble Andy didn't think twice about volunteering. Most of his crew that worked with him the night before was also involved in the search. He had promised his kids a day at Folly Beach, but with the rain and mist, and possible storm, they couldn't have gone to the beach anyway.

Andy's partner was Michael Graham. Michael was on his first assignment as a shore patrol officer but he was one of Andy's best men. He had the uncanny knack, or maybe even a six sense, for finding people. Although it was usually errant GI's, he just seemed to think like the person he was looking for. In this case though, Andy thought, he has no way of thinking like these folks. We don't know what's happening, who they are, or anything about their motives. Even so, Andy was thrilled that Michael had joined the search with him.

"Andy, you mind if I stop at Doughnut Heaven and get a thermos to go? I need something to crank my scooter."

"I could use a little myself, Mike; I'm glad you brought your thermos. It could be a long day."

"I hope not, Andy, I don't have any kids myself, but my heart goes out to the one that's missing."

"Well, Michael, my little Michele is about the same age as this kid so I feel compelled to find him."

Michael went inside and Andy stayed in the jeep looking at maps of the area. Although he knew Charleston like the back of a PT boat, Andy tried to imagine places that these child nappers might be. The Commander had not assigned any sections to anyone; just said for all to "Do your best and go on instincts. You might overlap, but that just means you're looking in the right places. The good thing is, since you are shore patrol, they aren't gonna get suspicious if they see you. We don't know they're on the run but neither do we know they're not."

When Mike went into Doughnut Heaven, Mamie was boxing up several dozen glaze covered doughnuts for one of her regulars. She looked at Mike, and kind of tilted her head back so she could see over her reading glasses. "Mike, what are you doing back here still in uniform, you said you were going home and get some sleep."

"Mamie, I planned to, but I got a call for a special assignment. There's a kid missing and I'm gonna have to work today, so I'm in need of some more coffee. Since I work again tonight you better put on a bigger pot."

"You keep coming, Big Boy, and I'll keep filling your mug. You won't find no dry pot in this place."

"Thanks, Mamie I'll be back."

"Jerry, you see any car that looks like what we're looking for? We should be able to spot it, there's hardly anybody out. I guess this weather has people staying indoors."

"Those people down there have enough sense to not be out in cars and here we are in an airplane low enough to look into the window and see who's driving. I've been terrified for so long now I think rigor mortis is setting in. If we see that car, I'll be able to check and see if he has enough air in the tires, we're almost below sea level."

"Jerry, if you look up, you'll see that the cloud cover is so thick, we couldn't go any higher if we needed to. Visibility is getting quite poor though, so I'm gonna make one more pass over the highway 17 area, and then we're gonna have to wait a while at the base. I guess some ham and eggs sounds good anyway. Take a good look while I circle this area." MB and Jerry didn't see any sign of the Packard and had to make plans to land. "Charleston Navy Yard, this is MB Huggins in Piper number Nov2514A. Do you read me?"

"Piper Cub Nov2514A this is Seaman Flynn; the Commander is at another part of the base for a while but he asked me to assist you in any way possible."

"Thanks, Seaman Flynn, It's so thick up here we're gonna have to come in for a while. Do you authorize a landing?"

"Absolutely, sir, the runway is yours at any time."

"Thanks, Flynn, we're a couple of hungry boys, so we'll be wanting you to point us toward some food."

"No problem, Sir, the officer's mess is right next door."

Jerry was pale faced in the back, and fighting airsickness. "Speak for yourself about that hunger, all I'm hungry for now is some of that fresh dirt, and I'm gonna taste it when we get down."

"You feds. I thought you were tough guys. Hey, look over at that small boat, those people are in deep trouble." MB picked up the microphone, "Seaman Flynn, cancel that landing for the moment and stay tuned to my radio. We just spotted a small boat with what looks like three people, and the boat is sitting low in the water."

"Roger, Piper, I'll be right here."

The rain was beating down, water was leaking in from a hole in the side, and the small boat was sinking fast. Sonny's arms were about worn out, but he was bailing water with the little cup as fast as he could. He knew Meggs and Richburg had to be exhausted too. They had been fighting the river for almost an hour and now they were still in the middle.

"Meggs, I don't see no way we're gonna make the other side in this piece of firewood. The current keeps pulling us over to the side where we just come from. We better get back over there and try and find another way to get to the other side."

"That sounds OK to me, but we're in a mighty swampy section over here. I hope we can get close enough to shallow water to get some land, my arms are breaking. I *wuda* thought after breakin' rocks for three years, I'd never get tired of pushin a little paddle, but I need a break, and we can't break in this river or we'll end up out in the ocean."

"Start paddlin' in that direction." Richburg made a motion with his head toward the closest trees, "let's try and make that downed tree over there. We can rest a while, and see what to do from there."

"Paddle harder! We gonna pass that tree if you can't help me get over there. Pull that paddle, Meggs. Play like that damn Gaskins is the water and beat that sucker bad."

"Push a little more and I may be able to grab a limb. Oh God! Richie, I'm falling, help!"

"Meggs, grab the end of this paddle, quick!"

"I'm trying." Meggs was right behind the boat and reaching but couldn't quite get his hand on it.

"Come on, swim to the back of the boat and I'll pull you in. Sonny reach out and grab him I've got to keep the boat from getting back in the current."

Sonny reached out, Meggs grabbed his hand, and Sonny was almost pulled in. Meggs gave a big push and grabbed the back of the boat. Now, they had to find another tree. Meggs was too tired to get into the boat, and no way that Richburg could keep paddling much longer. No way either that Sonny could keep on bailing. They were in one hell of a fix.

Michael was pulling in and out of hotel parking lots, restaurants, and any other places that he thought he might find the Packard. There were a lot of cars in the hotel lots, probably due to the tourists staying in because of the weather. The fishing boats were not out, and it was just dismal. If not for this operation Michael and Andy would be home too.

"Andy, I wonder what's going on with this caper. We don't have any idea why these people took the kid, and we don't have a clue as to what their plans are. Now that the weather's too bad to go on the fishing trip, what'll they do now."

"I wish I knew, Michael. The Commander said all of this could be just a mistake. They're not sure the kid was kidnapped, but they're not sure that he wasn't, so we've got to keep looking and hope we find him soon.

"There's a Packard over there by that restaurant. Sit here just a minute, that guy using the phone is skinny, and has on a suit. See if you can ease over and get a view of that plate without him seeing us. I'll try and see if anyone is in the car."

"What'll we do if it is him, Andy? Do we have the authority to detain him, since this isn't Navy business?"

"Well, if it is the car, there's no way that he's going anywhere. We'll sit on him if we have to until the Feds can get over here."

"Michael, we just struck blueberry pie. Look at that plate, A-55-321. Ease on over by the skinny guy on the phone. He meets the description that we have. Wait for him to hang up and then we'll hop out and ask him some questions."

"Dispatch, this is Andy Blackwell. Michael and I are on

Meeting Street at the Crab Pot Café. Tell Agent Means to get over here as fast as possible. We have the Packard in sight and we're watching a tall skinny guy on the phone. So far he hasn't spotted us, so we're gonna sit tight as long as he doesn't try to go anywhere."

"Roger, Andy, I'll give Agent Means your location right now."

"Thanks, there are no other people in the car, so get all the available folks in this area to start looking for the fat guy and the kid. Maybe they're on foot somewhere, or they may have another car, I don't know, but at least we've got the Clipper."

"Right. Hold on, Andy. Flynn hollered to Joe, "Sir, one of our units has found the Packard Clipper at a café not too far away, and they have a skinny guy in a suit in sight."

"Tell them to stay with him and don't let him go anywhere. What about the others, are they not there?"

"No, Sir, he says there is only one, the tall skinny guy."

"Get someone to ride with me Flynn, and I'm on the way. Call MB and Hamby, and if they can stay in the air, tell them to get over that area right away and start looking."

"I'll tell them, sir, but they're over a boat in the Cooper River that has capsized. They just called it in and I'm waiting for them to give me the details."

"What the heck are those folks doing out here in this kind of weather in a little boat. Heck, one of them is holding on to the back, and, by gosh, one of them is a kid. Visibility is so poor it's hard to tell, but I'm almost sure that that isn't Webb and McGloughlin. That means that probably isn't Sonny but we gotta get a Coast Guard cutter over here right away. We'll linger a while and watch, they're floating pretty fast and there's some rocks ahead they might hit."

"Seaman Flynn, this is MB Huggins, over."

"I read you, and we've found the suspect's car."

"Get some people over there, but right now we have to have a CG cutter here. Now! We're circling just north of the Cooper River Bridge and a small boat with two adults and a kid has capsized?"

"Roger, Piper, hold on, I'll get a cutter on the way immediately."

"Piper, I've got the Coast Guard on the way now. Are you staying there until the cutter arrives?"

"Roger on that, Seaman, these folks look like they might spill out at any minute. The boat's almost full of water and one of the men is hanging on to the back."

"I'll let you know the CG ETA in just a moment, Mr. Huggins."

"Right Flynn, do that, and tell them to shove on the steam. Look at that Jerry, that kid is holding one hand on that man on the outside of the boat and he's bailing water with the other. If that cutter doesn't get here soon his bailing won't make any difference. That water is pushing pretty hard."

"Jerry, there's a storage area right behind your seat. Pull it open and get those Mae West jackets out of there."

"There's two in here, any other place you may have another?"

"No that's it, but get 'em up here. I'm gonna go low in front of 'em. Wave the vests so they'll know that on the next pass we'll throw 'em."

"Ritchie, that damn plane has us spotted, and they gonna thrown us a life jacket."

"If he'll just do that and leave us alone, that'll be fine, but I don't want 'em to call in no cops to come and rescue us. I rather go down with the ship."

"Well, not me, Ritchie, I think breakin' rocks can't be no

worse than these rocks breakin' me. You done drug me over some rocks and stumps and my legs are hurtin' like crazy. What about you Sonny, you ready to get out of here ain'tcha?"

"Yes, sir."

"Well, if that don't beat all. The kid is polite even now."

"Watch it now, that plane is passing over and I guess will toss out the preservers. Heads up."

"OK, Jerry, the wind is gonna hit 'em, so throw it a little in front, then they can drift over to it."

"Here you go," Jerry tossed one of the jackets. It missed the target and there was no way they could get to it. Richburg tried to paddle over but the current was too strong. Even if Meggs was in the boat and paddling it would not make any difference now."

"They're coming back with another, Ritchie, try and get that one."

Jerry was so absorbed in getting the preserver into the boat he had gotten over his fear. He pulled himself outside the door, wrapped one arm around a wing support, and hung down low. He watched the boat get nearer, and as soon as he got in front of it he dropped it. It landed right beside the boat and Richburg grabbed it and pulled it inside. They had one but the other floated away.

"MB, this is Seaman Flynn, do you read me?"

"Loud and clear, Flynn."

"MB, the cutter is going to be arriving in about four minutes."

"Can't it be quicker? These guys are almost goners."

"He's full steam that way, sir, but his ETA is four minutes away."

"OK, Seaman, we'll circle over and watch 'em. Tell the cutter to look for us, we'll be right overhead."

"Roger, Piper."

"Gus, this is JT, I'm glad I caught you. That punk kid somehow managed to get away here in Charleston and we can't find him." JT was standing in the phone booth holding the phone with one hand and a cigar stub in the other. The stub was chewed to a nub.

"HE WHAT? DAMN! Can't you and Garland do anything right? How did both of you let a ten-year-old kid get away once you had him in the car?"

"We stopped to get some breakfast and he ran. We drove around the area but we can't find him. It looks like the Coast Guard is at the boat so we can't go there. I'm at a pay phone now on highway 17. Garland is in the inn, passed out from the medication."

"I should have had better sense than to get involved with a couple of idiots. Just stay the hell out of the way in that inn until one of my guys gets there. Where are you?"

"We're at the Night's Delight Inn on Highway 17, room 19."

"Well get your ass back there. Don't even think of leaving there until I get someone over that has enough sense to handle it. What makes you think he had'n already called the cops?"

"Well, if he were going to do that, I think he probably would have done it before we left. He didn't give any indication that he knew what was up."

"I don't know why in the hell I'm talking to you. You're too damn stupid to waste my time on. Now get back and stay there." Gus slammed the phone down, ranted and raved, and yelled for Dalton to bring him a double shot. "And forget the damn ice cube."

JT hung up the phone and walked back over toward the Packard. Andy grabbed Michael's hand and said "Hold up a minute and see if he goes to that Clipper. If so, pull up behind it and block his way." JT opened the car door and was startled when a navy Jeep drove up and two sailors rushed toward him.

"Hold still, sir."

"I'm in a hurry. Move that jeep so I can back out."

"I'm sorry, Sir, but you're gonna have to stay here with us until the FBI arrives."

"What do you mean the FBI, what is this about?"

"We're not sure, maybe you can tell us?"

"All I can tell you is that I have connections, and if you don't get out of the way you re gonna be swabbing decks for the rest of your life."

"We're looking for a young boy; you have any idea where he is?"

"I have no idea what you're talking about. Now get out of the way and move that jeep or I'm going to call the police."

"We are the police, sir."

"Well, you can see that I'm not a young boy, so go look for him. I have a sick person that I have to care for. I was calling in a prescription for him and I've got to go pick it up and get it too him."

"It won't take long, sir, and we'll take the prescription to him for you." About that time Navy jeeps started pulling into the lot, and in no time JT was surrounded by a dozen hefty SP's.

"May I sit down?"

"Yes, sir."

JT was wobbly and weak and his knees were about to buckle. He opened the car door and flopped inside. About that time, he heard a siren in the distance and soon saw the red flashing lights. What the heck would he do now?

"How you doing back there, Meggs? If we sink, this life preserver ain't gonna hold all of us and we're about under water."

Meggs didn't answer, he had taken in so much water he couldn't talk. Sonny was holding on to him but with the boat going down, he was falling over too.

Richburg pulled Sonny loose from Meggs, and said, "Okay, kid, this is yours. Take your life and make something out of it." With that Richburg put the jacket around Sonny. I'll just hold on for a while and then you can go alone, I ain't gonna go back to chain city. I rather face the sea devils." Richburg pushed Sonny out of the sinking boat, and held on long enough to make sure Sonny would float.

"Please, don't say that Mr. Richburg, this jacket is holding both of us. Hang on to me."

"Kid you're OK; I want you to be a role model for my kids. Find out where they are and tell 'em their daddy loved 'em." Sonny clutched onto his shirt, but Richburg took his hand, pried his fingers loose, and started swimming out toward the sea.

Sonny was crying, Richburg was swimming away to certain death, and Meggs was floating face down. Sonny was headed into deeper water, and he knew the plane couldn't get to him. He started praying hard.

"Seaman Flynn, where the hell is that cutter? We've already lost two of the three, and the third is getting into some rough water. He's just a kid."

"I talked with the skipper. He is in sight of your plane and only two minutes away. You should be able to spot him."

"I see him, but tell him to put all the coal on that he has, the kid needs some help fast. Tell him the kid is between him and us and for them to have someone ready to jump in. The jacket has come off of the kid, and he's just holding onto it. I don't think he has much strength left."

"He has divers ready, Sir, and they are on full alert."

"Thanks. As soon as they get him on the boat, we'll be in, clear us for a landing."

"You're cleared sir; I'll have a jeep pick you up on the runway."

Gus called the Charleston Longhauler's office and asked for Marty. What he didn't know was that Bob Johnson was listening to all of Gus's conversation. He signaled for another agent to get in touch with Mark and Pedro and let them know that Antonio has his Charleston crowd looking for the kid. "Tell him to alert Joe and Jerry. I've got to stay on the headset, it's hot right now."

"I'll get him the message right away, Bob."

Joe Means jumped out of the car before it stopped and rushed over to Andy and Michael.

"There's the Packard, Agent Means, and this is the skinny guy that was driving it. He tried to get in the car and Michael and I stopped him."

Joe flashed his ID and said, "I'm Agent Joe Means, are you JT McGloughlin?"

"I am, and I demand to know what is going on."

"Your demand can wait. My demand is to know where Sonny Sims is. He left his house with you this morning."

"He's back at the Inn. I came to get some medicine for Chief Webb."

"Which Inn?"

"I can't remember. I drove around looking for a drug store and I got lost."

"You have a key in your pocket, right?"

"No, I left the key there and told him to let me in when I knocked."

"Put your hands on the car, I'll just take a look."

Joe started to go through JT's pockets and JT put his arms down and said, "I want to talk to my lawyer. You have no right to search me. The FBI does not have authority in SC unless there is some federal crime."

"Oh really. Well first of all, we suspect there is a federal crime going on, and that gives me authority. But I tell you what I'll do: You look around the crowd of officers that have gathered here, and you can have your pick of state, county, or city police that can look for that key. Or, if you prefer these Navy guys here will be more than happy to do the search. Now, get your arms back on the car."

"My father-in-law is United States Senator Tom Furman. If you don't get out of my way your career will be over in the federal service."

Joe got nose to nose, "First of all, I advise you to shut up. Second of all, I'm looking for a missing kid; if Tom Furman has a problem with that I'll deal with it. Right now, if you don't raise your hands I'll have a few officers hold you down and take your pants off. Then we can look through your pockets without having to deal with you." Andy and Michael each grabbed an arm and Joe looked in his pocket and found the key to the Night's Delight Inn. "Well guess what? You were having a memory lapse after all. The key was right in your pocket and you didn't even know it. We're gonna have to take you into protective custody so you won't hurt yourself. Now get in the back of that car. We're going over to the Night's Delight and see your police chief friend. Have you got the kid there?"

JT glowered at Joe but didn't answer.

Joe motioned for Andy and Michael to put JT in the back of his car, and come with him. Seaman Partini had driven Joe over, he got behind the wheel and Joe got into the front passenger side. Andy sat on one side of JT, Michael on the other, and they headed for the inn.

Hannah was pacing back and forth. The phone cord was only several yards long so she was almost spinning in circles. "I have to speak with Senator Furman right away, you must know how I can get in touch with him."

"Ma'am I'm sorry, it's Saturday and the Senate is not meeting today. I'll leave him a message and he can call you Monday. OK?" Rita could tell by the tone of voice that the lady was not going to just leave a message.

"NO! That is not OK! I want to talk with him NOW! You get in touch with him and he had better call me right back. You tell him it concerns his son-in-law, JT McGloughlin, and that I have to talk with him right now. There is no one at the McGloughlin house and the Senator's son-in-law is missing. The FBI are looking for him and he has my son."

There was a long pause and then Rita said, "Let me see if I can find someone that knows where he is, Ma'am. Hold on just a moment." Rita rang the office of the Speaker of the House of Representatives and talked with his assistant, Nona Fairchild. She explained to Nona that no Senators were in her building, and how serious the lady sounded, and that the FBI was involved. Nona buzzed the Speaker, and said, "Mr. Rayburn, I hate to bother you but there's a lady on the line that is raving. She says that Senator Furman's son-in-law is missing and he has her son with him. Says the FBI is looking for him. Sally says she sounds for real. Can you talk with her?"

"Nona, I'm involved in some foreign affairs discussions

right now, are you sure this isn't one of the crazies that are always calling about such stuff as aliens and Martians invading us?"

"I don't think so, Sir, Rita has talked with all of the crazies, and she thinks this one is for real."

"Put her on."

Nona switched the call to the Speaker's office, Rayburn cleared his voice, and boomed, "This is Speaker of the House, Sam Rayburn, may I help you, Ma'am?"

"If you can get me through to Senator Furman you can help me. His son-in-law picked up my son this morning to go on a fishing trip, and they have vanished. The police and the FBI are looking for them."

"Ma'am, why is your son with Senator Furman's son-in-law? Why is the FBI looking for them?"

"I don't want to spend any more time explaining. I want to talk with Tom Furman and find out where my husband is. Senator Furman can explain all of the details to you."

"Let me get your name and number, Ma'am, and I'll see if I can find Tom for you. Are you sure the FBI is involved?"

"Yes, that is what I am saying; Inspector Stokes just left here. JT McGloughlin picked up my son at the house this morning and the agents are looking for them. Now, are you going to find Tom Furman?"

"If I can't get the Senator, I'll have someone call you back."

"Somebody better, I've got to find out where my husband is. He is on a secret war mission and Tom Furman knows where he is. I must get in touch with him."

"I'll try and find him. Speaker Rayburn hung up, and buzzed Nona.

"Nona, get a hold of Tom Furman, wherever he is. Tell him I have to talk with him right now. Also, tell Sally to get me J Edgar on the line. Drop whatever else you're doing and get on this now."

"Yes, Sir."

Sonny had taken in so much water that he was passing out. His grip came loose from the Mae West and he bobbled in the water face down. As soon as the cutter pulled up two seamen in life preservers jumped in beside him. One grabbed Sonny, and pulled him above water. They had tied lines to themselves before they jumped, and the other crew began pulling them back in. The seaman had to hold onto sonny's hair. He couldn't risk letting go to get an arm or a piece of clothing. If he missed he might go back under, and Sonny needed air more than hair."

Sonny was unconscious when they got him on the boat. A seaman trained in water rescue put Sonny face down, lifted his stomach and drained the water out. He then began pushing on Sonny's back 15 times per minute. Another seaman was feeling his pulse. "It's low, but it's pumping, but just barely."

Another cutter pulled up and the skipper told a seaman, "Swim over to that cutter and show them where to look for the other two while we take the kid to the hospital."

The seaman was diving over the side while he hollered, "Roger, Sir."

Joe had Seaman Partini stop at the entrance of the Inn. He got out of the car, looked back, and saw several dozen shore patrol jeeps and other police cars following. Joe asked the first driver to inform all of the others to stay put until he motioned for them to come in. He wanted to get into the room as quietly and as quickly as possible. He got back in and told Partini to pull near room 19. When they found it, he asked Partini to stay with the prisoner and he motioned for

Andy and Michael to come with him. Joe, Andy, and Michael got to the door, Joe inserted the key, shoved the door open, and the three rushed in. Garland was lying on the bed. Joe looked but didn't see the peace machine he had heard so much about. Garland had one hand in a cast and the other was in view."

Joe grabbed his boot, shook it, and said, "Get your fat ass up. Now!"

Garland looked at Joe, but he was so groggy and disoriented he had to let his eyes focus for a moment. "Who are you and what are you doing here?" Actually, Garland didn't know where he was.

"I'm agent Means with the FBI, where is the kid?"

"What kid?"

"Sonny Sims." Joe grabbed Garland's belt on the side of the waist and pulled the tub of lard to the edge of the bed. Joe was a world class weight lifter, and he was one of the few that could have dragged Garland Webb anywhere. "You and JT McGloughlin picked up the kid this morning. Now, once again, where is he?"

"He's with JT. They went to get somethin to eat. The kid was hungry. Now get out of my room."

Joe grabbed Garland by the shirt, perched him on the edge of the bed and got face to face, "Now! Let's get this straight. I'm looking for a kid and I'm not going to get out. McGloughlin is outside in the police car and that's where you're headed. Now get up, and let's go." Now!" Andy and Michael made mental notes not to ever antagonize Joe Means.

"I ain't going nowhere. I'm a police officer, you can't order me around."

"You were a police officer. Now you are a felon on the way to jail." Joe reached down, grabbed Garlands badge and ripped it from the shirt, pulling a big piece of cloth and several buttons off. Joe stuffed the badge into his own pocket, and said, "Now, you're a civilian, so get your ass outside. Now!" He pulled him to his feet and got chin to chin, "Do we understand each other?"

Garland didn't answer and Joe shoved him toward the door. Andy and Michael stepped back and Garland stumbled to the sidewalk outside. Joe grabbed him and on the way to the car, he shoved his head against the window of the car that McGloughlin was in. "There's your pal. Now, the first one of you that gives any lip is gonna lose it." Joe saw a city police Lieutenant, and said, "Can we use your jail?"

"Sure, I'll lead the way."

They were at the jail in minutes, and Joe asked the jailer to put them in separate cells. "I need to make a quick call to my supervisor, and then I want to talk with them one at a time."

"You got it, Sir."

Joe called Pedro's secretary, Connie, and asked her to "Find Pedro and have him call me at the city jail immediately. Let him know that we have the two suspects, but so far, no kid. I'm going to interrogate them now, and hopefully we'll know soon where the kid is."

"I'll have him call you right away, Joe. He's on the way to Charleston now with Mark."

"Commander, this is Ensign Amick, we have the kid that the Piper Cub called about but he's unconscious. We're on route to the hospital now and we'll let you know the kids name as soon as we get more information."

"Thanks, Ensign Amick, I'll relay this to the agents."

"Mrs. Sims, this is Tom Furman, I had a message that you

urgently needed to talk with me. I was taken out of a meeting with the Vice President, and a number of important Cabinet Members. What is this all about? It had better be important."

"You had better believe it's important. Your son-in-law picked up my Sonny this morning to go on a fishing trip and now he's missing. The FBI is involved but they won't tell me anything and they're asking a lot of questions about JT and Garland Webb. They think that your son-in-law has kidnapped my son. Now, I want you to tell me how to get in touch with Jack."

"Hannah. Are you saying my daughter's husband is a kidnapper? You had better not be saying that. If so, your husband will be home, all right, because I'll have him kicked out of the program he's in right now. You had better never even think anything like that again."

"I don't care what you say you're going to do; I want my son back. If the FBI thinks JT did it that is good enough for me."

"I'm talking in a few minutes with J Edgar Hoover. I'll find out what is going on but you do not call me again. If I choose to relay anything to you it will be through Ed Smith. Goodbye."

Hannah hung up the phone, cried a while, and then cranked the phone. Marylou Buddin, the town operator, answered immediately, "Number please."

"Marylou, this is Hannah, get me the FBI office in Washington."

"Hannah, is everything all right. I'm getting a lot of calls in and out of town, you just called for Senator Furman, and now you're calling the FBI."

"Marylou, Sonny is missing. The FBI has been here asking questions, and they asked for a picture of Sonny. I want to know what is going on."

"Oh, no, Hannah! Have you seen Tommy and Brian? I've got to find them. I'll have to close the switchboard if they're not at home. Please, Hannah, may I call home before I try and get the FBI."

"Of course, Marylou, I know how you feel, but please call me right back. I'll be here by the phone."

Marylou dialed her home number and prayed as it rang for the sixth time. Finally, a little voice said "Hello."

"Brian, is Tommy there with you?"

"Yes, Ma'am."

"Let me speak with him right away."

Tommy got on the phone and said, "Momma."

"Tommy, is Sonny there with you?"

"No Ma'am he's on a fishing trip."

"The police are looking for him; he isn't on the fishing boat. Do you know where he is?"

"No, Ma'am, he wouldn't let me tell you until he escaped, but Mr. McGloughlin and Chief Webb were planning on killing him, and he had a plan to get away."

"He what? You knew this and you didn't tell me?"

"He made me swear not to Mama."

"Well, now you're gonna make me swear. Lock the doors and don't even look out the window until I get home."

Marylou called Nell Moore "Nell, I have an emergency. Please come and relieve me right away."

"I'll be there in ten minutes, Marylou."

Marylou dialed Hannah's number, "Hannah, I just talked with Tommy and Brian, and they know something about this. Nell Moore is on the way here now, and she will get the FBI on the phone for you. I'll let you know right away what Tommy and Brian have to say about this."

"There's one of them caught on a low limb over there." With that the seaman secured his towrope and jumped into the choppy sea. He swam over to the body, dove under, got a hold on a belt, and tugged on the towrope. The other sailors pulled him over by the boat, and several jumped in and supported the body until they could be lifted out. The one that found him hollered, "This one is dead. If he hadn't gotten caught on that limb, he would have gone down."

The skipper radioed the other search boats, "We're taking this one to the morgue for ID so they can determine if this is one of the kidnappers they're looking for. Keep searching for the other body." With that the foghorns wailed and they headed for the base.

"Dispatch, this is Ensign Jacobs, we have a body we're transferring to the base, have an ambulance meet us at the dock. We need to transport him to the morgue and see if this is one of the fugitives."

"Roger, Ensign Jacobs, I'll get one rolling now and inform the morgue."

Gus paced the club floor. "Dalton fix me another double scotch." Tony was getting his men in Charleston together to look for Sonny, but Gus had no idea if the kid had already spilled his guts to the cops. "If we can get that kid, he has to be a goner in a hurry. We're already in too deep to worry about another murder charge. They can only cook us once."

"Here's your drink, Gus. What are you gonna do about Gladys' threats?"

"I don't know yet, Dalton, but I've only got until tomorrow. I'll do whatever it takes. I've decided that she knows enough to get a full-blown investigation goin, and that ain't good. I don't have much choice cept to call George Malini and have him settle for whatever it takes to get her off of my back."

"What if she takes the money and still talks to the reporter, or even the police?"

"One thing about Gladys, Dalton, she's good for her word. She's a bitch, but an honest bitch. If she takes the money, I think she'll stay quiet. Trouble is, I'll lose the club and everything else, but I don't have no choice. If I don't pay her, I'll lose everything and go to jail to boot. I'm gonna call George now and have him get a verbal agreement from her that if she takes the money she'll keep her mouth shut. Dial his number and get him on the line."

Dalton rang the phone and asked the operator for GA322 in Florence. When George answered, he said, "George this is Dalton, Gus asked me to get you on the line, but he just went to pee. Can you hold a moment?"

"Sure, Dalton." George didn't mind holding. When the phone rang he was reading the paper. He could hold the phone and read.

"George," Gus held the phone with one hand and zipped up with the other, "Have you talked anymore to Gladys?"

"No, you told me to wait until I heard from you."

"OK, I want you to call her and tell her that she has a deal. You have copies of my taxes so you know what I own; get my records out and bargain with her. Give her what it takes for her to stay off of my back and keep her mouth shut."

"Gus, are you in some kind of trouble? As your attorney I need to know."

"George, I just want you to do this now, we can talk about the other later. You're not my Boy Scout leader, you're my lawyer, so don't worry about what I'm doing and do what I'm paying you to do."

"Gus, I'll represent you as an attorney, but I'm not going to break the law by paying blackmail, if that is what this is."

"All this is, George, is a woman that's angry with me, and she wants to hurt me. Now, as my lawyer, represent me and get her off of my case. OK."

"OK, Gus, but if you have done something wrong I need to know about it now."

"I'll come over and see you Monday, but for now, get Gladys off my case."

"OK, but we talk Monday. Is that a deal?

"Right."

Joe called the Navy Base and got Jerry on the line. "Jerry get over here to the Charleston Jail right away. Tell MB to sit tight there at the airport until we see what's going on. We still don't know where the kid is."

"Right, I'll be there right away."

Jerry got a shore patrol officer to shuttle him to the jail. He walked into the small room while Joe was interrogating JT. Joe waved him in and kept right on talking to JT. "Now, one more time, I want to know where the kid is. You're in serious trouble and you're gonna make it tougher on yourself if you don't fess up and tell us what you've done with the boy."

"I told you already, we stopped at the Toddle House and he ran away; or maybe he was kidnapped. He told us he was going outside to drink his orange juice. When we finished breakfast and went out, he wasn't there. We were looking for him."

"OK, you're telling me that a ten-year-old that was in your supervision, miles from home, ran away, or was kidnapped, and you just looked for him? You didn't call the police?"

"I was on the phone trying to call the police when those big sailors started hassling me."

"Really, then why does the police department have no

record of your call? As you already know, you ended whatever call you were making and went to the car before the shore patrol stopped you."

"That's a lie, I started dialing and they came up and grabbed me."

Joe wrapped his hand around JT's tie and got face to face. "Now I'm starting to get very upset. When I get upset I do things I don't like. Jerry, go get Mr. McGloughlin a glass of water, and take your time getting back."

"Joe, are you sure you want me to leave?"

"Yeah, Mr. McGloughlin and I want to talk in private."

"Wait, don't go, this man is crazy. I want my lawyer. Get my father-in-law on the phone."

"If you don't tell me where the boy is, I'll call both of those folks and invite 'em to your funeral. Jerry, instead of the water, sit here and keep this gentleman company, I'll go and talk with his partner. McGloughlin, we're gonna find out what happened one way or the other. You'll be better off if you cooperate and help us find the kid. If your buddy in the other cell cooperates, he'll get the break you could have gotten."

"He's on pain pills. He won't know what's going on."

"Too bad for you both. I'll be back in a few minutes."

A police officer came in and said, "Agent Means, there's an urgent call for you from Inspector Stokes."

"Thanks, I'll be right there." He turned to McGloughlin, "While I'm on the phone you better hope I either have a change of heart or you have a change of story. If one or the other doesn't happen I'm gonna perform an experiment: I'm gonna see if that large Adam's apple you have in that skinny neck will pop out when I twist this tie." Joe patted JT's cheek and said, "I'll be right back."

Things were going hot and heavy now. While Joe was

going to the phone, another officer told him that the base had just called. "They think the person that was on the boat is Sonny, and they're pretty sure the dead guy is an escapee from the chain gang."

Joe picked up the phone, and said, "Hi Pedro, we've at least got a few things going on now."

"Joe, what's the latest there? Any news on the kid?"

"Nothing for sure, Pedro. We think we've found the kid, and we've got Webb and McGloughlin. When will you be here?"

"Mark and I are on the way now but we've got some big problems. J Edgar is furious. Tom Furman called the Director about this, and he's threatening to cut off our budget. You know the conference call meeting that J Edgar had planned for today? Well, it turns out that he was going to caution us to be very careful in this investigation. He was going to emphasize how important it is to not anger JT and Furman. As Hoover put it, he would like to save the kid, but he doesn't want the whole Bureau to suffer because of our efforts in this case. I tried to explain to him that we were dealing with a case where a federal agent has been killed, government weapons have been stolen, and a kid's life is at stake. You know what he said?"

"I could guess but maybe you'd better tell me."

"He said, 'Even though the Japanese have surrendered, we still have troops being fired on in some territories and we continue to have resistance from other foreign governments. Our agents are supposed to be working on matters of national security, not playing games that the local authorities can handle.' I won't have a job after this is over, and the bad part, maybe you won't either. He didn't relieve me of my duties yet so I'm going full blast on this case. I want you and Jerry to decide for yourselves whether or not you want to continue. You're risking your careers if you do. Mark has chosen to stay on the case."

"Pedro, you know full well that I am on this even if I get fired. I'm gonna find out what those SOBs have done. I think Jerry will say the same, but I'll give him the warning."

"Thanks, Joe, I knew you would say that. Mark and I will be there in about thirty minutes."

"Jerry and I are in the process of interviewing the suspects now, Inspector. They're not cooperating and It doesn't look like they will, but I'm gonna put pressure on. If I'm gonna get fired, I may as well go out in flames."

"Don't do anything that could make it worse, Joe. Just stay cool, OK."

"Right Pedro, you just get on down to the jail here. After you see these two you'll wanna kill them too, after you throw up."

"I'll see you in a few."

The jailer opened the cell door and he and Joe walked in. Garland was in a chair fast asleep. Joe shoved his head, Garland mumbled, and his head flopped back. Joe shook him some more, but it was clear that he was not faking. Joe figured he must have somehow gotten into some more of the pain pills. While Joe was on the way to have another shot at McGloughlin, he was told the county coroner was on the line. "Agent Means, this is Jim Dunbar, the coroner here in Charleston County, I have just examined a body that drowned and I'm told you have an interest in it. The body is that of an escapee from the Moncks Corner chain gang. He died of drowning."

"He was one of the two that was with a kid in the Cooper River, right?"

"Right. The kid's in the hospital, and he's only semi-conscious, but the doctors here have talked to a doctor in

Timmonsville. They've made a positive ID from several scars that the doctor, I think it was Dr. Holman, remembered that Sonny had. The kid'll be all right but he swallowed so much water he's not able to talk yet."

"I'm gonna send someone to the hospital now. Is your office nearby?"

"I'm right next door, Agent Means. You can have your person come to my office in the building on the left side of the hospital. I'll take him to the boy's room."

"Thanks. Agent Jerry Hamby will be there in just a couple of minutes. Meanwhile, have hospital security seal off that room. Tell them not to let anyone in except the medical staff."

"I'll have them set up security right away, Agent Means."

Joe banged on the door of the interrogation room and waved for Jerry to come out. "Jerry, we have an ID on the kid in the hospital. He is the one we're looking for, and he's gonna be OK, but so far, he hasn't been able to talk. Get over there now and get several of the local officers to guard his room. He was with an escaped convict when he almost drowned. My guess is that the two birds we have here didn't have the guts to kill the kid so they hired the job out to a couple of killers. Make absolutely certain nobody gets to him."

"I'll get right over."

"Oh, by the way, Jerry, I hate to tell you this, but J Edgar is raging. Pedro says that if you want, you can drop out of this case and go on home."

"J Ed has raged before. I'll call you from the hospital."

Pedro and Mark came into the room while Joe was questioning McGloughlin. Pedro said the hellos to Joe, and then smiled at JT. "Mr. McGloughlin, I'm Assistant Director

Pete Stokes from the Washington FBI Office. How are you this morning?"

"I'm not well at all, but I'm glad you're here. This thug that works for you has to be fired and I want it done right away. He has held me here for no reason, refused to allow me to call my father-in-law who is a lawyer, and he has made threats on my life. I want him arrested."

"Now, do you? You're really putting me on the spot, Mr. McGloughlin. Now, I have to decide whether I'm going to fire one of the best agents that the FBI has, or whether I'm going to take pleasure in watching you go to prison. Oh, my, what a dilemma."

"What do you mean? You know my father-in-law is a United States Senator, and he has oversight over your agency. Are you going to side with this thug and lose your job, or, are you, right now, going to give him the out?"

"Mr. McGloughlin, it may interest you to know that you can tell us what we ask or you can refuse. It really does not make much difference to us. You see we have tapes of your telephone calls to Gus Segars, and his calls to Antonio Felici. On those tapes they talk very plainly that your trip to Charleston was a ruse to throw the Sims boy overboard. We know that he overheard some of your dealings, and you may also want to know that the two convicts that you hired to kill him are dead. They drowned trying to drown the boy, but I'm sure you'll be happy to know that he is alive and well. He's in the hospital but he'll be out in a day or so. I'm certain that he will enjoy your trial. Since he is alive, you are facing only one murder charge, that of a Navy investigator. You may not have directly done the killing, but it came about from your conspiracy to steal government weapons; so, we plan now to charge all of you with murder. We also intend to dig up every acre of the area around the club if we have to. We've heard enough to feel pretty sure that our good friend from the Navy CID is buried there.

"You still want to call your uncle, or father-in-law, or whatever the Senator is to you? Oh, yes, he's your lawyer. Well, I suppose we could let you call him. Don't forget to tell him about the tapes we have implicating you in the attempted murder of the Sims boy. Of course—maybe he already knows.

"One other thing, your father-in-law may very well have the power to make me lose my job, but you know what? I'm gonna visit you in prison and show you my pension checks. They're gonna be a lot fatter than the five cents an hour you'll get for making license plates. I think I want you to make one for me that says, *'ha, ha!'* You have anything to say to this gentleman, Joe?"

"I think you've said it very nicely, Pedro. Let's ask the officers to gently place this nice man in a warm comfy cell and go get us some really fine Charleston cuisine.

"JT, it's been nice meeting you, and I'm sure I'll see a lot more of you. I'm sorry that you have an engagement and cannot dine with us at one of the local four star restaurants, but you enjoy your jail house grits. OK."

Joe and Pedro both kissed their hands and blew a kiss to McGloughlin. He just sat there and glowered.

JACK SIMS GETS FIRED
Chapter Nine

Jack Sims was at his desk, right where he had been for 36 straight hours. He was putting the final checks on a top-secret shipment—the return to the United States of every note, memo, scrap of paper, every piece of packaging and even the crypto machines that pertained in any way to two of the most powerful atom bombs in history. They had been sent to the Tinian Islands and, from there, dropped on Japan to bring about surrender. Jack had most of the details worked out, and had arranged to travel to the Islands and personally oversee the return of every piece of information that was used during the shipment of the bombs. The phone rang, and when Jack answered, Major Russell, from the base commander's office was on the line. Jack was a civilian but he was assigned to the base commander. "Mr. Sims, General Norton asks that you come to his office as quickly as possible."

"Thanks, Rob, tell him I'll be right there."

Jack was glad for an opportunity to stretch his legs. He walked right out the door to Base Headquarters, and Major Russell ushered him into the General's office. General Norton got up, met Jack at the door, shook hands, and asked him to have a seat. "Major Russell, get Jack and I some coffee."

"Jack I called you in for two reasons. One is to tell you that, in my mind, you have done an absolutely remarkable job in getting together these shipments to the Pacific Theater in an unbelievable short period of time. I also know that you have been working tirelessly to get all of the top secret related materiel safely back to Los Alamos. I'm well aware that you've been working almost around the clock, and you can be sure that your high degree of efficiency has greatly shortened this terrible war. The other news is, this message from The War Department: I was asked to give this to you immediately. Do you have any idea what it's about?"

Jack stared at the teletype; it was short and to the point.

> To: John Sims
>
> "As of 1130 hours, September 8, 1945, you are relieved of official duties. You will be given a set of travel orders and a train ticket by General N. Haskell Norton for your immediate trip home.
>
> Henry L. Stimson, Secretary, United States War Department."

"My God, Nelson, I can't believe this. I'm right in the middle of the project."

"I'm well aware of that, Jack. I called Secretary Stimson's office and he would not discuss it. Just said that it was orders and I was to give you the letter. I am to personally take over your project."

"Nelson, I know with you taking over the project it will be done efficiently, but I'm so heavily involved in this, it will still cause a delay getting all of the materiel returned to the states. Is there nothing we can do? Do they realize that we have to get this shipment back into safe storage in the US as quickly as possible?"

"I tried to impress that on Secretary Stimson, Jack, but he made it clear that there is absolutely nothing we can do. I was advised to inform you that you are not to speak with any political person about this. You are not to call any Senator or member of Congress. You are just to proceed home as soon as you get your bag packed. I'm puzzled, but we have no choice."

"Well, Nelson, I guess going home will be nice, but I would first like to have gotten that shipment back to the states. I know that they're in good hands with you though."

"Jack, after you pack, bring your bags back here. You're a good friend and I would like to take you to the train station myself. You're one of the best project organizers that I've ever seen, and I'll miss you, but these are the orders. Meanwhile, don't make any calls about this other than a family call."

"I'll call Hannah and tell her that I'll be coming home soon, then I'll pack. It'll only take me about an hour and I'll be ready to go. I have all the details arranged for the shipments in my safe; I'll bring them to you when I come back."

Hannah had been holding her hand on the phone all day. Before the first ring ended, Hannah was shouting "Hello!"

"Hannah, this is Doctor Holman. I just got a call from a Doctor Talbert in Charleston. Now don't panic, Sonny is in the hospital, but he's OK. Apparently he swallowed a little too much water and lost all of his food. He's quite weak, so they're giving him an IV. I have the number for Doctor Talbert at Roper Medical Hospital. Call him at SN334. You can confirm that it is Sonny and that he is OK. I'm positive it's him because of a few of the scars that I sewed on him. Call me back if there's further information that you need on his medical history."

Hannah was so flustered she just said, "Thank you, Doctor Holman," slammed the receiver down, and cranked the phone for the operator.

Nell Moore was still on the old Timmonsville switchboard and she placed the call for Hannah. The number rang right in Dr. Talbert's office and when his nurse answered, Hannah said, "Dr. Talbert please, this is Hannah Sims."

"Yes Ma'am, Mrs. Sims, he's right here waiting for your call."

"Mrs. Sims, this is Dr. Talbert, and I'm right here with a ten-year-old kid that Dr. Holman is certain is your son. He's doing fine, but we haven't been able to talk with him. Can you describe your son to me?"

"He's four-feet-six inches tall, weighs about seventy pounds, has light brown hair and light gray eyes. I'm sure Dr. Holman told you about the scars on his leg and arm. He also has a small purplish birthmark under his left arm, close to the armpit."

"Mrs. Sims, I am 100 percent sure that this is your son. He is going to be fine. He swallowed a lot of water, and threw up everything he had in his tummy, so we have him on an IV. He'll be in here at least until tomorrow, but his vital signs are very stable. Dr. Holman told me that you're a nurse so I can give you his vitals if you like."

"No, I'll take your word, Dr. Talbert, I'll be there in just a few hours."

"OK, Mrs. Sims, I'll take good care of your boy and when you get here ask for me, someone will bring you right to his room."

"Thanks Dr. Talbert." Hannah hung up the phone and as soon as she did, it rang.

"Hello!"

"Hannah! Honey, how are you doing?"

"Oh, Jack! I'm so glad you called. Sonny has had an accident and he's in the hospital in Charleston."

"What happened? How is he?"

"He's doing fine, and what happened is a long story but he

almost drowned. I just got off the phone with Doctor Talbert, at Roper Medical Hospital, and he assures me he's OK. I'm leaving to go down there now. Can you tell me where you are, and can you come home?"

"Honey, I can't tell you where I am, but I'm coming home today. I don't understand why but I've been terminated from this project. Now, I'm glad, so I can get home. I'm gonna call Tom Furman and have him get me a priority plane."

"I don't think that's a good idea, Jack."

"Why?"

"Well, JT McGloughlin was somehow responsible for Sonny almost drowning. Tom Furman is furious that I told him about the FBI investigation of his son-in-law."

"I guess maybe that explains why I got this paper relieving me from duty this morning. Hannah, he must have had me fired."

"Jack, I'm sure that he is responsible."

"I can't believe he would do such a vindictive thing. Even though the war is technically over, I was working on some things that must be done as quickly as possible. I can't tell you what I was working on, but I can't believe any Senator would jeopardize lives because of some personal matter."

"I'm sorry if I antagonized him in this Jack, but I had to try and find out how to get in touch with you. Furman was furious when I questioned him about his son-in-law."

"You did right, Hannah. I'll call Mendal Rivers and get a plane ride home; I need to be there as quickly as possible. He's one that has no fear of Tom Furman." What's the name of the doctor in Charleston?"

It's Dr. Talbert, at Roper Medical Hospital, and the number is SN334. I'll be there until Sonny gets out and can come home."

"I'll call Mendal from the Base Commander's office and

have him get me a flight to Charleston. I love you, and I'm thrilled that I'll soon be home."

"Same here, Honey."

Jack packed his bags and walked down to Nelson's office. "Nelson, as you know Mendal Rivers is a family friend. I'm not at all going to discuss anything about the real reason that I'm leaving here, but it turns out that my son is in the hospital in Charleston. I need to get there as quickly as possible. I'm going to call him and have him get me a flight to Charleston."

"Jack, I'll call Mendal for you. You have orders not to talk to anyone, and it could be construed that you were disobeying those orders, and that could spell real trouble for you. If I call, it will be a simple request for quick transport because of your son's illness. Mendal and I go back a ways, so plan on a flight."

"Thanks, Nelson."

Joe and Pedro signed several papers at the jail giving the Charleston Police Department authority to hold Garland and JT until they could get a judge to sign a warrant. "Joe, before we have our dining experience I'm gonna get my last hurrah in progress. Mark has called Bob Johnson and told him to get copies of those tapes to us right away. I'm gonna call Judge Weston C. Houck and get an appointment to let him hear the tapes. After he does, I believe we can get him to issue warrants for the arrest of JT, Garland, Antonio, Gus, Dalton Sellers, and I think we have enough information on there for the arrest of Cecil Gaskins as well."

"Sounds good to me, Pedro. I can't wait to make sure those two we have here, stay here. It was just a stroke of luck, that the two they hired to kill the boy got drowned in the process. Now, I would like to be the one to issue a formal arrest charge on our two friends here."

"Yeah, me too, Joe, we can only keep them awhile. If the Judge doesn't give us his backing they'll be out of there soon. I'm sure Tom Furman is working on JT's release right now."

"How long before we'll have the tapes?"

"Mark told Bob to get them here by the fastest way possible so we should have them in two or three hours, but I'm gonna try and make the appointment flexible. It's Saturday in case you didn't know, so I'll have to call him at home."

"No problem with that. As soon as J Edgar and our friend Tolson get through with us we'll no doubt have a lot of days in a row that will seem to be Saturdays."

Pedro borrowed a phone in Chief Howard's office, dialed O, and got the operator on the line. "Give me the number for Judge Weston C. Houck in Florence, please.

After a short pause, she came back on and said, "Sir, that is a private number that is not given out."

"Ma'am, this is Assistant Director Pete Stokes from the FBI. I must talk with him now. I'm calling from Charleston Police Chief Everett Howard's office. Please get the Judge on the line and tell him who is calling and from where. I'll wait here to hear from you."

"I'll get my supervisor, sir."

Pedro repeated the same request to the supervisor, and she said, "Yes, sir, just stay on the line, I'll call him and get right back with you."

Pedro cupped the phone and told Joe what was happening. "Cross your fingers that he's home and will meet with us today. I don't know him but his reputation is such that I think he'll see us and follow through. We need to get this done before he hears from JT's daddy-in-law. That would put a lot of pressure on him."

"Yeah, Pedro, especially if Furman calls J Ed and has him call the judge."

Pedro waved to let Joe know that the operator was back on the line. "Yes, Ma'am, I'm still here."

"Sir, the Judge is at the country club, but his wife is calling there and having him paged. She says that he's not been there long, and with the weather like it is, he's probably just sitting around telling golf stories. Can you hold on?"

"Yes, I sure can, and thanks."

While he was on hold, Pedro told Joe to ask the desk sergeant for the name of a good place, close by, to get something good, but fairly fast to eat. Joe walked out and the operator came on, "Sir, we have located Judge Houck and he will be on the line with you in about two minutes."

"Thank you, you are a credit to Southern Bell."

"Hello, this is Judge Houck."

"Judge, this is Inspector Pete Stokes from the Washington FBI office. I'm calling from Chief Everett Howard's office in Charleston. We have several suspects here that we think killed a federal agent and kidnapped a ten-year-old kid. We have surveillance tapes that I believe offer enough proof to issue arrest warrants. Would it be possible for you to meet with me this afternoon?"

"Can you give me a little more information, Inspector. What did you say your name is?"

"Yes sir, I'm Assistant Director Pete Stokes. I know you don't know me but I believe you do know Mark Hughley of our Charlotte office, and he will be with me. We've just found the kidnapped child, but as of yet, he has not been able to make a statement. He almost drowned and the killers that were hired to drown him were drowned themselves. The Coast Guard saved the boy and found one of the bodies of the killers. They, or at least the one that was recovered, escaped from the chain gang in Moncks Corner."

"I know Chief Howard quite well, if you will put him on the line that would be helpful."

"Judge, he's on the way here now. I'll have him call you and fill you in as soon as he gets here."

"If Chief Howard recommends that I see you, I will; if the weather permits I'm going to tee off, but I'll leave instructions in the pro shop to fetch me as soon as the Chief calls."

"Thank you very much, Sir, the Chief will be calling shortly. If the weather is like it is here, you probably won't be on the course by the time he gets here."

Joe found a good restaurant right down the street and Pedro left word for the Chief to come there as soon as he got in. "Pedro, I don't think food has ever smelled better, I'm starved."

"Yeah, but I've had so much coffee at the jail I don't know if I can handle much of that, but that onion sausage omelet sounds great.

The waitress came over and said, "Coffee, gentlemen," and before either could answer she starting pouring.

Pedro handed her his menu and said, "Yes, and I want to try that onion sausage omelet."

"I'll have the same except that I want green peppers with mine."

"I'll be right back with your order, gentlemen."

As soon as she left, Andy Blackwell and Michael came in. "I hate to interrupt your lunchtime breakfast, but I knew you would want to know this. Several of our shore patrol officers have found out that the Longhauler's Union, or at least some of the members, are looking for the kid. We don't know why, but they asked questions at a service station, and the station's owner happened to be the landlord of one of the shore patrol officers. The lord called him and asked him if that could be the kid he's looking for. We have them under observation and we have seen them talking to others that seem to be searching also."

Joe and Pedro looked at each other and both said at the same time— "Antonio. It's got to be."

"Thank you very much Andy that is extremely helpful information. Put them under surveillance and keep me informed. Thank goodness we have guards on the kid's hospital door. Excuse me, Joe, I'm gonna call Jerry and have him increase the alert."

"You better hurry back or I'm gonna eat your omelet." While Pedro was on the phone the Chief came in. He wasn't hard to spot; he had on a uniform with gold braid. Nothing like Garland's, but Joe knew it was the Chief as soon as he hit the door. Joe went over and introduced himself and the chief came to the table.

"Chief, thanks for coming over, we understand you know Judge Westin Houck. We need to fill you in on where we are on this kidnapping and suspected murder and have you call the Judge to set up a meeting with us. He said that if you recommended seeing us he would do so. It's in Florence but you'll be welcome to come with us if you would like."

"I don't think my going over will be necessary, but I'll surely give him the information you need him to have. I've already talked with my deputy chief and he's filled me in somewhat. What else do I need to know?"

Pedro got off of the phone and came over and introduced himself. He and Joe filled the Chief in with some other details, including the new info that members of the Longhauler's Union were looking for the kid. They also let him know about the Navy Investigator that was missing and thought to have been killed.

"As soon as you finish your meal I'll be glad to call him. You couldn't have a more helpful Judge; I don't think you'll have any trouble persuading him to issue the warrants. I will certainly recommend it."

Hannah drove to the hospital in Charleston as fast as she safely could. She went to the desk, told the operator who she was, and that she was looking for Dr. Talbert.

"Yes ma'am, he asked me to have you escorted to his office." She motioned to an orderly standing nearby, and said, "This is Mrs. Sims, please take her to room 311."

"If you'll just follow me Ma'am."
Hannah and the orderly got on the elevator and he put in a key that kept the elevator from being stopped until they were on the third floor.

When Hannah stepped off of the elevator she was met by a police officer. Before he could say anything, she said, "I'm Hannah Sims, I'm looking for my son."

"Come right this way, ma'am." He led her to the door of the room where another police officer was standing. The first officer, said, "This is Mrs. Sims."

The one at the door said, "I'm sorry to have to ask this, Ma'am, but do you have any identification?"

"Of course, I have my driver's license."

"Could I see it please, Ma'am; we have our orders."
Hannah took out her license and handed it to him. He read the name, date of birth, height and weight, looked up at Hannah, and said, "Please Ma'am, step right in. Dr. Talbert asked me to get him when you arrived. I'll have someone send for him now."

Hannah rushed over to the bed and the Mother in her hugged Sonny, while the nurse in her started taking his pulse. He was lying there sleeping peacefully. He had a tube in his arm, and a small cut over his eye, but otherwise he looked fine. She grabbed his hand, squeezed, and said, "Oh, Darling, Mother is here. You have been through so much, and I feel so guilty that you couldn't make me understand why you didn't want to go on that trip. Everything is going to be all right now."

Sonny was in what was normally a two-bed room, but it had been converted into a private room. Hannah hugged Sonny a while and paced the floor a while. A nurse knocked on the door, came in and said, "I'm going to take his vitals, and there's a phone call for you at the desk. It's long distance, would you like to have a phone brought into the room."

"Yes, please, I don't want to leave him."

The nurse gave an aide orders to bring in a phone and plug it up. As soon as Hannah said hello, she heard Jack's familiar voice. "Hannah, my base commander called Mendal Rivers and he has arranged a flight to Charleston. I'm waiting for the plane to get warmed up now, and I should be there tonight. Mendal's secretary called the hospital and they will have beds set up for us in Sonny's room. I've got to go now, but I love you. Say hello to my Little Buckaroo."

When Jack said that word tears welled up in Hannah's eyes. That was his favorite name for Sonny. Jack would hold Sonny when he was a small boy and sing "My Little Buckaroo" to him for hours at a time. She couldn't wait to hear it again. She squeezed Sonny's hand and he blinked his eyes. About that time Dr. Talbert came in and Hannah screamed, "Doctor, Sonny is waking up!"

Dr. Talbert felt his pulse and said "Sonny, can you hear me?"

Sonny had trouble with the bright light but he finally got

his eyes opened and said weakly, "Momma." Hannah burst into happy tears. She hugged and squeezed him while Dr. Talbert stood there and grinned.

"Mrs. Sims, I'll give you two a little time together and then I'll come back and make an examination. If he's OK to talk, the police need to interview him but I want to see how he feels first. I'll be back in five minutes." Hannah and Sonny embraced and both were crying but they were tears of joy.

`"Gus, this is George Malini. You sitting down?" Gus had to be sitting down. He had gone through so much Scotch that he was beginning to think the phone receiver was a set of bagpipes. "Yeah, George, what you got?"

"Gus, you told me to do what I had to do with Gladys, and she's been hard to deal with. She's getting almost everything you have except the club. She wanted no part of that. She'll get the house, the best car, and your amusement company. She said that you could continue running the amusement company with her accountant's supervision if you choose to, or she would sell it. She gave you that choice. She agreed to set you on a salary for managing it and after a period of time she may agree to let you take a percentage instead of a salary. She makes it clear, though, that you are her employee and she makes any decisions.

Gus said, "Just a minute, George. He laid the phone down, walked outside, screamed, cursed, and slammed his fist into the Lincoln that would no longer be his. He put dents in all four doors with his fists. His knuckles were bleeding and he was about to hyperventilate. Dalton said, "Anything, I can do, Gus?" "Yeah, get the hell out of my way!"

Gus picked the phone back up and told George, "Tell her OK, I'll sign any necessary papers on Monday."

George said, "Ok, Gus, I don't understand why you're

doing this but as your attorney I'll carry out your wishes. I'll see you Monday."

Gus spewed out a string of violent obscenities, kicked a pinball machine, and slammed the phone against the wall. Bob Johnson's ears were ringing.

Chief Howard gave Pedro and Joe the good news; Judge Houck would see them at his house at three p.m. Pedro arranged to have the tapes delivered to Florence, and he, Mark, and Joe headed for the Pee Dee. They arrived at the small one-man office above the post office at two o'clock. The agent with the tapes arrived fifteen minutes later. They placed them in the Magnecord reel recorder and started listening. Pedro made notes at places that he wanted to emphasize for the Judge. There were many. It was very clear that the fishing trip was a ruse to find out if Sonny knew about their hijacking operation. If so, it was also clear they planned to throw him to the sharks. They made no mention of hiring two convicts to do the job. Pedro, Joe, and Mark surmised that they hired them at the last minute because they chickened out.

"Anybody have any doubts that this is a conspiracy, and that the jail from which nobody escapes, behind the club, is where Investigator Parnell is buried?" There was unanimous consent that the Judge would be able to find no way but to issue warrants for the arrest of everyone but Cecil. He was mentioned on the tapes a few times but it was so vague that it left it open for interpretation. They would ask for his arrest, but even if not granted, they would be happy to get the rest of the bunch behind bars.

"Let's head over to the Judge's house." They drove over and pulled into Judge Houck's driveway. He met them on the porch and told them to come into his study.

"Why did you not tell me that Senator Furman's son-in-law is one of the suspect's in this case? And why did you not tell me that J Edgar Hoover has not authorized the arrest of these suspects. I'm going to listen to the tapes, but you fellows have put me in one hell of a hole. There had better be some very clear evidence there. Of course, I picked up the feeling from Director Hoover that I'm not the only one on the spot. He is very unhappy that you, one of his best supervisors in the past, have now gone off on a tangent. I have a recorder in my study, let's hear what you have."

Joe put the tape in and couldn't wait to turn it up so the group wouldn't hear his growling, nervous stomach.

Pedro had left instructions for Jerry Hamby to "Stay by the door of Sonny's room and, as soon as the doctor says he can talk, get some initial info out of him. Don't push him at this point, but get a feel for what he'll say, and call me at the Judge's house."

Dr. Talbert came out and said, "Mr. Hamby, Sonny is awake now, but he's very weak, I'm only going to give you a few minutes to talk with him. If he starts getting upset, I'll have to ask you to stop."

Jerry jumped up and said, "Yes, sir, Doc, if we can just get a little info to be sure we're on the right track that will be enough for now. I'll make my questions short and very direct." Dr. Talbert Okayed that and Jerry introduced himself to Hannah and Sonny.

"Sonny, I just want to ask you a few questions. I know you've been through quite an ordeal but it will help us immensely if you feel like answering. I know you're a Junior G-man, and I'm proud of that. Now, do you know anything about any hijackings of government weapons?"

"Yes, sir."

"Are JT McGloughlin and Garland Webb Involved?"

"Yes, sir."

"Did they bring you to Charleston today?"

"Yes, sir."

"Do you know the names of anyone else involved?"

"There is a man named Cecil, but I don't know him, and there is Gus Segars, and Dalton Sellers."

"Great, you're being a big help. Do you know anything about a Navy Investigator being killed?"

"I don't think so, but I did hear them referring to a jail behind the AMVETS Club. I got the feeling they had buried someone there."

"OK, do you know why you were chosen to go on that fishing trip?"

"Yes, sir."

"Could you tell me?"

"Yes, sir, they were going to throw me overboard but I got away first."

Hannah started hyperventilating at that point and Dr. Talbert asked a nurse to comfort her and try and calm her down.

"I only need a few more minutes, Mrs. Sims." With that Jerry continued "Now, Sonny, did JT and Garland personally hand you over to those two convicts."

"I don't understand?"

"Well, when you were picked up there were two convicts trying to drown you."

Sonny got very upset, and Dr. Talbert said, "We'll have to terminate this for now."

Sonny screamed and hollered. "No! No, please. They have to know Meggs and Richburg saved my life, they didn't try and kill me. Richburg gave me his life jacket and swam away, knowing he was going to die."

"Are you sure of this?"

"Yes, sir, I'm positive. They were not going to hurt me. They were just trying to get to the other side of the river to a friend's house. They were taking great pains to see that nothing happened to me."

"OK, just one more question for now. How did you get hooked up with those two?"

"I was running from Garland and JT and they found me hiding in the woods. They didn't have anything to do with Garland and JT. I swear. Mr. Richburg has kids of his own and he wouldn't hurt no kid. He wants me to go see his kids. Mama, I want to go see them as soon as I get out of here. Meggs and Richburg were nice men."

Jerry patted Sonny's head, and said, "OK, Sonny, that's enough for now. We'll need a lot more information from you later, but now you need to rest."

Dr. Talbert walked Jerry to the door then came back and took Sonny's vitals. His blood pressure was up, but that was good, it had been dangerously low earlier.

Judge Houck sat impassioned, listening to the tapes as Gus and Antonio talked about doing away with a kid. They also talked of the jail in the back of the club. It was obvious to the agents what they were saying, but the judge showed no emotion at all. He sat in stoic silence when there was talk of the little snitch being fed to the sharks. There was also no doubt that they were the hijackers of the government weapons, but still the Judge just sat there and stared. There were hours of tape but after thirty minutes the judge asked Pedro to stop the machine. "Gentlemen, I'm not sure that I hear any proof here. I certainly hear a lot of big talk, and bravado, but as far as anyone saying specifically that they planned to actually kill someone, I'm not sure it's there."

Pedro was not about to give up easily. "Judge this is the way these creeps talk, they think it's some kind of joke to kill a federal agent and even to kill a kid. Please, can we replay the part where they're going to feed a kid to the sharks? Then tie that to the farce plan Garland and JT used to get the Sims kid on the fishing trip. Add in the fact that when Sonny ran away they didn't even call the police. It doesn't make sense any other way."

"Well, you know we don't have Edgar's approval on this, and certainly we don't have Senator Furman's OK. We need proof, what else do you have?"

"Well, as soon as the kid wakes up, we have an agent there that is going to interview him. May I call and see if that will be soon?"

"Of course."

Pedro dialed long distance, gave the number for the hospital, and immediately got through to Jerry. "Jerry, what's happening? Any chance of seeing the kid soon?"

"Better than that, Pedro, I just walked out of there. He gave a statement, which his mother and Dr. Talbert heard, as well as a nurse. He confirmed that they are the hijackers, and they were going to kill him."

"Anything else?"

"Well the odd thing is, those two convicts he was with were not henchmen of that crowd. He just stumbled onto them while he was hiding from Garland and JT."

"But he did clearly state that they were going to kill him?"

"Very clearly that JT and Garland were going to, but he was emphatic that the convicts had absolutely nothing to do with it. His mother got hysterical."

"Will you tell that to the Judge?" Pedro handed the phone to Judge Houck, and said, "This is Agent Hamby, Judge, He has just interviewed the boy."

"Yes, Agent Hamby, this is Judge Houck."

"Judge, I can stake fifteen years of interviewing suspects on this kid; he is for real, and will make a star witness. He states assuredly that they were trying to kill him, and that they are hijackers, He knows where they have some of the bottles of hijacked whiskey, and he heard them talk of Dalton beating the driver with an axe handle."

"You are quite certain of this Agent Hamby? Could you be mistaken?"

"Judge, If I had any doubt at all, I would not say this; I am positive the kid is telling the truth."

"Thank you, Agent Hamby. The Judge hung up the phone and stared at a picture of himself and his wife with Senator Tom Furman. The Judge had his hand on a Bible and Tom Furman was swearing him in as a federal judge.

"Listening to these tapes, and Agent Hamby, gives me a feeling that you are correct. On the other hand, I have the direct call from the Director of your agency, and he tells me that you are off on a tangent. You have me in a spot. If I do issue the warrants and you are mistaken, then I have defied not only a U.S. Senator, but the Director of the FBI as well. On the other hand, if I don't issue these warrants, and something happens to Sonny, or some other person, I will feel responsible. Please wait here for a few moments, I'm going to walk around the block and think. I'll give you my decision as soon as I get back. Please make yourselves at home, and use the phone if you need to."

"Thanks, Judge, I do need to make several calls."

With that the Judge walked out and Pedro grabbed the phone. He dialed the hospital and asked for Dr. Talbert. "Dr. Talbert, this is Inspector Pete Stokes, and I'm in Judge Weston Houck's office in Florence. Is there any way you could allow Sonny Sims to get on the phone with the Judge? We need for him to tell Judge Houck who was trying to kill him so we can get warrants for their arrest. I know the kid is weak from this ordeal and this will be tough on him, but he will be a lot safer if we can get these crazy killers off the street. The Judge is walking around the block but will be back any minute now."

"Inspector, he's been through a lot but he's a tough little kid. Can you hold the line while I take his vitals again? If they're OK, and Sonny wishes to talk, I will allow it."

"Thanks Doc, I'll hold."

After a five or so minute wait Dr. Talbert came back on and said, "The vitals were fine and Sonny and his mother have agreed it will be OK. If he starts getting upset, I'll have to abort the call."

"Thanks so much, doctor, can you let me speak with Agent Hamby."

Dr. Talbert handed the phone to Jerry. "Hey, Pedro, what's up?"

"Jerry, brief the kid. I can't talk long now; the Judge is out for a few minutes. When he comes back, if he hasn't agreed to issue the warrants, I'm gonna try and get him to talk with Sonny directly. Start briefing Sonny now. Tell him if the Judge wants to talk with him, to tell him how he got involved. You do feel comfortable that he is for real, right?"

"No question in my mind, Inspector, I think he can make a convincing argument. He's a bright little kid, and he has seen some direct evidence."

"Just hang on to the phone, Jerry, and stand by. I hope the judge will OK this without further delay, but if not, maybe he'll talk with Sonny before he makes a decision."

The Judge walked in; it was misting rain outside and he was wet, but he had a smile on his face.

"Gentlemen, I'm not sure I'm doing the right thing, but my gut feeling is that you are on the same track the train is on. I'm going to issue the warrants. If I'm wrong, I can always go back to my law practice. What about you guys, even if you're right, you probably are in deep dung with J Edgar."

"We understand that sir, but it's part of the job. We feel we're doing the right thing, and we can't do otherwise. We were sworn to uphold the law, and even if we get canned, we have to do this."

"If you're right, and I think you are, I'll try and help smooth it over. I have some contacts in Congress other than Senator Furman. Of course if you're wrong, I'll be in the crowd smiling at your crucifixion. With that the judge sat down and picked up the phone. He dialed, and heard a voice—

"Hello. Hello."

Judge Houck hit the connection bar several times, and shouted, "Who is this?"

Pedro hollered, "Oh, no, Judge, we forgot Jerry. I asked Dr. Talbert to let Sonny talk with you if need be, and we had Jerry hanging on the phone. Let me tell Jerry that you won't have to talk with Sonny after all." He got Jerry off of the line and handed the phone back to the Judge.

Judge Houck put the phone down and asked, "Can any of you type? If so, we can go to my office right now and I won't have to try and find my law clerk."

"Judge, you can't be one of J Edgar Hoover's boys and not be able to type. Reports are the name of our game."

"Well let's go. I can't play golf; I may as well help you fellows commit employment suicide."

The desk sergeant buzzed Chief Howard and told him that he had a call from a Senator. The Chief picked up the phone and a pencil at the same time. He wanted to make notes of what the Senator had to say. "Yes, this is Chief Howard."

"Chief Howard, this is United States Senator Tom Furman. I understand that there is some misunderstanding there, and I am calling to clear it up. You are holding my son-in-law and I want him released immediately."

"Senator, warrants for his arrest are being transmitted here as we speak. If I let him go, I would have to re-arrest him before he got out of the door."

"Warrants are coming? From where?"

"I just got a call from Federal Judge Westin Houck in Florence, and he informed me that he is teletyping a copy of the order right away. The official copies are being hand delivered by federal agents. I don't believe I can let him go now, Senator."

"You do understand that I have considerable contacts in your city government and that you are causing big problems for yourself."

"I understand sir, but when I took this job I swore an oath to uphold the law. I took that to mean that even if a United States Senator tried to pressure me, I would still uphold the law. I do appreciate your calling, but I have to check the teletype and see if the orders are here. Is there anything you would like me to say to your son-in-law?"

"Yes, tell him that I said that he'll be out soon, and that the small town Chief of Charleston will be fired even sooner."

"Roger, Senator," Chief Howard said as he hung up the phone. He couldn't wait for the orders to get there. He was going to do the fingerprints and the booking personally.

ROUND 'EM UP, BRAND 'EM, AND PUT 'EM IN THE CORRAL
Chapter Ten

As soon as Judge Houck signed the warrants, Pedro was ready for action. "Joe, it's time to round 'em up, brand 'em, and put 'em in the corral. Joe knew that was Pedro's way of saying find them, fingerprint them, and put them in a cell. "I'm going to head for Charleston with these warrants. I want you to stay here, and contact all of Mark's crew. Order them to stay away from the Bureau phones. Get over to MB's house or at his airport office and have them stay in touch with you there. If I'm right, J Edgar will be calling and telling them that they are not to obey you and me. Tell them not to answer the agency phones under any circumstances. Call the others and have them pick up Antonio, Gus, and Dalton. Give them MB's phone number and coordinate from there.

"Since the Judge didn't feel there was enough information on Cecil to issue a warrant we'll have to build a case on him. He can wait, but I want a tail on him around the clock. As soon as we get the others in bar city I want you to go and lean on him. He doesn't seem to be a part of the Navy Investigators murder, nor the planned murder of Sims, so he may be the one we can turn. If so, and he becomes a witness, we can wrap this up quite quickly. The lab is still evaluating the prints and other evidence we took at the site of the hijacking. Hopefully, we can get proof of his involvement there."

"We can't prove it yet, Pedro, but we do know that he

hijacked a federal shipment."

"We'll get him Joe. Start making those calls, I'm heading for Charleston."

Sonny was sitting up in bed when the Charleston News and Courier reporter tried to get off on the third floor. The burly policeman asked what patient he was visiting, and when he said Sonny Sims, he was not allowed to leave the elevator area. He asked if he could speak with Mrs. Sims and the policeman agreed to ask if she would like to talk with him. She did.

Hannah went out into the hallway where the police were standing with the reporter, strolled over and said "I'm Hannah Sims, I understand you wanted to see me."

"Yes, Ma'am, my name is Bill Starr and I'm with the Charleston News and Courier. I understand that your son was kidnapped. Can you give me any details?"

"I certainly can, Mr. Starr. I want you to know that the Florence County School Superintendent and the Timmonsville Chief of Police kidnapped my son. Others are also involved and the FBI is in the process of arresting them. I also want the public to know that if it were not for the FBI agents on the case my son would have drowned and the people that were responsible for his death would have gone free. I also want the public to know that Senator Tom Furman is trying to get my son's kidnapers freed, and that he had my husband fired from a top-secret military project because I told him his son-in-law is a kidnapper. As long as I have a breath left in my body, I will work to either get him in prison, or at least get him out of office. That is my statement; however, before you leave, you must get everything I have said approved by the FBI. They are the reason my son is alive, and I will not cause them any grief."

The police officer asked Jerry if he would approve the statement and he said that any statement would have to be approved by Assistant Director Stokes when he returned from Florence. He ordered the deputies in the hallway to make sure that Mr. Starr did not leave the floor until the story was approved, or disapproved, by Inspector Stokes. They led him to a chair at the far end of the hall and told him to stay put.

Pedro rushed into the Charleston police station and the chief met him just inside the door. "Inspector, you have orders to call your Assistant Director, Fred Tolson, and you also are to call Senator Furman. You had better wait somewhere else while I get these two officially booked."

"I'll call them, but I need to use your phone first to see how the roundup is proceeding. Then, I'm going to see the kid in the hospital. After that I'll face Tolson's off-key music."

Pedro went into Chief Howard's office and called Joe at MB's home number. Joe answered and they both were pleased that things were moving along. Joe said, "I've got Mark's guys going after Antonio now, and I have the Florence Sheriff and several of his guys standing by and ready. We're going to the club as soon as I get off of the phone. We have a deputy watching the place and if they leave he is to follow. I'll call you as soon as we have them in custody."

"Go get 'em, Joe. You'll have to put them in the county jail so inform the sheriff that we need extra guards. These are killers."

"Right, the sheriff knows that, and he hates the guts of both of these two. Clyde Moody will volunteer, I'm sure, to guard them. He despises them too."

"OK, Joe, I've got the hornets swarming here but I'm going to see the kid before I make my last call. Later, I may be locked up with the others."

Chief Howard asked one of his officers to go with Pedro to the hospital. "Our guys know the short cuts; besides, you might need the company."

"Thanks Chief." Pedro got in the patrol car and in minutes they were at the hospital.

As soon as he got on the floor where Sonny's room was located the police officers told him about the reporter. Pedro went over and introduced himself. "Hello, I'm Assistant Director Pete Stokes; I'm told you wanted to see me."

"Yes Sir, I'm William Starr, with the Charleston News and Courier, and I have a story about the kidnapping from the mother of the kid. She won't let me release it unless you OK it."

"Let me see it." Pedro read it and chuckled. "Well Mr. Starr, I think the mother of a boy that has been kidnapped has the right to issue a statement. I have no comment, and if you choose to release it, I have neither approved nor disapproved. Understood?"

"Yes, sir." He couldn't wait to get to the office and type it up. He realized that this story would make the front pages of the national newspapers, since it concerned a powerful United States Senator abusing his office.

Starr got the story typed up and took it to his editor, John Monk. Monk read it over and immediately called the publisher, Bill McDonald. The three met and made a decision to print the story, but to also send it to Maggie Gallagher at the Washington Post. Maggie had been helpful to the Courier on several occasions and they knew she would give the Charleston News and Courier full credit for breaking the story. This would also get the story nationally a day sooner. As soon as John Monk rang Maggie, McDonald grabbed the phone. "Maggie, this is Bill McDonald with the Charleston News and Courier, how are things in Washington."

"Oh, hi, Bill, things are all fouled up here, so everything is going along normally. What's going on in Charleston that has you calling?"

"Maggie, we have a story that we'll publish in the morning and we want to give it to you simultaneously as long as you agree to give us credit. Is that a deal?"

"Of course, I don't see how I could refuse that. It must be hot for you to do this."

"As hot as a U.S. Senator shoving people around to get a suspected killer of a federal agent freed from jail."

"Sounds good, you want to get it on the wire to me, Bill?"

"Right away, Maggie. Then when your deadline comes you can put it out. I'm gonna hang up, transmit, and get back to getting it out in the early edition here. I'll send some follow-ups soon; there'll be a lot more coming on this story."

"Thanks, Bill."

Maggie got the story in her hands and smiled a smile that wet both of her ears. She despised Tom Furman. He was a sleaze bag as far as she was concerned. Each time he had been around her, in elevators of the capital, or other places, he had made some "accidental" move and let his hand slide across her backside. He made it look unintentional, but she knew better. It had happened too many times.

While the typesetters were laying type for the story, Maggie picked up the phone and dialed Hugh Munn. Hugh was J Edgar Hoover's public information director, and this was a story she wanted to get into quickly. Hugh, this is Maggie Gallagher, so how are you?

"Fine, Maggie, what gets you on the phone on a

Saturday?"

"I want to congratulate Edgar on the quick work your agents have done in South Carolina saving a kid's life from a gang of hijackers and killers. I also want to see what he's going to do about Tom Furman trying to use his influence to get these killers freed."

"Where did you hear this, Maggie?"

"I've got a story that will be running in the morning. It quotes the mother of the child that the gang tried to kill. She says that Tom Furman has gotten her husband fired from a top secret job and the firing will cause a lot of troops a delay in getting home. He is doing this out of spite because she is accusing his son-in-law of being one of the killers."

"Maggie, can you send me a copy of this right away? Director Hoover will want to see it and make inquires before he talks to the press."

"Can I count on you, Hugh, to get back with me first?"

"You know you can, Maggie."

"Ok, go to your wire machine, I'm sending it now."

"Thanks, Maggie.

Pedro went to Sonny's room, spoke with Jerry Hamby and Hannah Sims, and then he congratulated Sonny on his bravery. "Sonny, from what we have learned so far, you have really been through an ordeal. You are one special kid and I am so proud that one of our Junior G-Men is so brave. You are just the kind of person the Bureau needs for the future, and I hope that when you're older, you will become part of the G-Man team." With that, Pedro took off his FBI tie clasp, shook Sonny's hand, and presented him with his clasp. Sonny was beaming, and Hannah was so proud she was crying happy tears. Pedro said his good-byes, headed for a phone in Doctor Talbert's office, took several deep breaths, and called Clyde Tolson.

"Mr. Tolson, this is Assistant Director Stokes, I understand you wanted me to call."

"I expected the call hours ago, but that is of no matter now. The Director requested that I call and inform you that you are to be in his office precisely at eight a.m. If you cannot get a plane by that time, he suggests that you drive. In any event he is expecting to see you at eight a.m."

"Can you tell me what it's about, Mr. Tolson?"

"I believe that, as an agent of twenty-five years, you have sufficient intelligence to figure this out for yourself."

"I'll be there in the morning, Sir." Pedro hung the phone up and mused back over his twenty-five years with the Bureau. During his early years the agency was known as "The Bureau of Investigation." Hoover had the name changed, and the FBI was created. Pedro didn't always agree with Hoover, and certainly not in the current case, but he had to admit that the Bureau had made great strides in recent years. He had had a few bad times in his years with the Bureau but mostly they were good. Even if this meant the end of his career he wouldn't change any of his actions. Pedro had seen cases where Hoover had been angry before, and if he stayed with the Bureau, Pedro knew the best he could hope for would be an assignment in North Dakota searching for draft dodgers.

Pedro called all the airlines, and even with his priority status, he could get no flight. He then called the Navy Base, and asked if MB was still in Charleston. MB had delayed leaving because of the storm but now the weather was clearing. MB was on the runway making his preflight checks when he was called to the hanger for the phone call.

"MB, this is Pedro. Do you have access to a weather source between here and Washington?"

"Pedro, I just talked with the weather bureau and it's clearing all over the South and Northeast. I'm readying my Piper for the trip back to Timmonsville. What's up?"

"MB, can you fly me to Washington tonight? I have an urgent meeting with the Director in the morning, and there is no possibility of getting a flight out."

"Sure, Pedro, where are you now?"

"I'm at the Roper Medical Hospital."

"Well, get someone to bring you over and I'll file a flight plan. If weather conditions don't change, we're in luck. There's a fairly strong southeasterly wind, and if that continues, we should get there in less than six hours. I'll stay over and head home in the morning, I'm a tat tired from looking at clouds all day."

"Thanks, MB, maybe I'll hire you as a pilot for my law firm. I'll be right over."

Pedro said his goodbyes to Jerry and told him he and Joe would have to finish up the details as quickly as possible. "You may be ordered to leave soon."

Joe, Mark, and several other agents, along with local authorities, arrested Gus, Dalton, and Antonio. Pedro picked up a Washington Post the next morning, and saw the news.

J Edgar also saw the news. He had Tolson tell Pedro to wait in his office until further instructions. The wait was all day. Late in the afternoon, Tolson's assistant, Nadine, informed Pedro that he was to go home and await further instructions. The following morning when Pedro read the paper he was stunned. The papers were emblazoned with stories of how J Edgar had been in complete supervision of the arrest of a gang of hijackers and killers. There was a picture of Hoover, shaking hands and congratulating Sonny for his heroism. If you read it and didn't know the facts, you would never have known anyone but the Director was involved in the investigation. The other articles, of course, told the story of the hijacking, kidnapping, and murder. The story quoted Hannah Sims telling about her son being kidnapped by the son-in-law of a United States Senator, and how Tom Furman tried to get the killers freed.

Pedro was ordered to write an in-depth report of all details of the case, and to be available if he was needed. He never heard anything further officially from the Bureau about any aspect of the episode. He followed the trial in the newspapers and he knew that the report he filed was an important part of the prosecution. Hoover, however, told the Judge that Assistant Director Stokes was on another case and would be unable to attend the trial. Pedro received orders that he was being transferred to a newly created administrative position. His duties would be to recruit new agents from the masses of discharged military veterans. Pedro thought of ending his career, but with the Bureau so shorthanded, and saboteurs still in this country, he decided to stay and help staff the field offices with top-notch personnel. He could open his law practice after the aftermath of the war was over.

Joe was reassigned to Meridian, Mississippi. His new duties were to interview and investigate applicants for top secret security clearance: a job that was usually done by freshman agents. He, too, realized, that with most of America's young men still in uniform, his expertise was needed, even if it were not on the level he was used to. He filed a report on his activities in the investigation but he never heard any official comment about his work on rounding up the gang. Mark and the other agents kept their jobs, but each knew that they were on J Edgar's "most unwanted" list. One goof up would put them out. Sonny was a star witness at the trial.

Garland, JT, Gus, Dalton, and Antonio were all convicted and sentenced to life in prison with no chance of parole. Cecil provided information to the prosecutors and his ten-year sentence was commuted to time served while awaiting trial, and five years' probation.

Senator Furman received a lot of negative press and fought back at the newspapers and other media. He became a target for every reporter looking for a story, and many of the unknown deeds he had done in the past were delved into and exposed. He was re-elected, but only by a small margin, not the landslides he was used to.

Was he involved in the hijackings? Some evidence pointed in that direction, but so far, there has not been enough proof to make an indictment. The FBI and the military Investigators have never determined what happened to the paperwork assigning armed guards to the weapons truck that was hijacked. It led right up to the upper echelons of government—including a Senate Armed Services Committee. Unfortunately, the tracks melted before they reached a suspect.

Sonny, who was a Melvin Purvis Junior G-MAN before his abduction, is now making plans to become Special Agent Sonny Sims, reopen the case, and pursue leads on others not indicted—including Senator Furman.

ABOUT THE AUTHOR

John Aiken grew up and was educated in the public school systems of Timmonsville, South Carolina. John served in the United States Air Force in communications, and has been married to a former Southern Bell Telephone operator for 59 years. He graduated from the University of South Carolina and is an avid GAMECOCK fan.

He retired in 1996 from the State of South Carolina as a personnel administrator. Prior to joining the state, John sold Remington Typewriters and was an Employment Counselor for Snelling and Snelling.

He was a member of Columbia Toastmasters for 25 years and wrote a humor column for The Irmo News for three and ½ years. He resides in Irmo, SC with his wife and Maltese, Coco.

www.ingramcontent.com/pod-product-compliance
Lightning Source LLC
Chambersburg PA
CBHW020420110726
47899CB00006B/2062